THE SERMON OF LOSS

JH Tomen

ISBN:
ISBN-13:

This book holds depictions of chronic pain and OCD, both of which I have long suffered. But I write this in the hope that you can find healing as I have. Especially if you suffer from chronic pain, I urge you to seek out the works of the late Dr. John Sarno and Dr. John Stracks, both of whom - I say with no exaggeration - saved my life and taught me how to heal. If you live in Chicago - or if you live anywhere but have an internet connection - Dr. Stracks runs an incredible practice that is full of hope and healing.

Mental illness has long run in my family, but it's an incredible gift how far we've come as a society in recognizing this type of suffering. It is pain that never leaves you because it is you. But where my grandmother was simply swept under the rug for having 'spells,' I have had the benefit of incredible therapists and effective (maybe? still writing too many books…) treatment. Still, I want you to know that no matter what plagues your mind, you are good, you are beautiful, and you are enough. The mind, even when it serves as a prison, is a beautiful thing, and somewhere, behind our pain, is a connection to a universe of good. Even in the darkness, there will always be window, however faint, to remind you of the light.

I dedicate this book to all of us who suffer. Even in the depths of your despair, remember you are whole. Remember that there is a one-ness to us, that in every blade of grass swaying in the fields, there is a memory of each spirit flowing from the rest.
Most of all, remember that the cracks in you hold infinity.

et tui amóris in eis ignem accénde
renovábis fáciem terræ

Maps

THE MOTHER'S VALLEY
SEN'EL'SENG
SEN'EL'MEIN
PEN'DIL SOHN
PEN'DIL SELN
SEN'EL'TUL
PEN'DIL SING
SEN'EL'YULN
PEN'DIL DEYN
PEN'DIL YANE
PEN'DIL ZENN
BROKEN ARCH

* * *

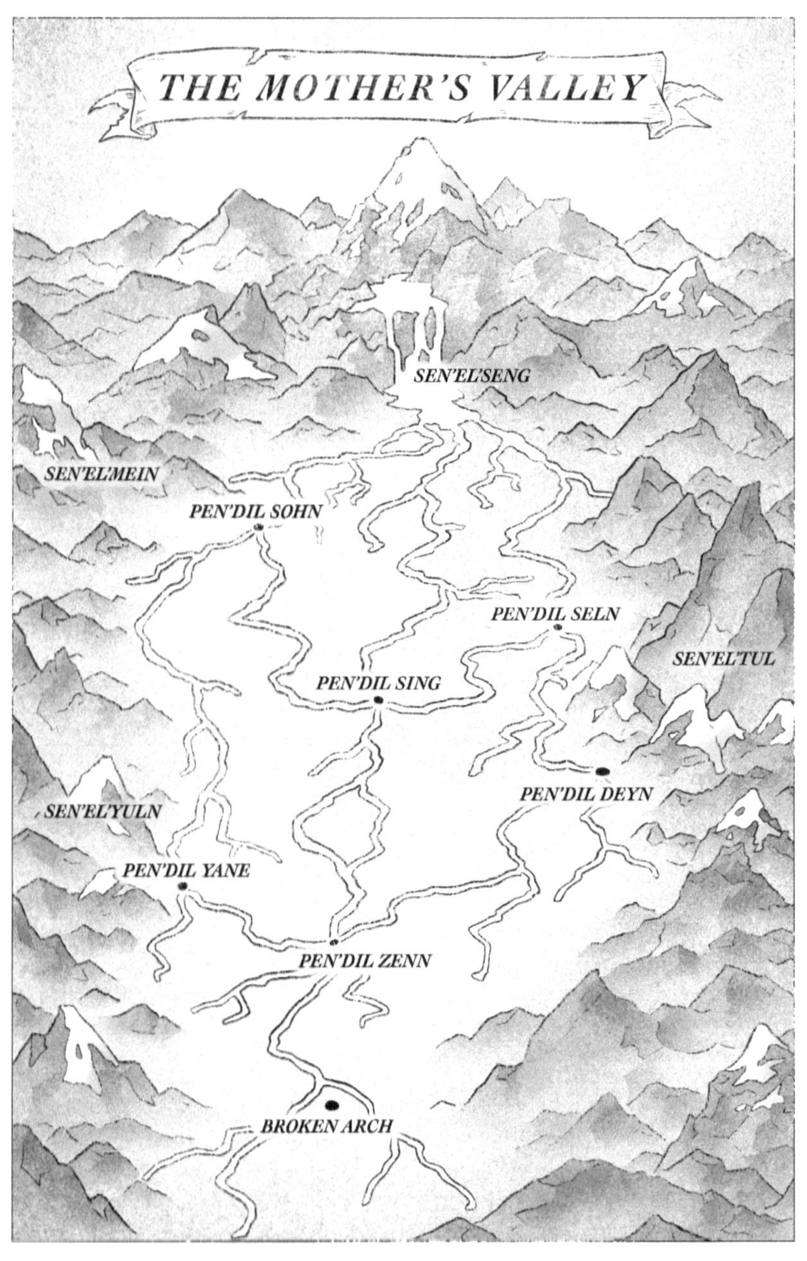

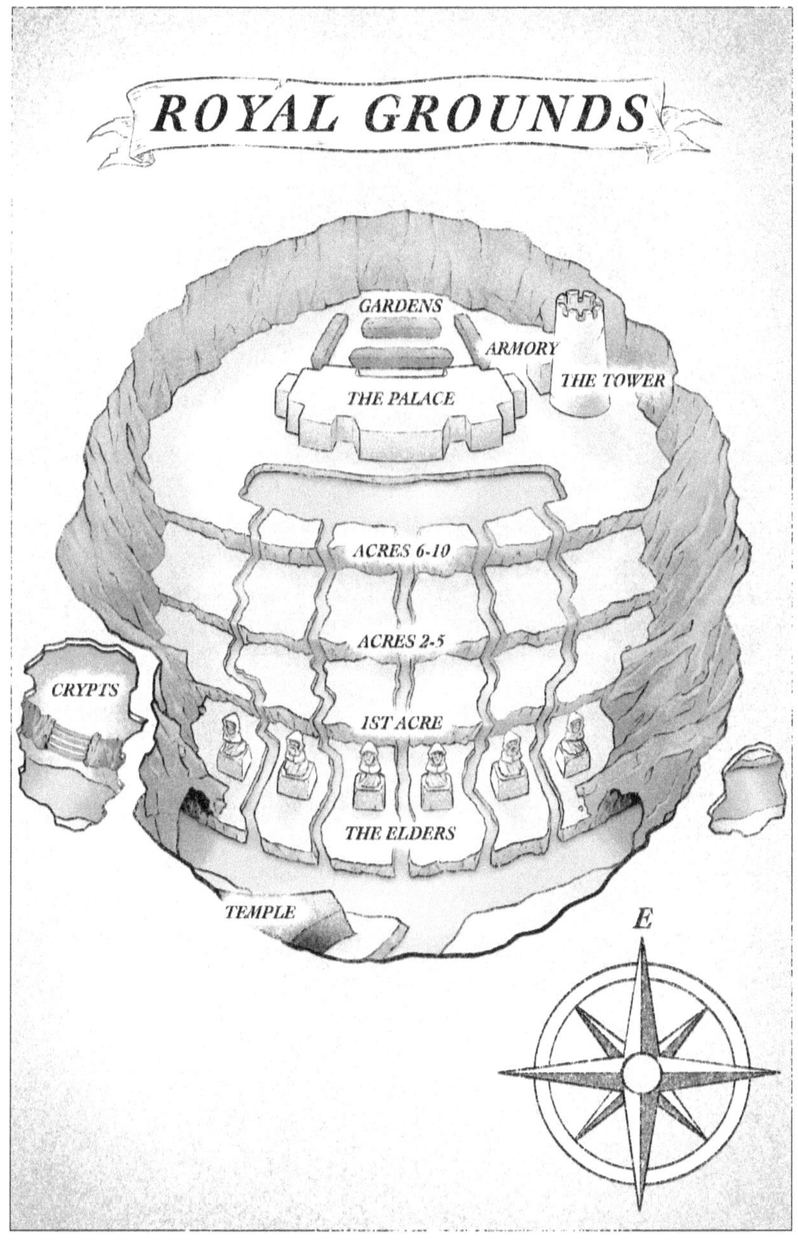

ROYAL GROUNDS
GARDENS
ARMORY
THE TOWER
THE PALACE
ACRES 6-10
ACRES 2-5
CRYPTS
1ST ACRE
THE ELDERS
TEMPLE
E

Prologue

Only now, as I survey the trenches of my heart, do I realize the depth of what I've lost. My heart is rent and my soul hollow, ripped apart by the tides I once called home. And yet, so sweet is the Mother's love that even as I choose death, I know She grants me life. It is only in the darkness that we remember light's sweetness, and in our yearning that our hopes can be fulfilled.

-The Sermon of Loss
excerpt from
The Odes by Entodal nol Serim

—:—

Part One

1

24th of Sund-z'ar : Middle of the Night : 984, 22nd Year of Iron
16 days until the 163rd Voting

Fire, blood, death, burning, bodies, death. Mother—

Teros clamped his eyes shut, shaking his head as he leaned against a streetlamp, his lungs searing. How far had he run? He opened his eyes, daring a look behind him. The street was empty now, but where was he? Not far enough. Never far enough. Why couldn't he get those things out of his head?

He focused on a good image of his mother, blocking out the one of her bleeding, dying. A memory? It didn't matter. All he could see was her face shining in the darkness. Putting him to bed maybe, her voice soft and cooing.

"My precious boy," she said. "My treasure." Kissing his head, pushing back his hair as she whispered almost to herself, "I will keep you *free.*"

That's why he ran, wasn't it? He had promised her: to stay safe, to look out for himself. But what did that mean without her?

Thoughts of those men came back, pushing through the door with their swords. And those…things. Things with masks where their faces should be, Mother lunging with a knife, the sharp crack of her skull. What was the last thing she said? "Pesrin sent you." So angry. Angry like when he was in trouble. But Uncle Pesrin was kind, wasn't he? He gave him candies, let him borrow books. But no, nothing could be kind about what happened to Mother. Why couldn't he unsee it? He clamped his eyes shut again, trying to will it away, but all he could see was fire.

Something in him had broken when she died, snapping like the rocks cracking during storms on the farm. Fire had leapt from him, become him, destroying those men, those things, destroying Mother's body, the room along with it. But in it, an opening, the cool air of night, the ruined room letting out onto an alley. And running, so much running.

Teros forced himself to keep moving, but he didn't know the city, had only arrived a week earlier… He focused on Mother's face again — the good face — banishing the ugly thoughts. *My boy,* she whispered in his mind. *Free.*

He looked about, trying to decide which way to go. He had run from Uncle Pesrin's house, turning…left? But what was left? What was anything? All he knew were the farms. Mother always said he'd been in the city as a baby, but that was useless to him now. He'd run past some grass. He remembered that grass, passing when they rode in from the city walls, when they moved away from Uncle Elin's. So, he was heading for the Un'weil, right? That was good, that was *freedom.*

He opened his belt pouch for a moment — a moment he didn't have — but it was calling to him, shining in the darkness. Hot shame burned his neck as he realized there was no food there. Mother had always scolded him for that, and now he was alone with nothing to eat. Still, it took some digging to find what he was really after. It wasn't his book calling to him or the letter Mother made him promise to carry.

Finally, at the bottom, he found it: Mother's ring. It glittered in the darkness. As he put it on for just a moment — the metal completely covering his smaller finger — it felt like she was there, like he could still touch her. And her face — the good face — became clearer in his mind. Good memories came back, times on the farm, times when they were happy.

He ran on, running as if something waited on the other side. But even if he escaped, Mother wouldn't be there. *Fire, blood, death, burning, bodies, death.* No. He shook his head, running as he held the good face in his mind, Mother's smile. That was all he needed: to keep her in his mind, to stay free. That was all that mattered. He was her treasure, and he would stay free. Free because she loved him, because she saved him.

My boy, my precious boy.

2

20th of Sund-z'ar : After 1st Meal : 984, 22nd Year of Iron
20 days until the 163rd Voting

—:—

4 Days Earlier

There was a shift in the air, and Keroes looked up to find a Masked One in the doorway to his office. He hadn't heard their footsteps approach, though that was often the case. They stood patiently with their hands behind their back, their thick golden cloak over one shoulder, no expression in their eyes beneath the porcelain mask. As Keroes looked for the Masked One's number, it spoke, revealing the familiar voice of 151.

"Keroes nir Sen'l," he said, "they're ready for you by the cave."

Keroes smiled. It was refreshing when a Masked One addressed him. 'Your Holiness' or 'My Lord Priest' was only right from commoners, of course, but the Masked Ones were a reminder of what this all was for, what his position was meant to uphold. And never was it more meaningful than on the day of the seeking ceremony, when the ancients might actually deliver him from his worries…

"Very well," he said, standing from his desk. The Masked One bowed, stepping into the hallway. As Keroes followed him, his personal masked guards joined them, forming a triangle as they moved through the tower. Their hands went to their swords as one, a lifetime of training honed into instinct. But it revealed a singular truth: behind all the ceremony, all the bowing, the Sacred Ones were raw power, like the river itself. But most importantly, they were his, and he would use them.

* * *

They exited the tower, the familiar walls of the city rising around them. It seemed to loom especially large on ceremony days, the weight of the people he served threatening to topple down into the palace grounds and crush him. The cliffs of the stone districts, choking with the poor and indigent, lifted above the other buildings as they blended with the massive mountains beyond. Still, there was promise in that view, too. The Mother's Valley was life, and he was here to keep her favor flowing.

He took a deep breath, looking for the god mount in the north. He could always feel Sen'el'seng, her power breathing life into the valley along the river. But as he turned toward the horizon, he frowned, a patch of thunder clouds approaching. That was far from a good omen for the seeking ceremony. Mists were common enough in the fall, of course, but they were well past Perat-tun when the storms were at their worst. He shook his head, quickening his pace. It wouldn't do to get the implements wet before the ceremony, not to mention what it would say about the outcome...

No one spoke as they crossed the royal grounds — not that Masked Ones ever spoke unless they had to. Still, that was fine by him with everything on his mind. It felt like he hadn't slept in weeks, a knot forming in the small of his back to remind him of his mortal weakness, of how little time he really had left. Even the crops did little to soothe him as they passed through the holy fields, their giant stalks seeming more a reminder of what he would lose if he failed.

Bloody Iron King! he thought, grinding his teeth. He immediately shamed himself for cursing — even in his mind — but what was a man to do when his world was on fire? The voting was approaching, and if he didn't do something, Bital nir Föhr would get an heir as warlike as himself, expanding beyond the basin until there was nothing left of Pen'dil Zenn, nothing left of tradition!

Keroes forced himself to suck in a deep breath, filling his mind with peace. None of that could scare him now. The gods, in their infinite wisdom, had answered. When he'd gone into the tower crypt for the first ceremony, the summoning, he'd almost thought they wouldn't, had been ready for the stones to reveal nothing at all as they had the past three tides. He'd upheld propriety in the ceremony, of course — gods forbid he ever became so lax! — but he'd been almost perfunctory, fatalistic even, as he poured the water into the cistern. But then...

He lifted his face toward what remained of the sun, closing his eyes as he basked in the memory of that brilliant glow. Even with clouds on the horizon, there was no question of the summoning omen: a soul — a powerful soul — had arrived, and the ancients would deliver him from all his worry. Rumors of powerful children were all well and good, of course, but only the ceremony could truly begin his search. And now that his Masked Ones were combing the western half of the city for the vessel, all he needed was the second seeking ceremony to tell him which soul was coming.

Sen'el'seng, he prayed, *Bringer of Life and First Daughter, may my prayers travel your waters. Send me someone who can save our people, who can keep our hearts pure and worthy of your favor.*

They reached the end of the fields, the crops giving way to the giant statues of the elders and the river beyond. The water surged past as they turned toward the caverns, the current seeming even more powerful than normal, especially for the end of Sund-z'ar. Why did the river seem so strong by the fields? It was almost as if it were excited for its brief stretch of sunlight between the sacred caves. Still...a good omen, perhaps? As the saying went, if the gods shed tears, they wouldn't need the river.

As they reached the riverbank, they met the rest of their party, ten priests and seven more Masked Ones, all carrying some implement for the ritual from the temple across the river. His head bishop put the striped cloth on his shoulders before bowing away, allowing him to take the lead. They said the king's crown weighed heavy, but what of the High Priest's stole? It was heavy work, watching over the kingdom as your "betters" made a mockery of everything you held dear. But not today. Today proved he had the one thing the Iron King did not. He had no armies and he wore no crown, but Keroes nir Sen'l answered only to the gods.

He led the others into the cave, the smell of life mingling in the air that blew through the gap in the stone. Keroes kept his pace slow at the head of the procession, chanting with the others as prayers flitted through his mind. As they crossed into the darkness, the rushing of the river filled his ears, leaving no gap between where the gods ended and he began. So, he chanted all the louder, his voice blending with the priests' as the caves filled him with their ecstasy.

How did the cave workers bear the sound of Sen'el'seng in their ears all day? Perhaps they simply couldn't hear the gods the way he could, but what a pity! How would it feel to spend your whole life tending to the bats or the moss fields, the sacred truth feet away from you without a way to touch it?

Thank you, he thought, praying again to Sen'el'seng. *Thank you…for choosing me.*

It wasn't long before they came to the crypts, the path beside the river widening into a broad cavern. For a moment, the tombs were almost invisible, the small crack of light at the end of the cave doing little to dispel the gloom. But with a nod of his head, the Masked Ones summoned Passion, flames jumping from their hands onto the torches ringing the sacred ground.

Keroes stepped up to the golden fountain in the center of the stone floor, the basin shimmering in the torchlight. The sacred names of the Elders — and the namesakes of their heirs — were etched into the metal. Föhr, Dek'rc, Irmun, Sen'l, Cosk, and Zi'yun, their legacy shining more brightly than the flames. He stepped onto the pedestal at the fountain's side, resting his hands on the rim as the others circled around him, the priests and Masked Ones mixing one beside the other.

For a moment, there was silence, and Keroes looked up at the crypts above him. It still took his breath away to see the resting place of so much holiness. Directly in front of him was the golden vault holding the bones of the Elders, the *immensity* of them almost too much to bear. The rest of the crypts were arranged in a V-shape, the ancients who'd served the Elders laid to rest on the left, while their progeny — the kings and dukes of the kingdom — stretched toward the mouth of the cave on the right.

He took a deep breath and began to sing, the others joining him. If he'd thought the echoes of their chants had been loud, the singing seemed to shake the stone, the roof of the cavern vibrating with their voices. The others copied him as he raised his hands, touching his forehead with the back of his thumbs. And as he placed his hands back on the basin, the Masked Ones summoned Flow, drawing two thin lines of water from the river behind them.

The Sacred Ones were careful, filling the basin without spilling a drop, the water weaving through the air like string. When it was full, he removed the rings from his fingers, placing them in the proper grooves along the edge. Able to move his fingers again, he reached into the pouch at his side, extracting a perfect pinch of sacred moss. As the singing reached a crescendo, he placed it in the water, its strands glowing blue in the darkness.

For a moment, they stopped singing, time standing still as the moss began to dance in the water. It swirled around the basin as the breeze worked its magic, the will of the Elders breathing through the stone. As it pushed toward the edge, he thought it might stop over House Sen'l, but at the last moment, it spun again, the moss coming to rest over the sigil of House Föhr, the house of the Iron King. He clenched his teeth, but he would never question the gods. Besides, the ceremony was far from over.

"It is decided," he said, taking the moss and raising it to his forehead. "Sing in thanks as we join the fire."

The priests sang the Song of Thanks, bowing their heads as the Masked Ones flanked him, climbing the steps toward the crypts. At the top, there was a smaller wheel, the sextants of the houses more carefully divided into the separate metals of each elder. He placed the moss atop the wedge of iron, directly over the sigil of House Föhr. As he opened his palms, the Masked Ones knelt, summoning Passion again as they extended their hands, the metal glowing under the heat of their flames.

The moss began to brown, and finally, painstakingly, it began to smoke. Keroes watched it carefully, ready for the answer from the gods. But as he squinted through the haze, the cavern suddenly darkened. For a moment, the sun was gone, the storm apparently having reached the palace grounds. It was as if night had descended, and his eyes widened, a shiver curving down his spine. He had never seen an omen like that, it was almost as if—

A burst of wind came from the depths of the cave, pushing the air toward the entrance. It carried with it the scent of bats, the musk of the chiroptary nearly overwhelming. And in that moment, the smoke flowed *away* from the ancients and toward the royal crypts. He had never seen such a thing, had only even heard of it happening once, in the Second Restoration some…what, four hundred years ago?

He strained his eyes, watching as the smoke swirled with an unfamiliar haste. And through the darkness, he finally saw its destination: the grave of Bitan nir Föhr, the Doomed Prince, the lost son of the Iron King.

"The gods have answered," he said quickly, his voice shaking. They had answered indeed, and in their words was his salvation.

3

Borash was drunk. But not the sleeping in an alley with a rat nibbling your toe kind he was used to. He was *good* drunk, like a bloody king, and for once, everything — including himself — felt right. The bottle of northern whiskey he'd found had him feeling so good, in fact, that he'd wandered east, the gleaming restaurants of the Wist Ristare rising up ahead. He'd pulled his good cane out of its hiding place, but he hardly felt his leg at all. As he passed through the park, invisible in the dim save for the glint of the lamplight off his cane, the fantasy almost felt real, like the old days when he could walk up to any restaurant and get a table.

Unfortunately, dreams were a luxury for the rich and the dead. As he stepped into the bright lights of the restaurants, he stuck out like a bat in the bloody palace, his beard and robes earning him more than a few glares. Even as he passed a fetching waitress at the Warbler — the girl having come out to the patio to seat some early arrivals — his gap-toothed smile only earned him a scowl and a hand reaching for a broom to shoo him away.

"Bloody vipers," he muttered to himself, shuffling out of view. Not that she could hurt him with that ratty old thing, but this wasn't the stone districts, and the man by the entrance with the cudgel would do a lot more than shoo. On second thought, maybe his leg *did* hurt just a bit… He shook his head, pulling the whiskey from his belt pouch. Unfortunately, there were only a few more mouthfuls left. When had it gotten so empty? He drained it, tossing the bottle into an alley between two restaurants. He'd need to scrounge up some more if his leg insisted on throbbing, but he should be able to bloody enjoy himself for one night at least.

He passed the next patio, an older woman frowning at him as she called to her waiter, pointing at where he'd thrown the glass. What did she have to complain about? Sodding alleys in the First City were cleaner than the king's privy, and a scullery maid would probably be out within the hour to sweep it up. He shot her a nasty look, hobbling along.

He made it to King's Square as the sixth meal bells began to toll, and he stopped, leaning against a lamppost to watch the crowds. He could see the entire Ristare, fancy men and women pouring into the streets from their shops and townhomes as they wandered toward the welcoming lights of the restaurants. A few even rode in actual wooden carriages, a bloody bounty of comfort compared to the ratty little moss nets everyone dragged around the slums.

For a single glittering second, he smiled despite himself. That was why he stayed in this loathsome city, after all. Even as all his memories turned bitter, the city still had a life to it he wouldn't find anywhere else. And besides, even if he went hungry two days out of every six, he still ate better than the bloody sheep herders in Pen'dil Seln.

He watched the crowds — staring at one fetching maid in particular — until he caught sight of an equally disheveled man across the way, leaning out from the curb as he shook his hat at passersby. He was too far away to hear, but it was doubtful there were enough coins in the hat to make a noise. He hobbled over, most of the precious rich folk subtly swerving around him.

"Ladik!" Borash called, raising a hand.

The man looked, scowling at the interruption. His face softened somewhat when he recognized Borash, though he didn't exactly smile either.

"Borash," he said, putting his hat back on with a regretful look. They both put their thumbs to their foreheads, bowing in the direction of the holy grounds.

"Do the gods grace tonight?" Borash asked. He wasn't usually one for formalities, but whiskey always made him talk like a lord. Ladik cocked an eyebrow, glancing at Borash's belt pouch as if his niceties might extend to offering him some food. He wasn't about to admit his pouch was bloody empty, of course, but what did Ladik think they were, flaming dukes?!

"Not exactly, no," Ladik said slowly, frowning when he realized he wasn't getting anything.

"Well, it's a hell of a place to put your hand out," Borash said. "What makes you think the bastards will pay up?"

Ladik shrugged.

"Can't do much worse," he said. "Tried Middle Field, but the Spill is paying for street guards now, and bloody blue coats at that."

Borash let out a slow whistle, shaking his head. That wouldn't bode well for him either — not that he was as desperate as Ladik. His friend glanced at the lords and ladies marching past, chewing his lip. He probably wouldn't get squat standing in bloody King's Square, of all places, but he didn't seem keen to miss the sixth meal rush either.

"Well," Borash said, touching his forehead again, "good luck."

"Yeah," Ladik said, already turning away as he pulled his hat from his head.

Borash moved on, continuing north. He could use something to eat himself, but it wasn't worth bothering until the end of the meal when the rich folk moved on. Begging was all fine and well, but if you were gonna live somewhere clam-fisted like Pen'dil Zenn, you were better off pilfering what you could. Not that Ladik was smart enough for that, poor fool. He'd likely get caught just smelling the damn plate.

He left the Wist Ristare, emerging onto the almost disturbing emptiness of the plaza above the royal grounds. The Bake Helm soared up to his left, filling the air with the smell of baking bread. Now those bastards had it made. Get to live a stone's throw from the palace — crown paying your rent, mind you — and all you have to do was watch bread bake. Why hadn't he chosen baking in school? Were the gods making sport of him, knowing he'd always get it wrong?

Still grumbling to himself, he hobbled over the king's canal and onto the marble viewing platform, the river audible as it surged through the grounds some fifty feet below. The guards on patrol eyed him but didn't move from their posts. As much as they wanted to keep the whole damn city for the dukes, you couldn't cut off every sodding sacred thing from the people. And yet, as he stared down at the pillars glittering in the moonlight, the Elders felt far from sacred. They looked like normal men, probably as corrupt as the rest, and they only reminded him of the life he'd been meant to have, the one the real gods — whoever those heartless bastards were — had snatched away. At least it was a decent view, even if it made him wish he hadn't finished his whiskey…

He looked up, hoping to see some stars, but, of course, the mists were rolling in, blocking the moon along with everything else. Bloody Sund-z'ar. What was the point of being out on a summer's night if everything was shrouded in fog? Meanwhile, he had to hear every pious bastard drone on about it being the god's breath of Sen'el'seng — "a blessing!" they told themselves. Easy for them to say with blessings coming out their ears! It's like they actually thought the elders were up there on the mountain, dancing about as they laughed at their descendants. What had bloody Sen'el'seng ever done for him? What had *anybody* ever done for him?

"Bastards!" he yelled at the statues, the whiskey filling him with a strange fire. "Sodding bastards, the lot of ya!"

He only got those two sentences out before guards were crawling out of the stones, surrounding him on the marble pavilion.

"Oy!" one yelled, knocking his sword against the railing, gold epaulets on his uniform. "Walk off or lose a hand, old man. Your choice."

"Apologies," Borash said quickly, stumbling backward, the whiskey's bravado washed away by fear. Ladik's brother, rest his soul, had lost a hand to the guards, and they hadn't exactly taken it off clean. He scrambled back over the canal like a rat, though it wasn't long before the anger returned. *Old man?* He was only thirty-five. Not that he looked like green moss anymore… Still, it made a man wonder. He was about the age when the older blokes in the alleys had started dying off, and it wasn't like he could afford a doctor if something happened.

He slunk away, grateful for the darkness even as his leg throbbed from the exertion. Old man indeed. He felt like that fairy tale from Pen'dil Sohn, the one where the man became a tree, too foolish to live and too stubborn to die…

By the time he made it back to the restaurant district, the whiskey was wearing off, and his leg turned stiff. He'd walked off the throbbing, so it wasn't painful exactly, but it was too soon to trust it, like the bloody thing knew it had power over him and was just waiting to dole out its punishment. Still, when he finally turned onto his favorite block, his heart couldn't help but lift at the bounty before him.

The rich folks called it the Menagerie — which was about as ridiculous as every other thing in this cursed city — but at least it was easy to tell the restaurants apart. Each one had a giant woven animal hanging off the side, staring down at the patrons as they ate on the terraces in bloody clueless bliss. He made his way toward the giant peacock where, thankfully, the early customers were already on their way out, quickly saying their prayers as they dropped hunks of food onto the offering altars.

The really fancy places had altars on every table, allowing the richest patrons to say their prayers in peace. It was the cheapskates who put 'em outside, hoping they could squeeze out some extra coin from a second seating. The beauty of the Peacock, though, was that the altars were even more out of the way, hidden by a screen of ivy just off the alley. You still had to dodge the glare of the doorman, but that was the case everywhere, and the ivy made it just easy enough that you weren't too likely to get your skull bashed in.

Borash stepped into the alley, sitting on a stack of boxes in a rare stretch of shadow. He waited for another couple to make their offerings before creeping back, standing behind a particularly thick clump of ivy to survey the goods. There were six pedestals carved into the shapes of the Elders, though they hadn't used metal like the nicest places. The statues had dials on their heads, each one turned to sixth meal so the offerings could be spread out instead of being jammed on Lord Zi'yun's head.

Not that the pious princelings had left him much to choose from… Bloody sixth meal. There was dandelion salad and boiled cattails next to amaranth balls soaked in bat's milk — which was enough to make him shudder. How was it that these pompous bastards could turn their noses up at a dying man while thinking royal milk from some sightless demon was a delicacy? Thank the gods he'd never ended up in the caves. It was almost enough to make him bow down and pray himself, a reminder there were worse places than the streets.

Still, even in their bad taste, he could tell the rich sods' food was quality. It gave off a kind of aura, shimmering with the power of the royal grounds, seventh acre at least — not that it mattered to anyone but those bloody masked things the king had prowling the city. Some bloody talent it was, too, knowing the price of things he was stealing. His teachers never had figured out how he could do it, even if it hadn't done him a lick of good over the years.

Putting his squeamishness aside, he started loading up his pouch. Just a handful from each pile, mind, enough to leave the altars looking respectable. He didn't need some axe-faced man with a cudgel hunting the stone districts for him all night. While he worked, he also shoved a few leeks into his mouth with a handful of baked clover. Even those tasted like the heavens, his taste buds giving way as he realized how hungry he'd been. No matter how much he liked to complain, in the end, anything, truly *anything*, was better than a bowl of moss to end the night.

He did up the clasp on his pouch and was turning to go when he froze. Across the street, unmoving in the shadows, was a Masked One, its eyes locked on him beneath its faceless mask. He wanted to run, to escape before the magic cut him down, but his leg throbbed, rooting him to the ground like a cornered rat. His mind moved like tar, reaching for something that could save him. Why was it just standing there? How much had it seen? The restaurants all had rooms upstairs where the things could eat if they wanted to, but you rarely saw them on the street. If only he—

The Masked One left, turning into the street as if it were going for a bloody stroll.

Borash gasped, clutching the railing of the patio as air finally rushed back into his lungs. He shook his head, forcing himself to hobble away through the pain, eager to be gone before his luck ran out. Like the old blokes used to say, only a fool stays in the cage when the door is open. And he thought the bloody palace guards were bad... At least they could only take one hand at a time. A Masked One didn't need permission to end you, could burn you for fun if it wanted to.

So why hadn't it done anything? Borash found his head darting around as he stumbled away, terrified he'd discover the thing following him. Perhaps it was... *No.* That sort of thing wasn't worth thinking about. It was probably just a late-stager. Everyone said the creatures weren't all there at the end, their stomachs turning to stone as their life drained away. This one probably couldn't even hold down enough food to waste magic on a rat like him.

He hurried down the street, the buzz of the whiskey well and truly gone. He headed back the way he came, suddenly grateful for the summer fog. He wasn't at the point of joining a temple or anything, but maybe when you were a bug, it really was a blessing when the gods decided not to squash you...

He had made it to the other side of King's Square — the odd, spindly trees of the park reaching up ahead — when he heard a moan coming from a nearby alley. The smarter part of him didn't want to stop, knowing he'd had enough trouble for one night, but the fool in him slowed, leaning on his cane as he stuck his head around the corner. There was a man on the ground, barely moving, though why the poor bastard would lay down in the brightly lit alleys of the Wist Ristare was beyond him. Shrugging, he was about to walk on when the man shifted, revealing his face: it was Ladik.

Borash rushed forward, nearly tripping as he scurried across the cobblestones. His friend's face was badly bloodied, his eyes barely visible under the bruising.

"Ladik!" Borash said, taking him by the shoulder. "What happened?"

The man coughed, forcing his left eye open.

"Bloody guards," he said, wincing as he tried to swallow. "Didn't like me begging."

He closed his eyes again, his head rolling to the side.

"Bloody giants, man," Borash muttered, trying to assess the damage. There was no pool of blood, so despite the questionable state of Ladik's face, he *had* seen worse. Bloody gods, but he had. At least Ladik had never been much to look at in the first place.

"Can you walk?" he asked, trying to feel the man's bones for anything obviously broken. All he got in reply was a groan.

"Well, you better pray you can," he said, "'cause you'll wake up in the caves if you sleep here."

Speaking of prayer... Borash looked at his food pouch, his jaw clenching. As much as it pained him, it was the closest thing they'd get to a doctor — sodding good-for-nothing priests. But all they did was feed you and say the prayers anyway. He unclasped his pouch, carefully avoiding the bat's milk as he pulled out an amaranth ball. He didn't like parting with the food so soon, but as Paps used to say, good things always left faster than they came. Ladik groaned again as Borash worked his jaw, but eventually, he swallowed. It took a moment, but as the seventh acre food went to work, Ladik's color came back a little, his blood seeming to *shift* out of the bruises ever so slightly.

"We'd better get walking, old friend," Borash said.

Ladik gave him the barest hint of a nod as he set his jaw, waiting to be picked up. And somehow, Borash got him standing, his bad leg behaving despite the other man's weight. They hobbled down the empty street, the darkness of the park drawing them in. He turned at every sound, sure those guards would reappear, but for once, his luck seemed to hold, and before more trouble could come crashing down, they were gone.

4

25th of Sund-z'ar : Before 2nd Meal : 984, 22nd Year of Iron
15 days until the 163rd Voting

732 sat in the darkness of the cave, meditating with her sword in her lap. She sat until she became one with the sound of the river, until she no longer felt the mask on her face or the golden cape coiled around her like a snake. Those things were still there, yes, but they were mere coincidences, passing away as they revealed the emptiness within her. And in that space, that internal silence, she felt…bliss.

Perhaps a human would find it strange, but in that state, there was no pain, no nausea from the Passing, no afterburn of Flow leaving her unmoored. It was a taste of what she'd longed for her entire life, the moment when she finally let go, blinking into darkness like a star as she floated to the place beyond.

She opened her eyes, the cleansing pavilion suddenly seeming bright despite the gloom of the cave. Bars of sacred metal — one for each Elder — reached up around her, glowing in the darkness as they lifted up, arcing toward each other and back down. Each metal on its own was loud, too full of its own Principle. But here, joined together, there was a special kind of stillness. The others sometimes referred to the pavilion as 'the cage,' but she only felt embraced as those arms reached up to block out the world.

She stood, her step lighter as she turned, heading for the exit. It would be second meal soon, and she still wanted to make it to the armory before her assignment came down from the captain — gods forbid it was as hard as her last one. She would serve wherever she was needed, of course, but spending ten days building that cistern had pushed her well past her limit, leaving her dizzy with the Passing. It wouldn't change how she died, of course, but the beginning of the end was almost certainly more frightening than the end itself.

She walked toward the river, popping a bit of tomato in her mouth and flaring it as it met her stomach. Flow surged into her mind, though the dizziness was thankfully gone. Still, she felt a twinge of regret at losing grapes on her last assignment. She had loved grapes. The other Masked Ones always said to never start with your favorites, but as much as it hurt, Viden had the right of it. If you were going to mourn, you'd better mourn early. She certainly wouldn't feel any regret when the tomatoes gave out.

As she reached the river, she nudged it with her mind, bending the water slightly to reveal the stone pylons beneath the current, just wide enough for her to step on. She took them one at a time, praying as she moved from stone to stone and thanking the sacred waters for their passage. Only Masked Ones could pass through the river, a gift from Sen'el'seng herself, a reminder of where her spirit would return when her vessel was spent.

Once she was past the river, she moved more quickly, her eyes having no trouble in the gloom with the power inside her. She stopped by the crypts for a moment, bowing her head against the stone as she faced the Elders. Some liked to touch their own crypt each time they passed, but she didn't see the point. She spared a glance for it, the crypt easily found in the seventh column and third row. But while her — his — old bones were sacred, the spirit was what mattered, and it was already inside her.

She emerged from the cavern into brilliant sunlight, the fog from earlier banished for the time being. She smiled under her mask, looking to the east where she could just make out the peak of Sen'el'tul. She could only see it on the clearest days, but it gave her hope, an omen of her own making. Perhaps this *would* be a good day. But as Viden always said, you didn't smile to avoid the bad days, you smiled because you knew they were coming.

As her eyes adjusted, she noticed a group of priests by the river, measuring the depth with their striped poles. They'd probably be ringing the bells for second meal at any moment, then. It came so early in the summer! Still, even if her meal was rushed, her other rituals were too important to skip. First, she walked across the length of the field, bowing her head to each of the Elder statues until she reached Zi'yun, the giant lithium pillar of her namesake glowing like the snow on Sen'el'seng. She carefully laid her sword in the grass before stepping up to the statue, resting her forehead just below his knee.

She closed her eyes, praying until she heard the whispers. She could never make out what they said, but the voices soothed her all the same, even if only she could hear it.

"Could be the Passing," Viden had said when she'd told him so many years ago. "Maybe don't mention that to anyone else — not that we aren't all a little touched."

Perhaps it *was* the Passing, though there was peace in that, too, looking your own death in the eye. Even more than meditating, though, there was…*power* in those voices, *possibility.* This was a sacred thing, where the gods and Elders merged, where her spirit could be safe. Perhaps it didn't change anything, but those whispers seemed… hopeful.

She took the central path back toward the palace, passing the green patina of Elder Cosk's copper statue. She walked through the Flow crops, the first acre nearly bursting with life: tomatoes the size of her fists, massive watermelons, her beloved grapes… Royal gardeners moved quickly from row to row, their golden robes and jewelry flashing in the morning sun as they rushed to finish whatever they were tending to before second meal. Still, most stopped to bow before hurrying on their way, their ranks knowing better than any other the power of the Elders — and the magic in their crops.

As she climbed the hill, a breeze picked up, no longer blocked by the plants as they grew smaller with every acre. She closed her eyes, breathing in deeply as the scent of flowers finally reached her from the palace. If only she could take off her mask and let the breeze blow through her hair until she felt like she was soaring, floating away like a dandelion to somewhere new.

She stopped, blinking. What an odd thought… She wasn't some initiate, a weak vessel itching to drop her mask. She'd been divined more than twenty years and raised fifteen! She shook her head, continuing up the path. She could feel the wind in her hair at the end, when she reached Sen'el'tul, but not before. Until the Elders were done with her, she was a Masked One, and she was theirs to use.

After her…aberration, she walked more quickly toward the tower. She normally liked to take her time by the palace fountains, sometimes even meditating by the lily pads, but she'd clearly had enough indulgence for one day. She reached the giant stone steps, a dozen other Masked Ones already moving about the grounds. Most were heading in like her, but some were already leaving, apparently skipping second meal with orders clutched in their hands.

As she walked through the doors, the bells began to ring, the whole city echoing with the sound. There were more Masked Ones inside, whispering in tight groups in the great hall as they drifted toward the stairs. No one spoke to her as she passed, though a few from her own cadre nodded. Most of them drank together the night before orders came in. Perhaps they thought she begrudged them their revelry, but she didn't. She simply didn't see the point. As Viden always said, different blades need different ways of sharpening. For her, indulgence only made it harder to be strong. The nights she *had* drunk had ended in tears, and they were better off forgotten.

She worked her way to the left, weaving toward the armory through the sea of people climbing to the mess hall. She was worried she might have missed her chance, but as she reached the giant metal door, it opened for her. She poked her head in, finding Pelona behind the counter, the old woman smiling warmly.

"See!" Pelona said, bowing deeply. "I told them you would come. They tried to rush me out, but I'd rather eat a cold second meal than shut the door on you."

"You honor me," 732 said, giving the woman a quarter-bow in return.

She glanced at the giant shelves behind Pelona, their racks covered in supplies as they disappeared into the darkness. All the other stalls were unmanned, everyone off to second, though she could still hear the clanging of metal from the smithy through the next set of doors.

"What'll it be, Sacred One?" Pelona asked.

"An eighth-satchel of dandeli—" 732 started to say as Pelona pulled a bag from beneath the counter, sliding it toward her.

"I know," she said, winking, "the usual. The others always ask for liquor, but not you. Always practical, you are, Eldest One."

Practical wasn't exactly the word her brothers and sisters would use… Still, it was impossible to deny the smile on Pelona's face. Even if she had no clue what 732 wanted the dandelion seeds for, she never wavered in her cheerful diligence. She opened the pouch, glancing at the clumps of dandelion fluff — not that she needed to check with Pelona. With the others working in the armory, maybe, but never her. Pelona never 'misjudged' the scale, never skimped on what was owed to the Masked Ones.

"Thank you," 732 said, bowing again.

"It's an honor, Sacred One," the older woman said. She reached into her belt pouch, sliding a brown rice ball across the counter.

"And this is for your friend."

Before 732 could protest, she turned away, waving behind her as she disappeared into the stacks. "A blessed second meal to you!"

732 ate her meal in silence, only her staff sergeant acknowledging her as she sat. She'd found a place in the middle, the other Masked Ones unconsciously organizing themselves by rank whenever they were forced together. The plates seemed to match as well, the youngers' piled high while the top brass ate next to nothing. Luckily, she could still eat most of the items from the buffet, the cinnamon peppers a good deal more palatable than the potatoes at first meal.

The food was already growing cold, the mortals in the kitchens barred from entering the dining hall while their masks were off. Not that she minded much. She barely paused to chew between each mouthful, her own meals meaning little to her these days. Besides, she'd rather be in a rush than go without her dandelion. She paused to grip it through her pocket, glad to know it was there.

She spared a glance at the ceiling, too, the only part of the dining hall she liked. Each section above the house tables was carved in relief, the stone brimming with images of each house's namesake Principle. House Zi'yun honored Place, of course, and amongst the grasses and weeds, she could also see her own dandelion poking through the rest. Such a peaceful carving, not like the Föhr table where tongues of fire spread from the center, or Dek'rc where Remembrance was shown in branching shards of ice.

Finally, with her bowl practically finished, the second bell rang, signaling the end of the meal. They all stood in unison, fitting their masks over their heads as they filed back to the buffet, dropping their leftovers into the open holes of the statues where they would be properly buried. There were six statues in all, arranged in a circle at the points closest to each house's table. As she dropped her food into the mouth of the Zi'yun Snake, she turned, finding the staff sergeant waiting for her. She put out a hand to accept her orders, but he shook his head.

"Higher-ups have something special for you today," he said, his mask ringed with gold. "Go ahead and see your friend; I'll send a runner when they're ready."

She nodded. There was no point in asking more. Like Viden always said, orders were like weeds; they'd pop up without you watering them. She left the mess hall, climbing to the eighth floor. When she reached the hospital wing, she stopped by the nursing station, frowning as she read the room chart. Viden had been moved to the tenth floor, facing the northeast. It was a nicer view, which meant the end was drawing near… Like everything with the masks, pleasure was only doled out in direct proportion to your pain.

Viden was unmoving in his bed, the sound of gentle breathing slipping through his mask. It was a beautiful room, probably the best in the ward, its high ceiling painted with glittering gold sigils, the brick seeming to glow in the light from the fireplace. And the window… She drifted toward it, taking in the view. She could see the Iron Barracks, soldiers the size of ants buzzing about, and beyond that, an endless horizon, the empty rocky plains stretching toward the towering mountains at the edges of the valley.

As she stared at Sen'el'tul, she held her breath, in awe of the bald mountain rising above the rest. It looked so close from the top of the tower… Her hand went to the dandelion pouch in her pocket, the hundreds of miles disappearing until only she and the mountain remained. *Remember me*, she prayed. Some would say praying to any mountain but Sen'el'seng made you a heathen, but she didn't believe it. They were all daughters of the Great Mother. And besides, she had left a piece of her soul there, the piece of her waiting for the dandelion

—

"Don't you have anything better to do than see a dying old man?" Viden asked, his voice like gravel.

She turned, finding his eyes on her, still bright despite his withering frame. She smiled, gently sitting on the edge of the bed as she took his hand.

"A son can't see his father?" she asked.

"Yeah, yeah," he said, a dry cough racking him for a moment. Still, he squeezed her hand tighter, showing he was really pleased. That had always been their way — vinegar and tenderness. And now she'd have to find a way to live without him…

"Pelona sent you a rice ball," she said, pulling it from her other pocket. "Just don't bite me if I help you eat it."

Viden chuckled, shaking his head.

"As much as I'd like to bite you, it's no use. Can't even stomach those anymore. I get a bit of gruel down in the mornings — bloody nurses — but it tastes like damned dirt."

"And how would you know what dirt tastes like?" she asked, cocking an eyebrow underneath her mask.

"Magic comes in many forms," he said, suddenly the wise teacher again. "Just wait until you try bat piss."

And perhaps she should… Always half-joking and half-teaching, his words were never meaningless, even if he acted like he was only trying to amuse himself. It reminded her of a time almost too long ago to remember, making her glance at Sen'el'tul again.

"Still thinking of your mountain, eh?" he asked. "I requested this room so you could look at it. Hell of a view, they tell me, not that I can see it."

Without waiting to ask, she took both his hands, dragging him to a seated position. He wheezed with the effort, but she swiveled him around, squeezing him tight around the shoulders so he could sit up and see.

"I'll be damned," he said. "It's gorgeous."

They looked for a long while until she felt a tear fall onto her hand, the water snaking beneath his mask and onto his shoulder.

"Thank you," he said quietly, barely above a whisper as he squeezed her knee. "You've been a good son."

Just then, there was a knock at the door, a nurse bowing his way in.

"Sacred One," he said, meeting her eyes. "Courier here to see you, from the High Priest."

She eased Viden back onto the bed, squeezing his hand one last time.

"I'll be back," she whispered, turning toward the hall.

Whatever her assignment was, she would finish it quickly. And when the time came, she would be there for Viden, holding his hand until the end.

5

25th of Sund-z'ar : After 2nd Meal : 984, 22nd Year of Iron
15 days until the 163rd Voting

That sound… Someone crying. But not just any old crying. It was blubbering, sobbing and muttering like his mother used to when she had her bad nights. The sound of the bloody world caving in, enough to ruin whatever sweetness was left of his dream, whatever sliver of light was accounted to him before the awfulness of the world came rushing back.

Borash woke up in his alley, already half sitting up. He immediately regretted it, though, his head splitting with pain as the morning light hit his eyes. But what was that bloody noise? If some damned bum had curled up in his alley, he was in for a throttling. He growled, pushing onto his hands and knees. His stomach wanted to heave — the 'good' whiskey a little too good — but luckily, he was too old for that sort of thing anymore. But the bloody headache… It had been a while since he'd felt this out of sorts.

Somehow, he got to his feet, forcing his eyes open. He wiped his face, taking out his flask and shaking it. So the bloody gods did love him! There was just a tiny bit left he'd somehow forgotten in his effort to carry Ladik home. It wasn't the good stuff — that had gone with the bottle — but he'd always drink rotgut in a pinch. He took off the top, draining the flask. It was hardly even enough to call a mouthful, but it felt like a bloody miracle with the hangover he was having. And maybe it would be enough to go back to sleep if he could stop that damned racket…

He looked around the alley, trying to pinpoint the sound. Like all the bloody cracks in the rock he'd called home over the years, the place was misshapen, carved haphazardly from the cliff face in the stone districts and left to fill with moss. There were deep notches in the stone walls every few feet and more than a few puddles with piles of crates and things besides. Still, he saw nothing. The crying had stopped again for the moment, but there *was* some kind of whispering coming from the other end of the alley. Now that he was awake, though, it sounded like…a child? Epsin's lad used to lurk around the place, but hadn't he scared him off well enough?

Borash stepped carefully on the wet stone, suddenly remembering his bad leg, though it felt oddly fine for the moment. You'd think it'd be protesting more given how heavy bloody Ladik was… Still, he'd hidden away his good cane again, and slipping in the damned alley would only add to his troubles. He followed the sound of the blubbering like a cave dog, inching closer until he zeroed in on it behind one of the larger piles of crates. He could make out snippets of it now between sharp breaths, the words beating out a strange cadence. *Mother* — the voice whispered — *boy…in…my…Mother.*

"Lad," Borash said as he came around the corner, "I thought I bloody told you—"

He froze, locking eyes with a boy he didn't know, looking like a cornered animal with his eyes wide and his face covered in tears. A memory forced its way into his mind unwanted: another face scared and hiding, covered in tears. Just then, a searing pain hit his leg, like demons gnawing on his bones, and he fell to one knee, gritting his teeth as the pain crashed over him.

"Are you okay?" a tiny voice asked him.

Borash looked up, blinking through the tears in his eyes to find the boy leaning forward, looking like he might reach out to steady him despite his arms still being wrapped around his knees. Borash sucked in a deep breath, not caring for the murky puddle beside him as he eased himself to the ground.

"Fine," Borash said, coughing before looking the kid up and down again. His face was dirty, but his robes were bloody purple kelo wool, and even with a few tears in them, they smelled like money. "What are you doing in my alley?"

"I'm sorry," the kid said, his eyes still wider than a bloody Yaneman's begging plate. "Where…am I?"

"Where you bloody supposed to be?" Borash asked. He hadn't thought it possible, but the kid's eyes widened even more, darting toward the mouth of the alley he couldn't even see through his pile of crates. On the run, then… Well, after the beating Ladik took the night before, he didn't want to be around when the kid's minders poked around. Still, something about that face… *No.* He couldn't get bloody sentimental now, although something told him the kid wouldn't move on without a bit of coaxing.

"Look," Borash said, "you're in the stone districts, lad, Föhr section, south of the well."

The boy narrowed his eyes, his head tilting to the side as every single word seemed to pass without recognition.

"Liana's Pub?" Borash asked. "Thelk Street?" Still nothing. "Bloody sages, kid, what the hell you doing out here, then?"

The boy reached into his belt pouch, fumbling with the clasp before pulling out a piece of paper. He handed it to Borash.

"Oh," the boy asked as he unfolded it, "do you know how to read?"

It was almost funny the way he asked it all innocently, even if it was the most offensive bloody thing he'd ever heard.

"You think I can't bloody read 'cause I live in the King's stone palace here? You think you—"

"Sorry!" the boy squeaked out, rubbing his hands together.

"Yeah, alright," Borash said, shaking his head. How had the kid softened him so quick? Like the anger melted out through his feet. Bloody rich kids, must get raised with a forked tongue to lace their insults with apologies. He furrowed his brow, trying to make out the letter. Not that he couldn't sodding read! But his eyes weren't so good anymore — especially after the night he'd had — and it'd been years since he'd had to read the bloody curly letters the rich called writing.

To whomever reads this letter, please take my son to the Duke of Identity, Lord Terik nir Irmun, at Irmun Pond. Please give him my second sealed letter, and you will be rewarded handsomely. And, please, if you have anything of the gods in you, protect my boy.

Kulawi nir Zi'yun

Borash looked up over the letter, his eyes widening like the kid's. A bloody duke meant more bloody problems — venomous bastards — but if anyone could give out a *handsome* reward…

"Your Mems wrote this?" he asked, holding up the letter.

A look of intense pain filled the kid's eyes, and he clamped his eyes shut, hugging his knees as he muttered to himself again.

"Alright, alright, don't worry about all that," Borash said. Seemed like a bloody yes anyway. Besides, the kid didn't find robes like that hanging on a damned clothesline. "What's your name, then?"

"Teros," the kid said quietly, looking up with fresh tears in his eyes.

"Alright," Borash said, sighing. "Well, I'm Borash. You know what this letter says?"

The kid nodded again.

"I suppose I can take you, but Irmun Pond's a long way off, and it ain't a cheap ride, either. You got any money?"

"No," Teros said, "but I have this."

He dug through his belt pouch again. When he opened his hand, there was a duchy ring in his palm, as long as his index finger and glittering with jewels.

"Put that away!" Borash said, dropping to his knees as he covered the kid's hand. He looked toward the mouth of the alley, but thankfully it was empty. "You can't bloody flash something like that around here, it'll get you killed."

Still, if that was just the start of the riches this bloody kid had access to… He swiped the ring, shoving it into his own belt pouch along with the letter.

"I'll hang onto these for you," he said. He shook his head, his mind whirring. Weren't many men he knew who would give him a ride these days, but maybe if he stopped by Maegin's, offered him a cut of the money…a small one, mind.

He opened his mouth to get the kid up when the lad's stomach growled, louder than the bloody Bake Helm on milling day.

"You hungry?" Borash asked.

The kid nodded. Borash cursed under his breath. He had nothing left after saving Ladik, but if he brought the boy back starving, you'd better believe the duke would wriggle out of the damned reward. Well, there was nothing for it, then.

He sighed, slipping off his shoe. He pried up the bit of moss he'd glued to the bottom, freeing up his last coin. He held it for a moment, letting the sun shine on it. He'd almost forgotten what money even bloody looked like… It was a fuller, more money than he'd seen in years, with eighteen seeds stuck in the little circle of enamel. Even with all the drinking, all the bloody slouching around, he'd promised himself he wouldn't spend this coin until the end. But this was different — this was an investment. The ring alone was worth a bloody half-stack, and that was after the pawn fee. He turned toward the pub, marching for the back door before he could change his mind.

"I'll be back, kid," he said over his shoulder. "Just stay quiet and don't move an inch."

Borash hobbled up the back steps of the pub, struggling not to slip on the slick stone. The door was covered in lime and more weathered than a riverman's wife — not that you could pry the crooked thing open on cold nights. Milerne kept it barred with a six-inch board, just like her mother always had. He knocked, stepping back as he did what he could to smooth his hair.

"Just a minute!" Milerne called through the door, her slippers shuffling against the stone. She pulled out the board, the door grinding against the misshapen frame. "We're just cooking for third, but you're welcome to come in and—"

Their eyes met, and the look of sheer exasperation on her face made him feel like a boy again, hiding from his mother and the wrong end of her broom.

"You know the rules, Borash," she said, hands on her hips. "Out by second and back after sixth."

He'd appreciated those hips rightly enough over the years. He'd hoped to join her in bed after her good-for-nothing husband fled for Pen'dil Sing, but a broken bottle had made it clear where she stood on that.

"I know," he said, swallowing the lump in his throat, "but I got a bit of a…er, situation. Besides, those were your Mems's rules, weren't they?"

"That they were," she said, "but she's also the kind one in the family, and I'm only barely foolish enough to let you lot keep sleeping out back."

"Oh no, you're plenty kind," he said, rubbing his hands together. "And how is your dear old mother?"

"Well enough," Milerne said, "and if you actually cared, you might stop by to see her. Now, I've good paying customers coming in front and back within the hour and I need you gone."

She nodded, making to close the door when he blocked it with his foot.

"Wait," he said, "I'm paying today, I swear." He held out his coin, which she eyed with suspicion. "I need food, and the good stuff at that."

"Why?" she asked. "What's going on out there?" She tried to look around him at the alley, but he shifted to the side.

"Nothing," he said, "not to concern you, anyway. Ladik got in a scrape again, but I'll set him right with some decent food — and we'll be gone before third, of course."

She met his eyes again, weighing him. Then, before he could change his mind, she took his coin and turned into the pub, waving for him to follow. He'd been hoping to at least save a bloody single out of the fuller, but apparently, he was already in the current, taking what the gods dished out and waiting for the pain to stop.

The pub was basically as he remembered it, though it had been bloody long enough since he'd been allowed inside. Like all good stone district pubs, the whole thing had been carved out: bar, booths, and hearth, all of it giving off a musty coolness. There was about as much lime built up inside as out since it was one of the oldest places in the neighborhood, but you could still see the pride in it: boars, flowers, and whirlpools carved carefully into the stone by the masons who'd worshiped the ground Liana walked on.

Milerne motioned for him to sit at the bar, and he eased onto an old stool while she fixed the plates. It was probably just leavings from second meal, waiting to be carried to the corner altar, but it still smelled like heaven. And to her credit, she was keeping it good and fresh, pulling things from the cold chest where a thick clump of radishes was still burning on the artifel's brass dial, filling the box with icy air. He'd never once seen her cold chest run hot, almost like the woman had a sense for when to change the radish. It wasn't unlike his own knack, in a way, like she could *tell* when it was spent...

He thought to ponder that more, but when she finally put a plate in front of him — garlic mustard beans with a bit of oat bread — he could think of nothing else. She'd always been an honest one — despite the reception he usually got — but she certainly hadn't skimped on him with that fuller. He could tell at a glance the food was ninth acre, probably the best she had, and more than good enough for the kid — and the pretend Ladik, besides.

"Thank you kindly," he said, taking up his bowl and slurping down his meal as quickly as it would go. Milerne shook her head, sighing.

"You'd be surprised what you can get when you're actually willing to pay."

"Say what you want," he said, pausing to breathe, "but I think you're soft on me."

She actually laughed, moving to wipe down the other side of the counter.

"That's one word for it, you bloody fool." She stooped beneath the counter, returning with a bottle. It seemed to gleam in the darkness, the amber color of whiskey lighting his soul like the angel of the caves.

"I'm sure I'll regret it," she said, sliding it toward him, "but you've more than enough money for a bottle, however you came across that coin."

"I'll have you know I came about it honest," he said, frowning, though the cloud passed quickly with the whiskey in front of him. He reached for it, like a treasure, when she slapped his hand.

"You save some for Ladik," she said with a sharp look. "And don't leave him waiting either. If he's as hard up as you say, I doubt he'd like you in here gabbing away with me."

"Right," he said, suddenly remembering the kid. Still, if he hadn't been sure about helping the lad before, he certainly was now. The ring alone would pay for a hundred whiskey bottles, and that wasn't even the full reward! He scooped up the other meal, heading for the alley with the whiskey tucked under his arm.

"Leave the bowls," Milerne called after him. "And be gone before third!"

He raised the food above his head as a goodbye, letting the door slam behind him. But as he listened, he could just barely hear a laugh sneak past the wood. Maybe she really was soft on him… And with a little money in his pocket, maybe he'd be a catch actually worth keeping in the net. It hadn't done him much good so far in life, but a man could always dream, couldn't he?

6

25th of Sund-z'ar : Before 3rd Meal : 984, 22nd Year of Iron
15 days until the 163rd Voting

732 hurried down the stairs of the tower. She'd stopped in her room for her best cloak — the one that had seen the least fighting, anyway — along with the rest of her things. Assignments usually began immediately, and it wouldn't do to be unprepared. Unfortunately, she hadn't had time to distill her new bag of dandelion fluff, but she'd grabbed one of her vials, adding it to the rest of her waist kit.

As she reached the throne room, she finally slowed, the guards outside letting her in with little more than a glance. Usually, they were prickly, jealously guarding their post. What was this assignment that they would be so prepared for her arrival? She'd been in the High Priest's throne room before for one ceremony or another, but she'd never been summoned by him personally. As she passed through the giant doors, though, the place felt transformed, with nothing standing between her and the immense presence of Keroes nir Sen'l.

He sat completely still as he waited for her, smiling as he looked on in full regalia. His dark robes poured off of him like water, becoming one with the brilliant blue tiles on the floor as they snaked toward the north, connecting him to Sen'el'seng and the opposing throne of the king. The throne itself was even carved in remembrance of the river, its back like roiling currents as it lifted behind him, the arms adorned with giant offering cups cast from each of the six metals.

"A good reminder, isn't it?" he asked, waving for her to kneel, his full-finger rings glittering with the gems of the six houses. "When I first ascended to my office, I was loath to enter this place, worried it didn't suit me. But this place…educates, like your mask, reminding us of who we are, of the purpose we serve."

She nodded, placing her sword before her on the floor as she knelt, sitting on her heels.

"732," he said, sizing her up, "a most sacred number — and a blessing in itself that we've seen your spirit twice. I'm told your vessel is one of the best we have, too. Trustworthy and…obedient."

She said nothing, watching his eyes, though they never changed, their deep black wells simply reflecting back the candlelight from the altars.

"Do you remember the war, Lord Curan?" he asked her, tenting his fingers.

Images appeared in her mind unbidden: giant fireballs in the sky, mixing with the stars; Viden holding her, dragging her away at the end; so many fewer returning than had gone.

"I do," she said quietly, her voice still deafening in the silent room.

"Good," he said, his gaze sliding above her head toward the north. "Many in this basin seem eager to forget." He gestured to the blue tiles beneath his feet, the river itself reborn in stone. "But we *are* the river, Lord Curan, and there may be a time when we must choose — between the sacred ways of our fathers and the profane dreams of men. Men who would march across the stone as if it were nothing, who would divert the blessed waters for themselves."

He no doubt meant the Iron King. Everyone in the tower knew of the king's water wagons, his experiments at the Hollow Well. Even as he'd used them to win against Deyn all those years ago, it seemed he wanted more. But what the king did was his own business. It was not her right to question, even if it *was* Keroes nir Sen'l's. Still, Viden had often warned her of moments like these. There was no snake in the Mother's Valley who didn't bite without a warning. So, she bowed, touching the floor with her forehead. She would be loyal, useful, even, if she could.

"Good," he said as she lifted her head, "I thought you might understand. The task I'm about to give you may be the most important of your return. The ancient ones gave us an incredible gift, and your work may well preserve it."

He picked up a bell and rang it. Another priest came through a door beside the throne, placing a scroll beside her before he disappeared. She left it where it was, keeping her eyes on Keroes nir Sen'l.

"A new spirit has joined us," he said, "and they have proven… difficult to apprehend. The gods told us of their arrival, of course, but when we went to receive them, there was an incident, a terrible explosion we are still investigating."

She felt her spine stiffen, her chest suddenly tight with fear. A deeper memory, deeper than the war, tried to resurface, but she squashed it, squeezing the air from it until it slumbered again. There was nothing for her in those memories; she knew why she served.

"Perhaps it is an especially volatile vessel, or — even worse — someone would like to see it escape our care, to use its power for themselves."

She sucked in a breath, no longer able to keep her silence completely.

"So you are as promised," the High Priest said, nodding. "I'm glad you understand. In our indulgence, we have lost balance, invited chaos into our world. But if vessels ever roam free again, it will be far worse than the war, it may be death upon us all. But however the boy escaped, this is an *extremely* important spirit, perhaps the most important since the Age of Disbelief."

The thought chilled her. Her teachers had filled her with history, but no time had received more attention than the Age of Disbelief. To think the 800s could have been so violent, could have spun so far out of control without Salin nir Cosk…

The High Priest gestured for her to take the scroll.

"In your instructions, you will find a description of the vessel, a boy. Report immediately to my chief of staff, 151, at the Seron Inn in the Föhr Middle Field. Beyond him, speak of this to no one but me. This is a grave task, Lord Curan, but I believe you may be the best we have to face it. I wish you luck."

She stood, holding her sword so tightly she thought the edge of the scabbard might draw blood.

"You have my word, Keroes nir Sen'l," she said, meeting his eyes one last time. "I will find the boy."

7

Teros stayed behind the crates, his eyes clamped shut. He tried to listen for noises from the street to make sure no one found him, but it was nearly impossible over the voices in his head. He could still hear Mother's scream, and he tried to bury it, covering it with the soothing coo of her good voice. *My boy,* she repeated, *my precious boy.* Slowly, her good face came back, hovering over him. *My treasure,* she whispered, warming him despite the chill of the alley. *My precious boy.*

He opened his eyes, the sound of footsteps returning from the pub. He blinked, rubbing his face as the older man reappeared, a bowl in one hand and a dark glass bottle in the other. The food smelled good, his stomach rumbling loudly again.

"You're in luck," the man — Borash? — said, offering him the bowl. "Milerne — the landlady, that is — set you up good and proper."

Teros took the bowl in his hands, staring at it like Uncle Elin had taught him. He began to hear the whispers from the food, and somehow, miraculously, they quieted the other voices in his head. He didn't know what they were saying, but they were soothing, and when he was done listening, he knew the food was good, ninth acre at least. It wasn't especially powerful, but it would be enough if he needed his magic.

"Well?" Borash asked, breaking through the whispers in his mind. "You gonna eat it or what? I paid good money for that food, and I ain't having this bloody duke accuse me of starving you for a profit."

"Sorry," Teros said, taking up the spoon and starting on the beans. "I was just seeing what acre it was."

Borash had been halfway seated against the other wall of the alley, the bottle in his hand, when he stopped, staring.

"Who taught you to do that?" he asked.

"My Uncle Elin," Teros said.

"Elin..." Borash muttered. "Odd, that."

Teros watched him for a while longer, but Borash only shook his head, waving for Teros to keep eating. He uncorked the bottle, and the sharp smell of alcohol filled the alley. It reminded him of Mother and the nights she and Uncle Elin spent dancing. He'd loved those nights, his bed cozy and warm, Mother sneaking in late to plant a kiss on his forehead before tucking him in again so he would fall right back asleep. She'd smelled like that, but better, like she'd had flowers mixed with the alcohol. Borash smelled...different.

He ate quickly, the food disappearing until he thought he might burst. Still, he ate as much as he could, his chest tingling with warmth as the food aligned with his body. Finally, the bells began to ring, filling the city with sound from somewhere far away. That would be third meal then, the other bells vaguely registering in his memory from when he'd been crying. This food was clearly from second meal, though, which meant Passion, combustion... An image entered his mind again, the fire exploding around him, Mother's body, him forced to—

Borash pushed himself to his feet, wiping his hands together.

"Well, come on, then," he said, stepping over to take the empty bowl. "There'll be crowds out for third, make it easier for us to cross the bridge."

Teros looked up, a knot forming in his stomach. He remembered a bridge from the night before, but hadn't he run over it to escape? If they went back, toward the fire, toward those men...

"Don't worry," Borash said, putting the bowl down on the crates and draining the last of his whiskey. "I'm sure you have your own problems with the rich folk, but we're just crossing into Middle Field. I got a friend over at the Cobalt Lock who should be able to help us with a wagon."

Teros nodded, putting what was left of the oat bread in his pouch before pushing himself to his feet.

"Will we be able to find an altar for the offering?" he asked.

"Never mind that," Borash said, waving for Teros to follow him from the alley. "The gods don't want from those without. Just keep up, and don't run off, either. You get yourself lost, I'm not coming to find you."

———

Borash stopped at the end of the alley, pulling his cane from its hiding place before moving onto the street, the third meal crowds surging around them. He turned around a few times to look for the kid, but he was always right behind him. At least he was obedient for a bloody rich boy… Still, he looked out of place all the same, his robes still too nice despite their tears and his eyes darting around like some outlander.

They made it up Thelk Street and were almost across the square when Borash finally realized the kid was gone. He stopped, grumbling as a tinker nearly ran into him with his sled. Still, it only took a moment to spot the boy, his purple robes obvious even in a crowd. He was standing at the edge of the well, staring into the water as he leaned against the stone wall. Squeezing his temples, Borash walked back and was about to yank the kid by the collar when he spoke in that tiny voice of his.

"Is this from the river?" Teros asked, reaching out to touch the water with a delicate finger. A washwoman gave them a dirty look, but she was dipping her basket in the damn well, so he gave her a dirtier one back, and she decided to mind her own business.

"What kind of question is that?" Borash asked, easing onto the rock to rest his leg. "Of course, it's from the river, doesn't bloody sprout from the stones."

Bloody rich kids. His parents probably burned a pound of grapes a day in their artifels, pumping water through their whole mansion as if it hadn't sprung from the Holy Mother's bloody teat. Hell, they probably washed their skivvies in it straight from the spigot — or their servants did, anyway.

"It's beautiful," the kid said, still looking at the water. "Reminds me of the farm."

Borash frowned, looking at him again.

"Where you bloody from, kid?" he asked.

Teros shrugged, looking back at Borash.

"Here, I guess. Mother said we used to live with Grandmama, but I don't remember 'cause I was only four. Until a month ago, we were living with Uncle Elin."

That name… Borash racked his brain, trying to figure out where he knew it from. Not that he could make sense of the farm bit. It was nothing but bloody stone and moss in the barrens, and farmers were even worse off than the blind men tending to the bats if you asked him. Unless he was from a bloody Duke's pond…

"Elin," he said again, the name sounding odd on his tongue. "Wait, do you mean the bloody Duke of Remembrance, Elin Dek'rc? He's your bleedin' uncle?"

He looked up sharply, realizing how loud he'd spoken. A merchant passing by gave him a look, but thankfully, he kept moving. Borash turned back, the kid nodding.

"I guess so," he said. "Mother said to call him Uncle, but I don't think he was her brother."

"Bloody death in the dark," he said to himself, shaking his head. "I've really rolled in the river this time."

He pushed himself up with his cane, beckoning for the kid to follow.

"Come on," he said. "One of those bastards is bound to be looking for you, and I don't intend to still be on the street when they do."

They turned up by the moss commons, the rows of worthless crops dotted with the poor taking their break for third meal. They made decent time through the warehouse district, though the kid did a fair bit of pointing and asking questions. It wasn't until they passed the bazaar that the kid started to drift away again, though a good yank on his collar set him straight. They could've gone that way, of course, but he wasn't about to risk his bloody meal ticket on the cutpurses in the bazaar, and the road to Maegin's was twice as long through the Guild Rows besides.

At any rate, his leg held up for once, and before long, they were passing the buffer park into the Spill. It was a shame how fancy it was getting. The stores were nicer, sure, but they were crowded enough west of the canal without a bunch of Middle Field lordlings colonizing the district. Besides, Ladik was right, there were guards everywhere — off-duty blue coats by the looks of them — and more than a few followed him with their eyes. But he kept his head down, and they didn't attract any trouble, his cane clicking against the stone until the bridge appeared ahead. He hardly ever thought about crossing the bridge into Middle Field — certainly hadn't the night before when he was drunk as a bargeman — but this time, it made his stomach knot.

The restaurants and shops hiding them moments before gave way to empty space, the pavers widening as they reached the foot of the bridge. The bridge arced high over the canal, and there were opposing guard houses on either corner, twenty feet high and made of stone. The uniforms of the actual bloody blue coats were visible, their pikes gleaming in the sun as they watched the traffic crossing. At least they weren't swords… Borash slowed for a moment, letting the kid catch up as he took him by the shoulder, forcing him to walk opposite the guard house.

"Don't say a bloody thing while we cross," he said.

The kid nodded, so he kept walking, turning the brass handle of his cane outward so he'd look at least a bit more respectable. Most of the guards were inside, their shadows moving behind the glass of the guard house. The one posted outside stood to the side, looking blessedly bored as he glanced at each passerby.

Borash tried to look straight ahead as they passed the guard, sticking to the middle of the bridge. For a moment, it almost seemed like they were going to make it. The man's eyes slid over them, but just before they were past him, Borash saw the man's head turn in his periphery. Borash tried to hurry, pushing the kid forward by the shoulder as he hobbled on his cane, but the damage was done. He heard the man's steps hurrying away, the door to the guard house opening.

"Bloody bats, I think he saw us," Borash said, his head turning in spite of himself. They were past the halfway point of the bridge, so he couldn't see inside the guard house, but the man had left the door open in his haste. "We need to hurry."

Teros looked at his cane but only nodded.

"Good, lad, good," Borash said, doubling his pace — or trying to, anyway. It'd been a decade since he'd run anywhere, so a quick walk would have to do, but at least his leg was holding. For a moment, he thought of sending the kid off to hide somewhere, but what would be the point of that? Either he'd lose the bloody reward, or the blue coats would torture the kid's location out of him. No, as Paps used to say, the only way out was out.

Soon, they were off the bridge, passing the canal park on the other side. The park had a path through the grass, but there was nowhere to hide, the bloody weeds from Pen'dil Seln no higher than his waist. No wonder the damned rich folks liked to grow it so much, made it easier to track the poor sneaking over from the Spill. Instead, they hurried to the corner, turning left on Trison Street, passing a block of apartment buildings with the merchant school on their right. He bloody hated Trison Street, but for once, his memories of the school had no hold on him. Instead, he studied the apartments, looking for a gap in the walls where they might find a hiding place.

"In there," Borash said, pointing as he finally spotted a deep-looking alley. They started toward it, but just then, a wave of blue coats came around the corner, waving at them and shouting.

"Bloody gods," Borash swore, yanking the kid toward the alley. His legs kept working, thank the Sacred Mother, but just like when he'd finally lost his business all those years ago, he knew deep down that it was over.

They hurried into the alley, but unlike the one he lived in, there was nowhere to hide. Clotheslines spread overhead, but the walls were smooth and the walkways empty.

"Don't these damned people have any bloody crates to store?" he asked no one.

"Oy!" came a voice from the mouth of the alley.

Borash sucked in a deep breath, forcing a smile onto his face.

"Yes, officer?" he asked, turning around. There were a half-dozen of the murder-loving bastards, flanking an older guard with a grey beard and gold epaulets on his shoulders — a captain, maybe?

"So you got bloody ears, eh?" the captain asked. Unlike his men, he had a sword, the hilt covered in scrollwork. "We been yellin' at ya for half a block. Don't you know it's a crime to disobey the Duke's Guard?"

"My apologies," Borash said, bowing low. It took a good deal of effort not to wheeze with his heart pounding, but he kept his voice steady. "I didn't hear ye, I swear it. My nephew and I are just in a hurry, is all."

"In a hurry to an empty alley?" the captain asked.

He was only a few feet away now, the rest of his men blocking the exit in a prickly-looking crescent shape. Behind him, Borash could see the towers of the Merchant School rising into the sky, their roofs shaped like the peak of Sen'el'tul in the distance. He felt like a student again, the headmaster stripping him down for one thing or another. He'd never stopped being that bloody boy, really, bowing and scraping to every damned bully he came across. Still, he smiled.

"I admit," he said, "it does look a bit funny." He pointed to the Merchant School. "You see, I attended the school back in the Second Copper. My nephew wants to attend as well, and I thought I'd show him the old dormitory. Can't seem to find the entrance, though, it—"

The captain put up a hand, chuckling, though the sound was dry, sinister even, his skin crawling at the sound.

"Save it," he said. "The way I see it, you're a sodding bum despite your," he waved his hand back and forth, "fancy words. But this kid ain't your nephew, and he looks an awful lot like the wanted poster I been given. Awful big reward, too, though I don't know how you got your dirty hands on him."

Borash's temples began to pound, his mind racing. He glanced at the kid, his own face frozen in terror. He almost gave him up right then and there, but as the kid's eyes met his own, that cursed memory flashed in his mind again, of that other child, scared and hiding. And suddenly, he knew he couldn't do it. No matter what it cost him, he couldn't bloody do it. He looked back at the guard.

"Well, maybe not my nephew, exactly," he said, reaching carefully into his belt pouch, "but there's no reason for any trouble. I'm sure we can work something out."

He pulled out the kid's ring, the gemstones glittering in the hazy sunlight.

"You think we can be bought, eh?" the man asked, his thin veneer of humor disappearing.

"No, no," Borash said hurriedly, "just something for your trouble."

The man sighed.

"Well, the kid's worth ten times your little trinket there, and turning him in ain't no bloody bribe. It's our due for serving the king."

As their eyes met, time seemed to slow down and speed up at the same time. Borash felt his stomach twist with fear, but he felt a fire growing, too.

"Take the boy," the guard said, waving for his men to step up. "And kill the old man. Drop him in the Stones when you're done."

The group split into two without needing to be told, half toward the kid and half toward him. The kid tugged on his sleeve, tears flowing as he started to mutter again, his tiny voice echoing in his mind, pulling up those other cries, that other face. He was watching those men, but his mind was somewhere else. Something finally boiled up inside him, rushing into his head, making him feel lighter. A wind seemed to lap at his back, the gusts so strong he thought he might just float away. For a moment, the guards hesitated, looking scared. Could they feel the wind, too? Still, he could barely grab hold of the thought, a strange haze filling his mind.

"Go on, lads," their leader urged them, pulling his sword free.

"Grab the bloody child."

The men moved toward them, step by step, the captain forcing his way to the front, his sword gleaming in his hand. He raised his hand to swing it, to end Borash's pathetic little life, but in that moment, the fire boiling up inside him hit its peak. He could take no more — *would* take no more.

"No!" he roared, putting up his hands. In a fraction of a second, not even the span of a breath, reality came apart. Fire leapt from his hands, the air shimmering as the light blinded him. It was the most fire he'd ever seen, like a warehouse going up in flames, filling the alley, blocking the sun. But then, just as quickly, it was gone, and the alley was empty save for seven charred corpses, their bodies reduced to smoking bones.

Borash staggered, a searing pain tearing through his head. He blinked, but his eyes wouldn't cooperate. He looked to the side, reaching for the kid — begging the gods spared him that awful heat — but he was nowhere to be found. The kid…he… He felt himself falling, though it felt more like floating, the wind behind him growing stronger, cradling him. He fell, into forever, and all was darkness.

8

25th of Sund-z'ar : After 3rd Meal : 984, 22nd Year of Iron
15 days until the 163rd Voting

732 moved quickly through the Wist Ristare, those still on the street giving her a wide berth. Even as she tried to walk, though, she kept rolling her right shoulder. It was a bad habit, and certainly not one befitting of an emissary of the throne. And yet, even when she managed to stop, she couldn't help but grind her teeth. The words from the High Priest's scroll kept circling through her mind, tying her chest in knots.

A child, low-level noble in the Zi'yun line. 8 years old, dark hair shaved on the sides. Volatile, destroyed a building in Little Baronet to avoid apprehension. Last seen at the house in question on Deris Street, south of Orit. Believed to have fled through the alley.

She turned left toward the Children's Temple. 151 would be waiting for her at an inn in Middle Field, but she wanted to stop by Little Baronet to see the damage first. Perhaps it wasn't necessary, but it felt like something was pulling her there, like a cave fish on the line, summoning her in the darkness. She *had* to see it, had to know what she was up against, and then she had to stop it.

She blinked back tears, remembering the day she ascended, the wind and fire she'd thrown at Viden, almost killing him. He'd taken her in his arms, shushing her. She could still hear his voice that day, its sweet cooing, a sound she tried to replicate in the darkness on the hard nights when sleep was hard to find.

"It's alright," he'd whispered, holding her close, the porcelain of his mask cool against her face, his blood wet against her clothes. "Just be glad it ain't yer family, child. But I'm here, and I'll be your family now."

She shook her head. It had been so long since a new vessel had come, and even longer since there'd been an incident while taking one into custody. They needed to save this child and free its spirit before something awful happened. She may serve the king, but *this* was her purpose, to protect the basin and guard the magic so life could continue here, so everything she loved could carry on.

As she sped along the outside of the park, a woman passed her, walking just as quickly in the other direction, towing a child by the hand. In her haste, she almost didn't register them, but something about the child broke through her thoughts. She spun on instinct, burning the potato wedge in her stomach as she flared Permanence, locking their feet to the stone. The woman cried out, spinning her head around.

"Sacred One," she said, her eyes wide. "Please, we didn't—"

732 didn't hear her, her eyes on the child who was still facing the other way, struggling to uproot his feet from the ground. She held all six magics in her mind, watching him for any ripple of power. Still, it had been ages since a fight between Masked Ones, and even longer since Viden had trained her in dueling. Would she know the ripple for what it was? Children often drew magic with the body and not the mind, giving little warning of what was coming. She drew Identity, a ripple of wind wrapping around them, at least providing something to protect any passersby.

In a moment, she was in front of the child, one hand on her sword as she grabbed the child by the chin. She froze. It was a girl, no older than five. Her hair was shaved on the sides, true, but this was not the vessel. The girl's eyes filled with fear, her chin shaking in 732's hand. Her mouth tried to open but no words came out. She let go as if burned, the girl's face an ugly reminder of things she'd rather forget.

"I'm sorry," she said to the mother before continuing on her way, releasing the magic with the wave of a hand. Behind her, the little girl began to wail, but she would be fine, wouldn't she? Better to be frightened than chosen by the gods. That little girl would still have a mother, a life. Still, as she moved toward Little Baronet, the tops of the mansions rising ahead, she couldn't help but feel the dozens of eyes following her. And even as she kept her eyes straight, her stomach churned, filling with bile from far more than the potato.

Finally calmer, she reached the Seron Inn, the two-story building like a plaything shoved between the mansions. She had stopped by the scene of the explosion, though it had told her little beyond the shivers it sent up her spine. Still, this child *was* powerful. The guards who'd let her into the building said the space had been a dining room, though there was little trace of that now. The stone had been blasted in all directions, and she suspected even the skeletons they'd removed would have been little more than ash.

To use that much Passion, though, the child would have had to pull energy from everything in the room: the hearth, the candles, even the heartbeats of those around him. And that should be nearly impossible for a vessel without training. She ground her teeth again, a dull ache climbing up her jaw. The High Priest had suspected the child had help, but if that help was more than human… She shuddered, pushing it from her mind. She had work to do, and filling her mind with nightmares would make it no easier.

She must have looked like a storm cloud coming up to the inn, though, because the man waiting for her by the patio — presumably the owner — began to bow the moment she turned the corner.

"Sacred One," he said, his forehead shining with sweat. "Thank you for honoring my inn with your work today. There aren't many inns in the city, of course, but we pride ourselves on being the most comfortable for you and yours, Your Holiness."

She nodded, and he turned quickly, gesturing for her to follow as he guided her around the side of the patio. There were a few guests finishing third meal, but the tables were emptying out as the waiters scurried about to clean them. Against the side of the alley was a door embossed in gold. When they reached it, the owner bowed again.

"A private entrance for you, Sacred One, ensuring you won't be disturbed. Is there anything I can get you? We've already served your associate, but if there's anything you'd like, I can have it sent up the dumbwaiter in just a moment."

"No," she said, "thank you."

"Of course," he said, his head still bowed as he backed away. "Simply ring the bell if you change your mind."

The door was heavy — solid gold, maybe? — and behind it was a wide stairway leading to a sun-filled room above the porch. As she turned the corner on the landing, she found 151 waiting for her. He was sitting at a table large enough for a platoon with a pile of food before him, his mask sitting by his plate.

"732," he said, nodding his head, "I've been expecting you. Would you like anything to eat?"

"No," she said, stopping in the middle of the room with her hands behind her back. There was a roaring fire opposite the windows, and it combined with the sun, baking the air like the royal greenhouses.

"Suit yourself," 151 said, taking up an enormous river crab claw and sucking the marrow from it. "I dare say it's our due for our service to the crown."

732 said nothing, though she looked around the table. There were more than a few things her body could no longer tolerate, though the High Priest's chief of staff seemed to have no such issues. Perhaps she ought to be jealous, but she felt only disgust as she looked upon this man's life. He still used magic for the rituals, same as the rest of them, so the Passing would come for him too, eventually. It wasn't a life she'd choose. As Viden always said, if death was coming, why choose the diaper over the knife?

For a moment, 151 almost seemed to have forgotten her, completely absorbed by his crab. But after a minute of cracking and sucking, he met her eyes and frowned, dropping the shell onto a pile of other bones.

"All business," he said, wiping his hands together as he stood. "I suppose I shouldn't be surprised — your reputation proceeds you."

He came around the table, though he didn't take up his mask, leaning over a map. She stepped up beside him, the western half of the city appearing before her with little red circles of wood arranged in several places.

"I trust the High Priest has given you the report?" he asked.

"Yes," she said, though she didn't mention stopping by the house to see the explosion.

"Well," he said, "this is where I've had tips from ducal guards." There was basically no rhyme or reason to them, the red dots scattered all over. She narrowed her eyes, looking at 151. "Precisely," he said, chuckling. "As you can tell, most of the tips were useless, the guards eager to get a reward. They know to only give the information to me, though, so I wouldn't worry about a leak. Besides, even though they know they're looking for a little rich boy, they don't know why."

He reached into his pocket, holding out a silk kerchief. There was a crest on it, though not one she recognized. He shook it at her, so she took it, placing it in her pocket.

"This is my personal crest. We should split up for now, but if you need anyone to answer your questions, just show them my sigil. I've covered most of the warehouses in the Föhr, so you may want to head north."

He went back around to his seat, reaching for a fried bat wing.

"Leave word for me here if you need me," he said. "I'll be in and out. But do use your flare gun if you get into a scrape. We can't talk about our mission, of course, but there's no reason for you to go without assistance if things get…complicated."

She nodded, turning to go. There seemed to be little chance of him leaving much, but at least she'd know where to find him. That would make it her mission alone, of course, though that was probably for the best, anyway.

"Oh, and 732?" he called as she reached the stairwell.

She turned, his eyes on hers despite the ding of the bell to his side, signaling another delivery from the dumbwaiter.

"If we fail, it's both our heads."

She nodded, heading back down the stairs and onto the street.

9

11th of Curis-gul: Before 1st Meal : 961, 14th Year of Copper
23 Years Ago

Borash stood on the edge of Mer'n Hill, looking out at the glowing lights of the Nord Ristare. The sun was just starting to rise over Sen'el'tul in the east, though the never-dimming lights of the inner city didn't seem ready to give up the fight. He looked back toward home, the brick box indistinguishable from the others in the predawn light. Still, Mems would be up by now, tending to the awful wound on Paps's side. Beyond the house, the windmills on the top of the hill were already spinning as if nothing had ever happened, the stones grinding grain for the Bake Helm caring little if one of their caretakers had been crushed in the gears a few days before.

He took a deep breath, setting off down the hill. He refused to move on like nothing had happened, like their family wasn't slowly running out of food. He would find a way to help, to find something to eat. Mems would be angry — always going on about his studies — but what if Paps didn't get better? He'd heard them arguing at night, and he knew there'd be no merchant school if they couldn't pay the dues.

"Twelve is old enough to work," Paps always said in the same serious voice, his voice gravelly with drink. But he was right. Eyri was five already, and he knew his parents had been saving up iron to have another child. They could always send one of his siblings to school, but if they didn't have enough to eat, they'd have a lot more to worry about than some silly school. He pulled his robes tighter around his chest, walking faster to beat the cold. It would be a long day away from home, but if he didn't come back with something, the cave witch could have him.

* * *

By the time he made it down the hill, the Nord Ristare was already thronged with people, most of them workers trying to find a restaurant paying for odd jobs. A few had men unloading crates for first meal, the workers frantically scurrying under their loads while the waiters — and cart drivers whose loads were being handled — watched on warily. Borash stood in one or two of the lines of men waiting to offload crates, but the drivers invariably waved him off when they saw how young he was.

Finally, walking past Queen's Square, he stopped. The bell for first meal would be ringing soon, and he had nothing to show for his efforts besides the ache in his stomach that had been brewing since he'd skipped fifth and sixth the night before. He sat on the curb, looking up at the golden statue of Seray nir Cosk. The queen's thick hair glowed in the morning light, and her eyes seemed to watch him, measure him. But she no doubt found him wanting, her smile suddenly more mocking than joyous.

Would he ever find a wife so beautiful? Would he find a wife at all? Once, he'd thought he would, Mems filling his head with dreams: merchant school, guild membership, the kind of home that would attract a beauty the same way Paps had done so many years ago. But now, the possibilities of life seemed to be closing in on him, reducing to nothing as his dreams drifted away.

And if his dreams were slipping away, what would happen to Eyri? His sister would no doubt be asking about him by now — amongst the million other questions she asked every day, the words spilling from her mouth like the sacred river itself. 'Borash, how do butterflies fly?' 'Borash, why don't tadpoles sing when frogs do?' He smiled despite himself, though it only made him wish he'd earned something to take home to her, to buy one of her favorite sweets from down the hill. But it made him worry too…

As often as he heard his parents argue, he heard them whispering about Eyri, too. Her strange fits, the days she had to spend in bed, unable to play. They tried to hide it, rushing him out of the house whenever she had a 'spell.' But she was…different, his sister. Everyone could tell, even if they didn't know why. And if his parents didn't have the money to protect her, who would?

"Won't find much work laying about," a voice said behind him, shaking him from his dream.

Borash turned, finding an old man watching him as he leaned on a fine-looking cane.

"Come on," he said, beckoning for Borash to follow. "If you sweep my patio, I'll see it's worth your while."

Borash hesitated for a moment, but the man didn't slow — his gait surprisingly strong for someone with a cane. He got up from the curb, hurrying to catch up. When he was finally walking beside him, the old man looked him up and down, smiling.

"Where you from, lad?" he asked.

"Mer'n Hill," Borash said.

The man looked in that direction, though the hill was barely visible past the rooftops of the square.

"Good place," he said, nodding. "Altitude makes a man honest — something my bloody waiter could apparently use a bit more of."

"You...own a restaurant?" Borash asked.

The man laughed.

"You could call it that," he said, gesturing with his cane.

Suddenly, Borash noticed the tiny restaurant in front of them. It was wedged between two much larger places, though it was still charming. It had yellow paint and ivy growing on trellises around the patio.

"It's a small place," the man said, "but I'm the only shop on the square with Pen'dil Seln lamb. Problem is, my fool nephew's my only waiter, and the bastard didn't show again."

He paused, pointing to a broom leaning against the edge of the patio.

"Well, get to work," he said, "and we'll see about your pay."

———

Borash put his head down, sweeping like Paps had taught him in the mills, working in straight lines and never letting the dust get the better of him. It was a wonder a restaurant like this could even get this messy, but it *was* open to the air, and the dry weather in Curis-gul didn't offer much to tamp down the dust. Also, looking at the state of things, maybe that waiter was out more often than not...

He worked until the bells rang, and then he worked some more, carefully staying out of the way of the patrons who piled in for first. Eventually, his head down to scoop up another pile, he felt a hand on his shoulder.

"You did good, lad," the old man said, unsmiling but clearly satisfied. "Let's get you paid."

He led Borash through the indoor dining room — reserved only for the coldest days of the turning — and into a large stone enclosure full of meat hanging from hooks. The floor was lined with artifels, the dials flashing blue as they kept the room startlingly cold, a heap of raspberries running them in the corner. He couldn't help but stare at it all. He'd never been in a restaurant before save for the pub on Mer'n Hill, and they only went there on holidays besides.

"Do you do your own butchering?" he asked the old man, hobbling ahead on his cane.

"Have to," the old man replied without turning around. "Nobody in this damn city knows how to do mutton proper."

Perhaps the man was from Pen'dil Seln, then… He'd never met a foreigner before — wouldn't even know what to look for — but Paps said everyone who moved to the city never left, so maybe the man wouldn't have an accent anymore, old as he was.

Beyond the butchery was the kitchen itself, the massive room done up in brick with three huge ovens built into the left-hand wall. There was another man in the room, middle-aged, who was sweating profusely as he pulled racks of lamb from the fire, cursing all the while. This man, on the other hand, had a thick accent and was speaking what must be Senal.

"*Piles courush tali nerift,*" he muttered to himself, shaking his head as he laid the lamb down on a long stone table behind him.

"My cousin," the old man said, "our chef." He took Borash by the shoulder, urging him to sit on a stool at the corner of the table. The chef eyed him for a moment but only nodded, turning back to his meat as he began hacking at it with a cleaver. The old man went to a counter beside the oven where he fussed with something.

"*Septo crona veri nel,*" the chef said to the old man. He was holding a pepper, which he looked like he might want to murder had the thing been alive.

"Speak Zenil, cousin," the old man said without turning around, "we have a guest."

"These peppers are shit," the chef said, laughing. "Clear enough for you?"

"Clear and colorful," the old man said. He finally turned around, a large plate of food in his hand. It was the first meal selection from the patio but heaped high, potatoes and lamb shank with roasted beets and a thick wedge of bread. He set it down in front of Borash with a flourish.

"Your payment," he said, leaning back against the counter beside the oven.

Borash looked down at the food, his stomach twisting with hunger. He forced himself to swallow, looking up at the older man.

"No…uh, money?" he asked.

"Afraid not," the older man said, giving Borash a sad smile. "Got a business to run, and a bit of sweeping certainly ain't worth coin."

He turned, reaching into a cabinet by the ovens where he pulled out a half-dozen more uncooked potatoes.

"But I'm sure you got family," he said, placing the potatoes in front of Borash. "Might as well help where you can."

Borash looked at the potatoes, nodding slowly. He glanced at the chef, who was still quietly cursing his peppers.

"What if I cleared the plates from first?" he asked. "I could probably find some better peppers in the market, too."

The old man laughed, shaking his head.

"It'd take a hell of a merchant to find decent peppers in this *keristal*," he said. His cousin looked up, laughing at whatever that word was in Senal. The old man locked eyes with Borash, the same sad smile returning to his face.

"Look, kid," he said, "I get it. You seem down on your luck. Back in Seln, I was poorer than poor, almost ate my cousin here once. But this world runs on coin, and if you want some, find yourself a trade. Go to the merchant school if you can scrape it, and when you're done, I'll let you sell me all the bloody peppers in the basin, alright? But for now, eat your fill and take what you can to your family. It's a good deal, and more than you're gonna get anywhere else."

Borash nodded, his cheeks hot with shame. A bit of sweeping really wasn't much, after all. And the food was a kindness, it… He looked at the plate, tilting his head as the look of it struck him. It looked strange, like the special jar Mems kept above the stove at home for emergencies, or the meals they had on birthdays. This was fifth acre at least, and a far deal nicer than anything he'd eaten in months.

"Thank you," he managed to get out, meeting the old man's eyes before he tucked in, grabbing the bread and dipping it into the morning stew. It was a kindness this man had done, but he was right about the rest, too. He needed a trade, a way out. He was sick of being hungry, of worrying about Eyri. Whatever it took, he'd find a way to change his life. And one day, when he was rich, he wouldn't have to sweep for a bit of food.

10

Teros knelt over Borash, the older man's breathing coming in ragged bursts. They were shaded by a tangle of laundry lines, but even when the sun did slip through, he didn't look good, his color gone. Teros looked over the edge of the roof, taking in the damage below, the burned husks of what used to be men. He grimaced, clamping his eyes shut, trying to push away the memory of Mother dying, the fire as he ran away.

I will keep you free, her voice said in his mind. *My boy, my precious boy.*

He nodded his head, returning to Borash. She was right, they needed to keep running. After that much magic, more guards would surely come. But how to wake him? Mother had sometimes felt sick after using the Principles — in a way that went beyond the Passing — but never like this. Perhaps this was Borash's first time, perhaps he hadn't known…

"Paps," Borash muttered, his eyes still closed. "Gotta… Before third… Eyri wants…"

"What was that?" Teros asked, leaning closer. Borash let out a ragged breath again, overpowering him with the smell of whiskey.

It had to be the whiskey, then… But what had Uncle Elin said about that? Uncle— The man's face was gone, the memories inaccessible. He could still see Mother's face, thank the gods, but the rest… He blinked, sitting down on the rooftop as the dizziness overtook him for a moment. He had used a great deal of wind to get them on the roof, flaring huge amounts of Identity. The magic lingered in his mind, clouding his thoughts with the Passing.

Keep you free, Mother's voice said again, urgent.

Yes, he had to hurry. He clawed open his belt pouch, taking out his book. The leather cover was worn, the pages dog-eared in many places, but what was he looking for? It was no use, his mind unable to think through what he was missing.

He closed the book, biting his lip. Suddenly, a strong breeze blew over the rooftop, flapping the laundry on the lines. He looked in the direction of the wind, toward the west. The false mountains of the stone district lifted up across the canal, and beyond that, endless fields of stone, stretching toward the horizon and the giant peak of Sen'el'yuln.

He remembered that mountain… He focused on it, his eyes locking with its snowy peaks. A memory bubbled up. Standing in fields of wheat, far from here, far from all this awfulness. The wind whipping through the fields, everything golden in the sunlight. His Uncle was there, his face finally coming back into focus. Uncle Elin.

"Feel the wind, lad," his Uncle said, his voice so familiar and yet so distant. "Lean into it, until you think you might fall."

Where was Mother? He remembered the house, its giant tiled roof only just visible above the wheat. It was the height of summer, the plants stretching far above his head, though Uncle Elin stood even taller. She had told him to hide his magic, hadn't she? But this was Uncle Elin…and he was smiling now, something he almost never did.

"Come on, lad," he said, warmth entering his voice for once. "I know you can do it."

Mother always looked so worried, the lines by her eyes growing deeper every season. But she was so beautiful still, so perfect. Still, she smiled the most when Uncle Elin smiled, her worries seeming lighter. She always sighed so much, especially when she thought Teros wasn't looking, when she got those letters from the city, brought to her by one of the blue-clad guards.

He had let the wind lift him, feeling his body entwine with it as he soared — if only for a moment, climbing into the sky until the house was visible below. He had seen Mother in the window then, the whites of her eyes wide and afraid, even from across the field. He'd lost the wind then, falling to the earth in a heap. But Uncle Elin had been clapping, picking him up and spinning him around. It felt good to be loved, to do something for Mother. She worried too much. She…
Another memory came to him: Mother waking him in the darkness, shushing him as he asked questions. Rushing toward a carriage, a

maid leading them through the fields by candlelight.

Teros put a hand to his chest, his heart beating much too quickly. How had he never realized? It was his fault they had to leave the farm, his fault they came to the city. His fault…that Mother died. But why? It was just Uncle Elin. Had someone else seen? Had someone told the priests? He started to breathe too quickly, clamping his eyes shut.

"No, no, no," he said to himself, tears welling up in his eyes. "Mother. I'm so sorry."

He pulled his knees to his chest, rocking himself against the stone of the rooftop. His teeth were clenched together, his lungs refusing to gather air. His memories were free now, the Identity burned away, and the dark thoughts came freely to his mind, surging like a flood. *Fire, blood, death, burning, bodies, death. Mother.* But then…her voice.

My precious boy, she said. *My treasure.* Yes, he had to think of her voice, remember her good face.

His lungs relaxed just a fraction, allowing him to suck in a deeper breath. He opened his eyes, the world still there albeit blurred by tears. He looked to his left where he saw Borash, still muttering in his sleep. He needed to wake him; they needed to be away.

He got on his hands and knees, crawling toward his book. When had he dropped it? Still, his memories intact again, the words on the page had meaning once more. He could hear Uncle Elin's voice in his mind, their late-night tutoring sessions guiding him through their lessons.

"Remember this diagram well, lad," Uncle Elin said. Teros turned to the page by memory. This one was in color, painted in the center of the book across two pages. Six overlapping triangles, wide in the middle and narrowing to points at the edges. The symbols of the Elders danced around the outside, and the insides were filled with foods, sources of power for the various magics.

"Peppers are great for fire," Uncle Elin said, "but not whiskey, never whiskey. Take it from me, lad, alcohol's power isn't worth the cost."

Teros glanced at Borash, the older man looking almost as gray as the stone he lay on. Teros crawled toward him. He hesitated for a moment before putting Borash's head in his lap. What if he didn't wake up? He would have another death on his hands. First Mother, and then this man, a man who was only trying to protect him, who was apparently as magic as he was.

Teros grabbed his canteen, gently tipping it into the older man's mouth. Borash coughed, thrashing about before spitting out the water, the precious liquid wetting his robes.

"Food will kill you, but it's the only thing that'll save you, too," Uncle Elin said in his mind.

Teros reached into his pouch again, pulling out the leftover oat bread from the tavern. He soaked it in water, as he remembered Mother doing for the farm dog when it was old after it had lost its teeth. The older man's beard was scratchy and greasy, but Teros took him by the chin anyway, placing the bread in his mouth before working his jaw. This time, the unconscious man swallowed, with none of the kicking from before. Immediately, his color looked better, and after a few more tense minutes, he opened his eyes.

"Kid?" Borash asked in a hoarse voice, his eyes half-opened.

As the clotheslines fluttered again in the breeze, the sun hit Borash's face, making him wince.

"What happened?" he asked. He seemed to realize he was still on Teros's lap and rolled onto his side, hacking drily. As the coughs subsided, he lifted his head, looking around the rooftop. "And where in the bloody caves are we?"

Teros merely pointed toward the edge of the roof in the direction of the palace, the mangled bodies.

Borash struggled to his feet, shuffling toward the edge. As soon as he looked below, however, he staggered, retching over the side. Finally, he turned toward Teros, strands of spittle stuck in his beard, his eyes red.

"So that fire…" he said, putting a hand to his forehead. "Was I?"

Teros nodded.

"No," Borash said, shaking his head. "That isn't… Why would I?"

Teros carefully stood, carrying the book toward him, the page still open to the diagram. Borash's eyes struggled to focus at first, but then he frowned.

"What is this?" he asked, his usual gruffness replaced by fear.

Teros pointed to the triangle of Passion, curly etchings of fire rising around the list of fuels.

"Garlic," Borash muttered, "mustard, nutmeg…"

"Whiskey," Teros said, pointing again. "It's why you're so sick."

Their eyes met, the older man's brows weighted with worry.

"So I…" he said, feebly pointing to his chest.

Teros nodded.

"My Uncle said everyone has a little, but some have a lot. Mother could make the water dance. But Uncle Elin said people in town pretend it isn't so."

The memory filled his mind, a good one, banishing his fear for a blessed moment. Mother at the pond on Uncle Elin's land, the morning light glinting off the sacred water. Mother smiling down at him, waving her hand as she made the water jump in growing rings, crystalline rainbows lifting above the mist. A good face, a good memory.

"Wouldn't that make me a demon, though?" Borash asked, looking down at his hands as if they might sprout claws. "You either wear a mask, or you come from the dark ones, not much in between. And those men…"

He looked in the direction of the alley, putting a hand to his mouth as he swallowed hard.

"I don't know what demons are," Teros said, trying to meet his eyes. "But I think there's ways to not be either. At least, that's what Uncle Elin said. And… I've done things I don't like, too. But sometimes, you have to keep yourself safe. You have to—"

"This the same Uncle from before?" Borash asked, cutting him off.

Teros nodded.

"We have to go then, kid," he said, groaning as he got to his feet. "More people than I thought are gonna be after you." He glanced toward the bodies again. "And a hell of a lot more after me."

Borash walked back to the edge of the rooftop, looking down at the alley below. He turned back, eyes wide.

"There's a crowd down there now, kid. We really gotta go."

He stopped, staring at Teros.

"How did we get up here?" he asked.

"The wind," Teros said, pointing to another triangle in the diagram.

"Not a dream either, then…" he muttered under his breath. He walked over, snapping the book shut in Teros's hand.

"We need to get you some new clothes," he said. Walking along the clothesline, he pulled things down at random, shoving them into Teros's hands.

"Put these on," he finally said. The garments were rough, mostly brown. Not rough like the rags Borash wore, but nothing like his purple kelo either. Still, he obeyed, slipping off his belt pouch before pulling the robes over his underclothes. Borash took a robe for himself but didn't put it on, simply draping it over his shoulder.

"Never leave fruit on the tree," he said.

Then, Borash snuck to the edge of the roof again, looking down.

"Dropped my bloody cane," he said, glancing at his leg. "Just gonna have to hope it holds out. Come on."

He waved for Teros to follow, setting off along the rooftop in the other direction.

"Do we need more wind?" Teros asked.

Borash waved him off, walking quickly along the stone.

"There!" he said finally, pointing. There was a catwalk between the buildings, an iron walkway spanning the gap in the rooftops with iron pipes underneath.

"Bloody bastards in school always took more baths than any lord," he said before leading the way over the alley below. Teros gulped, trying not to look down as they crossed. It was different to be up high without the wind beneath you. Still, it had to be better than more fighting, more dying. He stole a look below and saw the crowd was growing, their voices carrying, though no one seemed to notice them pass. And soon, they were gone, with nothing left behind but scorched bodies and a broken cane.

11

25th of Sund-z'ar : During 4th Meal : 984, 22nd Year of Iron
15 days until the 163rd Voting

Borash led the kid across the rooftops, snaking their way between the buildings. He probably ought to be thankful for the catwalks keeping them off the street, but the bloody things also gave him an awful case of vertigo, the mountains seeming to ripple in the sunlight, bending forward and pulling away. He shut his eyes, trying to ignore his stomach as he put one foot in front of the other. The bells had rung for fourth, and they had little hope of eating again until they reached Maegin.

Still, shutting his eyes was a mistake in its own right, those strange dreams bubbling back to him from when he'd gone under, the pitiful face in his memories clearer than ever.

"Hey, kid," he said, glancing over his shoulder. He'd been muttering to himself again over the first couple of rooftops, though he'd stopped now. "You ever have, um…strange things in your head?"

"All the time," Teros said quietly.

Right… Maybe that wasn't the right question to ask a bloody *sorn'l* who talked to himself.

"Sure," Borash said, "but I mean from…the magic?"

Was that what he was gonna bloody call what he'd done? If he really had done it… He kept hoping it was the kid rubbing off on him, but he'd seen *fire* come from his own hand. He grimaced, shaking his head. He'd heard plenty of stories about demons, but never how you became one. Maybe it was just like this, a wretched man with nothing left but the caves calling to him.

"Oh," Teros said, finally looking up, "I suppose you mean the

Passing?"

"The what?"

"The Passing," Teros said again. "Serat the Wise called it 'the bitter root,' and 'the death beneath the current of life.'"

Borash stopped, wiping his forehead as he looked down at the kid.

"Where you learn a thing like that? Sounds like poetry."

Teros patted his belt pouch where he'd stored that strange book of his.

"It's in the *Laws of Faith*," he said, shrugging.

"And you memorized all that?" Borash asked.

"Not all of it," the kid said, looking at his feet. "Uncle Elin always said I wouldn't grow without knowledge, but I did try. I guess—"

Borash cut him off.

"Don't mind all that," he said. "But speak clearly for me, lad, you're saying this magic'll kill me?"

Teros blinked, looking up at Borash like he was a damned moss bear.

"I...um... Yes, I suppose so," he said. "But not right away. It takes a long time. But that's what the Passing *is*."

He fumbled with his pouch, pulling out the book and opening it to that strange diagram again.

"See?" he said, pointing, though, of course, there was nothing to see but a bunch of gibberish. Still, as the kid outlined another triangle with his finger, Borash leaned in, trying to focus his eyes on the damned thing.

"This is the Prism of Passion," Teros said. He pointed to a symbol at the base of the triangle. "You summoned the fire by using the whiskey, but the burden of Passion is burning." He pointed to another symbol in the center of the triangle. "It'll fade soon, but you might feel angry for a while after you summon fire. I always do. Uncle Elin said you can harness Identity to reverse it, but you would need grain."

Grain? Prisms? Flames and burning? Borash shook his head. They'd burn *him* when they realized what he'd done. He gulped, wishing for a fresh drink. He could still see those men's faces as the fire reached for them. He hadn't known he would burn those men, *couldn't* have known what would happen when he lifted his hand. But he did remember feeling angry, so terribly angry. Those men were gonna kill him, weren't they? He'd been beaten, spit on, and lied to, but those men meant to do worse than that. He hadn't had a choice. They'd left him no choice.

He sucked in a breath, shaking his head. He could work his way out of this; he just had to stay positive. Like Paps always said, you don't leave a coin in the street just cause you're cryin'. Blasphemies aside — not that the gods had ever done anything for him before — if the kid was right and he could be something more than a demon, then maybe he could still use this to his advantage. After all, if the sodding Duke of Identity wanted this kid for his magic, maybe he'd have use for a man as well. And maybe he could do more than line his pockets, maybe he could get back a fraction of the self-respect the world had been so content to claw from his hands.

"*Do* you have any grain?" the kid asked, looking at him with concern.

"What? No, of course not," Borash said, blinking. "You ate up my last coin in the alley, and I don't go carrying around clumps of wheat like a bloody courtesan."

"Oh, sorry," Teros said, frowning as he put his book away. "I just thought it might help you feel better. My oat bread woke you up."

The kid looked like he'd been kicked, his eyes all swollen like he might bloody cry.

"No, lad," Borash said, awkwardly patting him on the shoulder, "it's nothing." He couldn't go getting on the kid's bad side and screwing up this deal. Besides, the lad *was* impressive, memorizing all that gibberish. Not to mention being magic himself…

"Just try not to mind me when I get angry," he continued. "Just like my Paps, I guess. Not to mention that…er…Passion stuff you mentioned. Really, you're a smart kid, I never could've memorized all that."

Teros looked up, a shy smile on his face.

"Thanks," he said.

"Now come on," Borash said, tilting his head toward the north. "We'd best get off these rooftops before someone sees us. But you can tell me more about that book of yours while we walk."

He moved on, the boy's tiny voice trailing behind him, full of things he barely understood. But it was better than silence, better than thinking about dead men or awful dreams, and for that, he was truly grateful.

———

After reaching the last rooftop in the row, they scurried down a stretch of pipes into Cobalt Park. The Dek'rc warehouse district stretched up before them, its imposing walls hiding an army of buildings belching smoke into the air. Still, through the haze, he could make out the plaza ahead where the Barge Lock was thrumming with people. Maegin was that way, and hopefully a way out of this mess with his hide intact.

They slipped into the crowd, the kid already blending in a lot better with his new clothes. Still, the lad looked about like an outlander, staring at the squat little houses in the Guild Rows and the tall walls of the wool mill. At least near the Barge Lock, even an outlander wouldn't look out of place... As they reached the square, he could already spot dozens of foreigners: Sohnmen with their staves, Selnmen covered in so much wool they looked like sheep. There was even a Yaneman, his voice rising above the crowds as he stood on a box telling his stories, his colorful braids twisting around him.

"And then," the Yaneman bellowed, "Meris found the key of riches, its handle glowing with all the colors of the ancients."

He shook his arms, his robes shining as they caught the light. Teros slowed, trying to watch, but Borash tugged him along.

"Never mind that," he said, trying to keep the lad from running into a pack of dockworkers. "Every story from Pen'dil Yane's the same: the gods care, the young ones win. It's all rubbish."

"You don't think the gods care?" Teros asked, looking up at him. "Mother always said the gods cared enough to give us the valley, they just wanted us to decide what to do with it."

"And a whole lot of good we're doing with that," Borash answered, frowning. He'd just killed a bunch of men with the gods' own magic, hadn't he? If the gods cared, they'd hardly do a thing like that. It was like a bad dream, like a bloody vision from the Giant Lands. He shook his head, pushing it from his mind. Those men were gone, and he needed a drink, nothing more.

"Now keep up," he said as he waved for the kid to follow, pushing back into the crowd.

They cut directly across the square toward Maegin's, taking them past the Lock, the giant crack in the ground covered in nets and straddled by cranes lifting supplies from the boats below. The crowds grew thick where workers were spilling onto the streets from the cavern steps, squinting in the sun as their eyes adjusted to the light. They carried thick bundles, most of it trash — unfit for the sacred river, but apparently just fine to burn in the forges already covering the square in smoke.

Borash glanced down at the river as they passed, a massive longboat from Pen'dil Sing filling the entire northern dock. Like everything from Sing, it was crowded beyond belief, another two dozen sailors moving about the deck. And at the edges were a handful of their strange magicians, perfect balls of fire in their hands as they tended to their torches. He'd always wondered how they did it, lighting the way through the darkness of the caverns, their secret pathways faster than any other basin's. But now, looking at that fire, he felt something… familiar, like the shimmering air was calling to him, like it—

He stopped, clamping his eyes shut from a sudden wave of vertigo, though that only made the kid bump into him, his stomach lurching as he tried to catch himself with his bad leg. He turned, glaring.

"Watch it," he snapped, "you could've knocked me in the damn river!"

Teros glanced at the cavern and back.

"But…the nets?" he asked, raising an eyebrow.

"That's beside the point," Borash said with a huff, turning back toward Maegin's. He pressed ahead, ignoring the strange fires below. Still, he couldn't help but look with longing at the sailors as they dropped their bundles, walking toward the Inten Wist with their foreign passes at the ready. He'd never drunk better than in the Intens, the places nearly drowning in exotic liquors from all over the valley — not to mention the generous sailors, their coin slipping out just a bit more freely than other men as they tried to forget how much they missed their families. And gods on the mount, could he use a drink right now…

He would have liked to keep grumbling to himself, of course, but it only took another minute to walk across the square. And as they entered the alley that led to Maegin's, he found himself smoothing his hair, his chest suddenly tight as his dirty fingers tried to make sense of the rat's nest on his head. Perhaps there was no point — he was no stranger to feeling unwelcome, after all — but these people knew him, and that always hurt worse. Restaurant owners always hurled the same anonymous curses, but these men knew his mother's name, knew the same folks he had back in the day, their barbs far more deadly in their specificity.

"Look sharp now, lad," he said to the kid, leaning over for a second to adjust his baggy robes from the clothesline. They'd desperately needed a way to blend in, of course, but did the kid still look the part? Maegin would probably only give him a moment to explain himself — albeit possibly at knife point — and the kid would have to look appealing enough to make them just a hair more interested than hostile. He leaned over, licking his hand to straighten the kid's hair, anything to—

"Borash?" a voice asked, startling him.

He turned, finding bloody Small Jerin, of all people, staring at him with wide eyes. He had a bolt of fine cloth in his arms, his merchant ring on his finger. Jerin was a good head taller than him now, but he'd always be Small Jerin, his face as youthful as it'd been when they were boys. Borash himself looked a little worse for wear after his years on the street, of course, but he was getting mighty fed up with everyone he used to know looking like they'd seen a cavern ghost when he appeared.

"Jerin," he said, nodding quickly. "Uh…good to see you mate, been a while."

"Yeah…" Jerin said, shaking his head. "You…aren't here to see Maegin, are ya? Pretty sure he still has a price on your head."

"Small misunderstanding," Borash said, waving his hand. "Though maybe you wouldn't mind breaking the news that I'm here? I…uh… got something interesting for him."

Jerin looked at the kid, raising an eyebrow.

"Oh, yeah?" he asked. "And who's this then?"

"I'm T—" Teros started.

"Tarik," Borash said quickly, jumping in. "My nephew. You remember my cousin Kieray, right? Moved off to Sing when we was lads?"

Jerin opened his mouth, looking doubtful, but Borash plowed ahead, the lie blooming like a flower in his mind.

"Yeah, well, she's done pretty well for herself — husband does some trade with the bloody Wheat Duke, of all people. But the boy here's a scholar — gonna study at one of the ponds — and she asked me to get him there in one piece. Sent some coin for his care, too, of course, and I figured Maegin might give us a ride for a good price."

Jerin frowned, looking between him and the kid.

"Maybe…" he finally said slowly. "Wait here."

He disappeared through the gate, closing it behind him.

"Why'd you tell him my name is Tarik?" the kid asked, looking up at him.

"Best not to tell people too much," Borash said. "People are looking for you, remember?"

"Oh…right," Teros said, looking at his feet. He began mumbling to himself again, but Borash ignored him, his palms starting to sweat as he waited.

Maybe it was a mistake to come here. But what else was he supposed to do? If he took the kid somewhere else, they'd either turn him in to the guards or try to get the money for themselves. At least this way, he could try to stick by the kid, see what he could get out of the whole situation — assuming the entire thing didn't blow up in his face.

There was a sound of grinding metal, and Jerin reappeared at the gate, a giant brute of a wagon guard at his side.

"Alright," Jerin said, "Maegin said he'll see you. But for your sake, none of the usual nonsense, alright?"

"Sure, sure," Borash said, nodding as he followed the men inside. Still, it was hard not to gulp as he was swallowed into the warehouse yard, a lifetime of mistakes suddenly towering over him. And somehow, he had the feeling he wouldn't escape in one piece when they fell.

12

25th of Sund-z'ar : After 4th Meal : 984, 22nd Year of Iron
15 days until the 163rd Voting

Teros followed Borash into the wagon yard, his friend, Small Jerin, holding the gate open for them. The large man who'd come out with him looked scary, like the guards at Uncle Pesrin's house — those awful men who'd been there the night when Mother… No, he couldn't think about that; he had to be strong. He balled up his fists, sucking in a deep breath.

As he passed Small Jerin, the man flashed him a smile. Maybe these people were different, nicer… At least he was still with Borash. For all his gruffness, Borash seemed like a good person. It was almost as if they had been meant to find each other. It wasn't surprising that Borash could use the Principles, exactly — Mother had seemed to think they all could in one way or another — but what were the chances of them finding each other when he needed help most? It had to be Mother watching out for him, knowing he'd need someone strong. After all, what had made him choose that alley to hide in, of all places? He looked toward Sen'el'seng, hoping he could somehow see the shimmer of Mother's soul. *Thank you,* he thought, pretending the sun was her shining face.

He fell in next to Borash as the other two men led the way. Borash gave him a sharp look, putting a finger to his lips. He nodded. He could keep a secret. He hadn't told anyone about Uncle Elin's lessons on the farm for all those months. He would prove to Borash he wasn't a baby, and then maybe he wouldn't be angry with him all the time. But still, he felt safer now knowing Mother had sent him, and feeling safe helped the bad faces drift away, making him feel as if he'd be able to keep his promise.

The wagon yard was busy like Uncle Pesrin's pond on harvest days. Men moved in every direction, crossing between the giant warehouses as they loaded things onto real wooden wagons: crops, jugs of wine, baskets of grass. The warehouses were dark, but he could still see piles of even more goods looming in the shadows. They turned the corner of the L-shaped yard, revealing a group of men sitting at a long table, large stacks of paper in front of them straining against their paperweights in the breeze.

Teros felt for the wind in his mind, feeling the traces of Identity it carried. Like Uncle Elin said, it was always good to know where the wind was, where you might find your freedom. But as soon as he looked at the man in the middle of the table, he forgot about the wind, freezing under the glare of those dark eyes. The man smiled when he saw Borash, but it wasn't a happy smile.

"Maegin," Borash said, bowing. He didn't seem like he did it often, grunting with his bad leg shoved out to the side.

"What is it this time?" Maegin asked, not even returning the bow with a nod. "I think your last scam was passing off some vinegar you stole, no?"

"Right, er…sorry about that," Borash said. "Like I told Small Jerin, though, I'm here for family."

He put his arm around Teros, nodding in his direction.

"We're just looking to book a fare on one of your wagons. Mother wants him at Irmun Pond by the end of the week."

"Irmun Pond," Maegin said flatly. "And you want me to believe you have real money to pay for this fare?" The man beside him at the table chuckled, twirling his mustache.

"Well, not on me — we spent the boy's coin on lodging. But the Grain Duke will pay it when we arrive."

Maegin sighed, squeezing his temples.

"Borash," he said shaking his head. "You know the only reason I ain't broken every bone in your body is out of respect for your father. But if you keep coming to me with this nonsense, I swear—"

"No, no," Borash said, putting his hands up. "I swear it to you, Maegin, look." Borash took Mother's ring from his belt pouch and held it out, the gems glittering in the light.

"We can't pay with this," Borash said, "it's too important to his Mems, but we can….er….use it as collateral."

Maegin looked at Teros, those cold eyes like ice, like a well of

Permanence rippling in the darkness. Teros looked back, feeling suddenly like he couldn't move.

"This true, boy?" Maegin asked, his face unmoving.

It wasn't, of course. But Teros wasn't a baby, either. Like Mother had said when they left the farm for Uncle Pesrin's: "Men only need to know a bit of the truth. Just let Mother speak and all will be well."

He could feel Mother now, watching over him, could hear her voice, whispering beyond the wind.

I will keep you free, she whispered in his mind.

She had brought him to Borash, and she would get him to safety.

"Yes," he said quietly, staring into Maegin's eyes.

"Hmm," Maegin grunted, running a hand over his beard. He looked to his left at the man with the mustache. "We have been trying to get Irmun on that bloody silver contract. Maybe doing him a favor would finally crack him."

"I suppose," the man said, shrugging.

"Alright, Borash," Maegin said, turning back to them. "We have a team going south in the morning. They got a full day of stops in the east end, but they'll finish at the Zi'yun guard post outside the city — which is as close as you'll bloody get to Irmun Pond without wings. It's a whole day's walk from there with that leg of yours, but if you can keep your hands off our goods for a night, you'll have your ride."

"Thank you, Maegin," Borash said, bowing again, "thank you."

Maegin cocked his head toward one of the warehouses, and Small Jerin ushered them away. They moved quickly out of the wagon yard, the other men resuming their work, but Teros could still feel Maegin's eyes, following him into the darkness.

———

They spent the next hour in a small room above the warehouse, the sun slowly slipping lower, cutting through the room with golden beams that lit the dust floating through the air. Teros tried to read his book by the window while Borash lay on the floor. The older man seemed to be good at doing nothing, but he didn't look happy either… He stared at the ceiling with his jaw clenched, his eyes barely even blinking. Every now and then he'd sigh, his chest deflating with the effort.

Finally, he rolled over with a groan, digging through his pockets until he removed a metal flask. He muttered to himself, "Bloody demons," the only thing Teros could make out as he took a sip, wincing.

"Ugh," he said, wiping his mouth with the back of his hand. "Tastes bloody awful."

"Is it whiskey?" Teros asked.

Borash looked up, blinking, a frown on his face.

"It… Why? Does it make a difference?"

Teros closed the book, folding his hands together. He didn't want Borash to get mad, of course, but…

"Well?" Borash asked, sitting up. "Out with it, then."

"Um, well, it's the Passing. It doesn't just make you dizzy; it'll make things taste bad. You'll be able to stomach it for a while longer, but like me, for instance, I can barely swallow wheat anymore."

Borash ran a hand over his face, staring down at his flask.

"Bloody gods, kid, I don't know what I regret more, drinking my life away or ruining the only damned thing I like." He looked out the window to the south in the direction of that alley. "Not to mention all these sodding things I can't stop seeing."

He shook his head, taking his flask and tilting it to his lips again with an even deeper grimace.

"I guess it ain't much worse than a hangover," he finally said, though there were deep lines around his eyes.

"It…gets worse," Teros said quietly.

Borash looked up, looking like he might want to cry.

"How much worse?"

"It'll take time, maybe a few months of burning whiskey, but if I eat wheat now, I'm sick for days," Teros said. "And if I want to use Identity, I have to burn something else."

"I think I'd better read that book of yours," Borash said, "maybe if I —"

There was a knock on the door just before it opened, Small Jerin sticking his head in.

"Hey, gents," he said, hefting a glass bottle in his hand. "Maegin said you're welcome to dinner, but I thought I'd come with a little something, too. Just for you."

He passed the bottle to Borash, who looked blankly at it in his hand.

"What's this for?"

"Well, Maegin seems mighty excited about the whole Duke thing — not that he'd let on, mind you. But I figured if I made your journey a bit more, uh…tolerable, give us a better chance of things working out."

"Thanks," Borash said quietly, looking up. "It's…uh…whiskey, though, or…?"

"Vodka, I'm afraid," Jerin said. "I remember what you like — unfortunately for me — but we only got the good stuff in browns. Nobody'll miss a bottle of the clear."

Borash nodded, relief on his face as he slipped the bottle next to his bedroll.

"Alright, then," he said. "Thank you, really."

Jerin nodded, waving for them to follow into the hall and back down the stairs.

"So," Borash said stiffly to Jerin's back, "I didn't know you were working with Maegin. Doing alright for yourself?"

Jerin shot him a look over his shoulder, a scary one like the kind Uncle Pesrin would give Mother when they tried to pretend they hadn't been arguing before dinner.

"Maegin wasn't my first choice," he said quietly, "but you didn't leave me a lot of options, did you?" Still, as he met Teros's eyes, he softened.

"I suppose it's alright, though," he continued, turning. "Got to keep my grain business with Maegin's loans, and I'm part of his guild now — or whatever you want to call it. I get a good freight rate so long as I give a discount to his men. He's after Irmun for the silver trade, though I wouldn't mind getting my own contract out of it if I can. I guess it's good you came along when you did."

They reached the bottom of the stairs, the hum of voices coming through the door to what must be the mess hall. As Jerin opened it, gesturing for them to go in, Borash stopped, turning to his friend.

"Listen, Jerin," he said, wringing his hands. "I…uh…about before…"

"Yeah?" Jerin asked, his eyebrows raised.

"It's…uh… Thank you."

Jerin grunted, weaving between the crowd of other men from the warehouses as they piled around a giant wooden table. Teros stood by the wall, eyeing the scrum of workers. There were just so *many*. Jerin returned with two large plates in his hand, tilting his chin toward an open spot.

"Come on then, lad," he said to Teros, dropping a plate down in front of him. "If you're shy around these bastards, you'll never eat."

Teros nodded, clambering over a tall bench that left his feet well off the floor. He glanced at the giant man seated next to him, a guard dressed in leathers — something rare enough in the city — with a beard reaching all the way to his plate. The man looked in his direction, chuckling as he passed him a large brown jug, nodding to an empty cup. It turned out to be cider — though he struggled to pour it — the amber liquid glowing in the candlelight. It was different from the wine he'd drank with Mother, but that was a good thing, something to keep his mind off his memories.

Finally somewhat settled, he took a deep breath, looking down at his plate. Surprisingly, the food was mixed with mid-acre crops, glowing with a shimmer that bent the air around it. It was fifth meal, but luckily there was no wheat, the plate piled instead with plump oats and a glistening peanut sauce. Only then did he realize how long it had been since he ate. He quickly took a large scoop with his spoon before stopping, the food just before his lips.

Was he meant to say his prayers? He always did with Mother, bowing their heads together as she recited the Odes, her voice beautiful as a bell. Even though they'd lived in so many places, had placed their offerings on so many altars, he'd never missed a single meal with her in his whole life. Today, without her, he hadn't prayed once, though he hadn't eaten since second either... In fact, the warehouse didn't even look like it *had* an altar. He shut his eyes, trying to hold back the tears.

I'm sorry, Mother, he thought, praying she could hear him. *When I get to the pond, I promise I'll pray every single day.*

He tried to picture her smiling, pushing away the bad face, imagining she was there with him. He held onto it for dear life, listening to her whisper in his mind.

My precious boy, she said. *My treasure. I will keep you free.*

He shoved the spoon into his mouth, the sweetness of the sauce rushing through him, sweeping away his worries. He opened his mouth to take more when he noticed Borash frowning at him. Borash opened his mouth, but a man called his name from the end of the table, saying something before everyone laughed.

Borash rolled his eyes but raised his glass, shouting out a toast. A few of the men looked at him funny, but then they all drank. Even Teros held the heavy cup in his hands, drinking down the bitter cider. And afterward, the men seemed to laugh more. They seemed to forget they had glared at Borash, that Maegin had been so mad at him. And then, it was easy to eat. Borash still looked worried, tipping his flask into his cup, but Teros shoveled the oats into his mouth, his hunger suddenly ravenous. Everything would be okay. Tomorrow, they would get on a real wagon, and they would ride to the south, to safety and the future Mother promised.

THE END OF PART ONE

A Respite

—:—

Serimh pressed his eye into the spyglass, straining to take in the details of the pillars from his window. The crack in the Pillar of Knowledge was definitely longer, wasn't it? But how much longer? A scientist shouldn't have to bloody guess. If only he could go down and take his measurements, but that would mean explaining to the guards what he was doing — and why he wasn't spending every minute of every day on their superiors' bidding.

He paused to listen as he heard footsteps passing outside his room. He was well-practiced by now at dashing back to his desk, but it also wouldn't do to waste energy if no one was coming. It was like being a hungry bird. They would fly away if a cat appeared, sure, but they never moved for squirrels. Why use your wings when you didn't have to?

Still, even he had to admit he wasn't going to get any useful measurements this way. He sighed, snapping the spyglass shut as he returned to his desk. He picked up a vial, eyeing it in the candlelight as he wrote down some measurements. Those bastards wanted serosine? He'd drown them in the stuff. It was no business of his if they killed every Zennan in the valley. What he wanted was so much bigger than that. War was a thing of generations, but metals, mountains — *chemistry* — were forever.

He looked over his shoulder once more before he reached to the side of his desk, lifting the false panel so he could access his diagram. He jotted down some additional measurements, adding some notes to the side. Why did kings always insist on being brutes and fools? In the serosine they only saw swords, but he saw a pattern. Beautiful, inexplicable, unfathomably complex — but a pattern all the same. Why was serosine a cobalt alloy? Why was pure cobalt neutralized by lithium when serosine wasn't? Why were the densities of the two so similar but their properties so different?

He had few answers, though the grid hidden in his desk still made him smile. Science was a dance, and questions like these — and the patterns they eventually created — were the truest joy in the world. It was in dancing with the universe that you found your true self, found the connections between yourself and the stars — no, the *gods*.

Everyone knew that no human could enter Sen'el'seng. But as far as he could tell, only he knew about the mountain's effect on magnets. At least among men that still lived... The Elders had hinted as much in their writings. But they also seemed to have left out as much as they included. Why? Could only he sense that they were keeping secrets? They'd passed along enough metallurgy to ensure Pen'dil Deyn thrived without leaving behind enough to escape the basin's clutches. When he finally discovered why, he was sure he'd find a way into the mountain and up to the realm of heaven. And more importantly, he'd find a way out of his current predicament, returning to the path the gods had set out for him.

Serimh added one last marking before snapping his desk closed again. Then, he took up the vial, holding it steady as he relit his burner. He was a man of truth, yes, but even truth required toil. He would make his swords, he would earn his bread, and then he would leave this world behind.

———

Pen'dil Yane - Time Unknown

—:—

Aitesi began again, walking in a circle around the giant Pillar, trying not to miss a single word of the *Ode to the Distant Star*. She twirled a finger through her braids — a bad habit she was supposed to have stopped — the blues, purples, and greens of mamin's old threads keeping her calm. Still, Entodal nol Serim — Wise Father though he may have been — was decidedly not a poet, and his words were probably the hardest to string together in the entire repertoire.

"It was only then, when I...saw her face and touched her essence that I knew how lost we were. Forsaken in the Giant Lands, children of...another god, unknowing and..."

She paused to look at her sheet, cursing under her breath.

"Uncaring of our heart's true desire!" she cried out, smacking her forehead. Why could she never remember that line? Bloody second stanza.

An old fish vendor rolled his cart around her, smiling as he passed. She smiled back, bowing her head. Of course, he probably thought she was a source of hope — another acolyte studying the ancient verses, hoping to spread the wisdom of Pen'dil Yane beyond the basin, blah, blah, blah. But if she couldn't pass the entrance exam, she'd never even become a bard's assistant, let alone a wind sage.

At least it was still early. The fishmonger was the first vendor at the square, the sun not yet above Sen'el'tul. That should give her another hour. Even if it was another hour of trying to force foolish old words into her brain, it was an hour that was hers alone, an hour she could be free of the backbreaking work in the spider silk weaver's.

She stopped her circling, sighing as she stepped closer to the Pillar of Self, gently resting her forehead against it. Even in the predawn light, the zinc seemed to shimmer where it cracked through the chalky white oxide on its surface. Why did the sages make you memorize the repertoire *before* teaching you to master the wind? The sages had the best memories in the world, and they said the magic helped them retain almost any piece of information. So why not just give her the magic and then see if she could memorize these damned stanzas?

She squeezed her eyes shut, taking in a deep breath. It wouldn't do to be sacrilegious in front of the Elders. Not to mention mamin... How long had her parents been dead? Four years? She'd spent so much of it studying it was getting hard to keep track. Or her memory really was going... Still, she wouldn't ever let mamin catch her not saying her prayers.

"Dear Elders," she whispered. "Please help me."

Then, she quieted her mind, and thankfully, the voices returned. She couldn't tell what they were saying, but they seemed to have a rhythm — the perfect rhythm to remember the poems. She smiled, starting again as she recited the Ode from the beginning. Somehow, she knew that this time, she wouldn't miss a word.

PART TWO

13

732 ground her teeth beneath her mask, forcing herself to write down the man's words — useless though they may be. She ought to be closer to finding the vessel by now, the attack in the alley only proving how dangerous the boy was. She'd gone back to the tower only briefly, conducting her debrief interview before returning here. The priests, at least, seemed to sense the urgency of her task. The man who usually handled her cases had been replaced by someone else, and he…had not been gentle. But she had nothing to be ashamed of, right? She was doing everything in her power.

"So, you also saw no one in the alley when you arrived?" she asked.

The guard met her eyes beneath the mask, immediately looking away, looking for his friends where they stood in a tense group by the door to the bridge. 151 was in the opposite corner, murmuring with the captain of the guard, his slimy voice the only other noise in the guard house.

"I…uh…no, Sacred One," he said. "It was empty when we arrived — save for the men who had…"

He grimaced, but she pressed on. She had seen the bodies, of course, but it was nothing to be squeamish about. She'd seen men immolated with Passion before, and they were all the same. These guards were missing the point entirely. The disturbing part was not the fire, but who had done the burning.

"And the older man they were chasing," she said, "describe him to me."

"Well," he said, "like the others said—"

"I don't want the others," she said. "I'm asking you. Describe him."

"Forgive me, Sacred One," he said, putting a thumb to his forehead. "He was a beggar. Older, in his thirties, maybe? He had a mangy beard. I only saw him for a moment, the guards on the bridge at the time came in and told us to look as they passed through. Said they noticed the kid with him."

"And you saw his face?" she asked.

He opened his mouth, perhaps about to object again, but he sucked in a breath.

"Yes," he said.

The vessel could have been involved with the fire, true, but the statements they took on the street had described the fire like the sun itself. And while the guards had retched at the sight of their fallen comrades, she had knelt down, inspecting what little remained of their lieutenant's cloak. The brass buttons had been completely melted, reforming into brittle disks where they had pooled against the cobblestones. It would have taken at least five chul'uns to do that, and even a volatile vessel shouldn't be that powerful... So, who was helping this child, and why had they taken off their mask?

It was a terrifying line of questioning. Even when the Passing made her bones ache and death loomed around every corner, she was thankful for her mask. They wielded the essence of the gods, the magic of the ancients, and to think of that power held out of bounds... Was it even a man? She knew well enough the stories of demons, of the myriad ghosts haunting the stone barrens. But which was worse? If it was human, they'd need food to make their power, and that meant access to the armory. She knew the others were corruptible, but if so much of the sacred food was on the streets, it would mean the cracks were already well within the foundation...

"Perhaps I'll just—" the guard began to say, breaking into her thoughts as he moved to join his fellows for first meal.

Without hesitating, she filled him with Permanence, rooting him to the spot as his eyes widened. It was standard practice to root anyone they had to interview, but she'd thought the guards worthy of some additional courtesy. Clearly, that had been wrong. The ducal guards never wanted to deal with the crown, true, but they should still know the difference between the sacred and the profane.

Even though the guard should have known — should have seen others similarly rooted by Masked Ones — he still tried to fight his bonds, squirming where he could. But unlike the woman on the street earlier, she had put the Permanence into his muscles and bones, burning two entire chul'uns into his lower half. Moving his own body would feel like fighting a boulder, like *becoming* one.

"We have not yet finished," she said gently, putting a hand on his shoulder to stop his struggling. "Please, describe the man from the bridge again, in as much detail as possible. Tell me if—"

"732," 151 said loudly from across the room. She turned, finding a new guard had joined him and the Captain, a scroll in his hand. She left the guard where he was, moving over to stand at attention.

"Sir," she said, not looking at the Captain, though he seemed to tense as she approached. Was it having to be near two Masked Ones, or was there something about 151 that made him more palatable despite his mask?

"We have a tip," 151 said, gesturing to the guard with the scroll. "Go ahead, soldier."

The guard cleared his throat, stepping forward and delicately offering the scroll to 732. She took it, stowing it away.

"Man came by, said he wanted to leave a tip," the guard said. "Heard there was a reward and left his address."

"Where?" 732 asked.

"Cobalt warehouse district," the man said.

She felt her stomach sink. It was one of the busiest places in the city, with plenty of the upscale wooden wagons that could get a man — and a child — across the city in a matter of hours, let alone the boats at the lock headed for every basin in the valley.

"Please investigate," 151 said, "I'll stay here in case another tip comes in."

She nodded, already heading for the door.

"Wait," the frozen guard called behind her, but she didn't look back. 151 could free him, assuming he still remembered how the Principles worked. And if this tip turned out to be false, she'd have more questions when she returned.

14

26th of Sund-z'ar : Before 2nd Meal : 984, 22nd Year of Iron
14 days until the 163rd Voting

Borash winced, another bump in the wagon sending a jolt of pain through his leg. They'd been riding in the blasted thing since sunrise, and the roads never seemed to get any smoother. Bloody king and his bloody roads — probably spent all the money on his damned water wagons. Not that the army cared about anything in their own basin. They probably couldn't even feel the cobblestones in those sodding clouds on wheels!

"Are you alright?" Teros asked, looking up from his book. Always reading, that one. They were both wedged between a bunch of crates, but the light from the back of the covered wagon was apparently good enough to see by.

"Fine," Borash muttered, squeezing his forehead. Not that the hangover helped. He drank more than normal the night before, afraid of dreams more than anything else. He'd dreamt all sorts of terrible things anyway, of course, even if the worst dreams — and one face in particular — hadn't come back. Still, he did feel somewhat better even with the little sleep he'd gotten. He felt off-kilter, true — those men's faces burned forever into his mind — but he *was* still himself. He hadn't woken up with claws, hadn't been pulled to the caverns in the night. So, he wasn't a demon, but if he was a man…

When he opened his eyes again, he tried to see what he could of the kid's book, even though it was upside down. If he was going to accept the magic — and a hell of an *if* that was — he ought to learn something about it before they reached the duke. But it only made him realize how much he didn't know… How many others had the Principles?

How many other tricks — like bloody Milerne's artifel — were really tied to it? And if it were true, then why all the talk of demons? Why the insistence that the only ones worth—

He clamped his eyes shut, shaking his head before that face came back. He could think about that later. For now, he had to learn something. If he wasn't useful by the time he reached the duke — or even worse, if the man stiffed him — he'd need this magic. To have a life again, to have something no one could take from him. He *needed* it, plain and simple.

He shifted, leaning forward a bit to try and see the book, but that only made his robes tug against his gut. The damned thing he'd stolen from that rooftop hardly fit. Not that the bloat from the whiskey helped any… Still, it only made Teros notice, the lad looking up.

"Do you want to see?" he asked.

"No, no," Borash said, waving a hand. "Don't even know what I'd do with a book that thick."

He looked back out the back of the wagon, letting out a sigh.

"Although…" he said, turning back. "Seeing as how I'm getting you safely to the pond, maybe you could answer a couple questions for me?"

"Sure," the kid said, closing the book and holding it to his chest. "Uncle Elin always said it was good to teach people things, that knowledge *needs* to be known."

Borash frowned. Imagine having the bloody Duke of Remembrance for your sodding uncle. Not that it made him want to learn any less. Maybe this was the edge those bastards had kept on him all along. Maybe this was the only thing separating who he was from who he'd been meant to be.

"How do I…do it on purpose?" he asked. "What I did with the fire." There, he'd said it. A thousand blasphemies in a single breath. But in spite of all the dreams, he wanted to know. Even when the world cracked in two, a man would find himself looking in the hole.

Teros looked at him for a moment before nodding, muttering to himself as he dug through his belt pouch. Finally, he pulled out his hand, revealing a long, flat stone about the length of his palm. It glittered in the sunlight and seemed to have dozens of hairline cracks crisscrossing its face.

"This is my practice stone," Teros said, smiling down at it. "This is how I learned Permanence — that's what you use on metal and stone. Since we already ate first meal, I think you could try to call the

Principles…um…on purpose."

The kid sat up, leaning forward with his hand outstretched, gesturing for Borash to take the stone. He hesitated for a moment — the thing even *looked* magical — but he needed to learn this, needed to find a way out of the hole his life had become. He took it, holding it in both hands, the stone cold against his fingers.

"The most important thing to learn," Teros said, suddenly sounding much older, "is that the stone doesn't *cause* the magic, the Principles do."

"The Principles," Borash repeated under his breath, still staring at the stone. He hadn't had much use for religion on the streets, but only a fool could forget the basics seeing as how they worshipped one Elder or another at every bloody meal.

"When you brought out the fire," Teros continued, "you used Passion, which comes from Iron. But you weren't *creating* the fire; you were telling the air to burn. Do you understand what I mean?"

Borash finally looked up, his face feeling numb as he remembered — *really* remembered the fire. The awful heat of it, those men, the way he collapsed afterward. But he felt he did understand in a way. The fire had been foreign, bizarre and terrifying as it escaped his control, showering his face with heat. And now, behind the fear and guilt, he felt a new…*hunger*, a desperation to learn more. He nodded.

"Good," Teros said, nodding. "That's the most important thing."

He gestured to the stone.

"Now, you have to *look* for the Principles. The most important one for stones is Permanence. Can you see it shining?"

Borash looked down at the stone, but it just looked like a rock. He frowned.

"It's just shiny," he said.

"Take it out of the sun," Teros said, gesturing to where the edge of the canvas shaded the inside of the wagon.

Borash did so, blinking as he thought his eyes were playing tricks on him. Even in the shade, the stone seemed to have a glow about it, a sort of…dancing light. It was actually just like the tiny glow he got from food, the one that told him which acre a meal was from. So that meant…

"Have I always been able to see that?" he asked, looking up at the kid.

"Probably," Teros said. "Practice stones are easier to see, though." He moved his finger over one of the cracks in the stone. "They've had fresh lines of Permanence made and broken over and over, which leaves a trace. But everything has the Principles on the inside — you'll see them everywhere once you're used to it."

"So it *is* like the food," Borash said, more to himself than anything. Still, the kid nodded.

"Do you still have that vodka from your friend?" he asked.

Borash reached into his pocket, pulling out his flask. It was growing worryingly empty — and he'd long ago abandoned the bottle — but there was still some left.

"Pour it into your hand," Teros said.

And waste the bloody vodka? Borash opened his mouth, almost telling the kid to roll in a ditch before thinking better of it. He took a deep breath, undoing the cap. He could always suck it out of his hand when they were done, right?

He poured a small drab into his palm, blinking at it in the light before he remembered to move it to the shade. But sure enough, as he looked at it, he could see the glow.

"So this is…"

"Permanence," Teros answered. "Vodka comes from potatoes, right?"

"The good stuff, sure," Borash said. "But I guess this ain't complete swill, after all."

Unwilling to risk it any longer, Borash carefully brought his hand to his lips, savoring the burn of the vodka, warmer than the sun — and less likely to burn you besides.

"So," he said, licking his lips. "How do you *know* it's Permanence, aside from the potato thing?" He'd always known the acre of food, true, but you knew a potato was a potato 'cause you weren't a bloody fool. The glows, however, looked the same to him.

The kid nodded, flipping through his book before he turned it around for Borash to see.

"It's the way they dance," he said, pointing to a diagram. There were six squiggly lines, like the strange words they wrote in Pen'dil Seln. He pointed to one on the top left. "This is Permanence. Can you see it?"

Borash looked between the book and the rock, and oddly, it *was* sort of similar in a way. Still, it seemed he could see all the others too, bouncing about beneath the Permanence, like gnats darting to and fro.

"What about these others?" he asked, trying to lock his eyes on just one.

"Every Principle is always present," Teros said, "but they'll have different amounts. It will also take more effort to use a Principle that's hardly there. You might need more chul'uns and then—"

"Wait, wait, wait," Borash said, waving a hand. "Enough talking, I want to try it."

"Okay," Teros said. For a kid who muttered a lot, at least he shut up when you wanted him to.

Borash held up the stone, its spidery lines glittering in the sunlight again.

"What do I do?" he whispered, keeping his eyes on the dancing lights.

"Crack the stone," Teros said quietly. "Take the power in your stomach, the energy that matches the Permanence, and break it. Feel the stone's Mind, and tell it to be different."

His stomach… He looked at the kid, but Teros only nodded. Borash closed his eyes and found…something. There was a warmth to his stomach he hadn't noticed before. And oddly — though maybe it was just his pulse — it seemed to shift along with the light on the stone. Suddenly, without him wanting them to, they seemed to merge, the pulsing in his stomach reaching for the stone.

"Tell it," Teros said again.

Borash reached for the stone, the shape of it rising in his mind. He could feel its outlines, sense a sort of…memory, the lines along its surface holding a pattern. He could sense the way it wanted to hold together just as it might break with the right nudge. He just had to tell it, just had to—

Break, Borash thought, the heat in his stomach suddenly seeming to flare. There was a loud crack, the stone splitting in a burst of light. He dropped it in surprise, his eyes widening.

"It…it worked," he said. But as he bent to pick up the stone, his head spun violently. Suddenly, he felt heavy, like a boulder he would never pick back up; like he'd fallen in the river, the light fading from the edges of his eyes.

"Kid," he rasped, fighting to breathe with his lungs doubled over.

His vision blurred, but he saw the kid reach for his belt pouch.

"You need Flow," the kid squeaked, scrambling toward him. "Think of a stream, imagine yourself in the water, floating. Don't let yourself get heavy."

Borash tried to do as he said, but his mind couldn't focus, every image he thought of disappearing just as quickly as it came. The kid grabbed his shoulders, and a fresh wave of warmth came over him, the weight disappearing from his muscles. He gasped, bolting upright as he clutched his chest.

"What in the cave witch's milk was that?" he asked.

"The Passing again," Teros said, breathing heavily himself, his eyes wide. "I…uh…thought it would be alright with breakfast, but I think maybe the vodka made it worse."

"Bloody gods," Borash said, running a hand over his face. He'd thought being angry and nauseous was bad, but this… "Is it always like that?" he asked.

"First time is the worst," Teros said, "until the end anyway. Uncle Elin always liked to say, 'everything gets better before it gets worse.'"

"Great," Borash said, chuckling in spite of himself. "Can't wait to see what the others are like."

"Permanence is the scariest," Teros said, a haunted look coming to his face. "The others really aren't so bad."

Borash opened his mouth to ask another question when the wagon suddenly halted, the drivers calling out orders. They'd made nearly a half-dozen stops already, crisscrossing the eastern half of the city. Maegin had offered them a ride, sure, but he'd never said it would be a quick one. A day wandering through town just to have a day's long walk waiting for them from the outpost… Footsteps approached, one of the giant wagon men coming around the back.

"Need the salt fish," he said — grunting more than speaking, really — as he pointed at one of the barrels behind Borash. "You gonna help this time?"

"Sorry," Borash said, shaking his head, "leg's still hitting me something awful."

He'd actually tried to help at the first stop — if only to keep the men from glaring at him — but he'd dropped a crate when his leg acted up. Not that they'd seemed to believe him… On the other hand, apparently taken with the kid like every other bastard on the wagon team, the big oaf smiled at Teros.

"Come on, lad," he said, holding out a hand, "I'll help ya down."

Teros thanked him, more or less floating down with the giant man holding his weight. He pointed Teros to the front where he could talk with the other men before jerking a thumb at Borash.

"Get scarce."

"Gladly," Borash said, groaning as he dragged himself over the lip of the wagon bed. Magic or not, it seemed his bloody joke of a life wasn't ready to let him go without one more kick in the shins. He limped after Teros, muttering to himself about stones and passings and every other cursed thing the gods seemed fit to send his way.

15

26th of Sund-z'ar : 2nd Meal : 984, 22nd Year of Iron
14 days until the 163rd Voting

732 moved quickly through the streets toward the warehouse district — or as quickly as the crowds would allow. The bells had rung for second, and it seemed like the whole city had come out to block her path. Even as the crowds noticed her mask, parting like the river around a boat, her destination felt impossible to reach. Desperation tingled along the muscles of her shoulders, urging her onward. Who was helping the vessel? And what could possibly be worth forsaking the Elders? If you wielded the magic, death would always come. To deny that, to seek profit, was only wishing death on all you once held dear.

She saw one of the king's giant wagons passing through the crowd and slipped behind it. People still moved readily for the crown, at least, and the wagon guards actually bowed to her, no doubt happy to have the extra protection if only for a few yards. Still, she couldn't help but stare at the thing, such a singular reminder of the war. The wagons were so much bigger than she remembered, at least ten feet long and five feet wide, the entire thing more or less a cradle for the massive metal tub inside where the sacred water sloshed about. She would always remember the first time she saw them, lined up by the dozens as they tried to keep their men alive on the march to Deyn.

Finally, they reached the other side of the square, nodding to the guards as she slipped into the shadow of the warehouses. Alleys snaked off in every direction, though the tip had at least specified where she was to look. The place was called Maegin's, and luckily, it was close to the barge lock. She took the first left but stopped, coming up short as she found two large guards waiting for her by a metal gate. Their hands were tight around the ends of clubs, their stances prepared as if they'd been waiting for her. She looked up, catching a shadow disappearing from the rooftops. Waiting indeed…

"Is this Maegin's?" she asked, her hand going to her sword.

"Aye, Masked One," the man on the right said, his eyes unwavering as he watched her. She could do without bowing, of course, but from this man, the lack of her proper title felt…dangerous.

"I have some questions for your boss," she said.

"I'm afraid that's not possible," he answered.

They grew silent for a moment, tension filling the air. Perhaps they thought if they were quick enough, she would be easy to deal with? She could always sense when men were considering violence, their minds teetering over the precipice. Suddenly, the man on her left shifted his stance, his foot sliding in the dust as he prepared to swing. She opened her palm, a large flame appearing as she burnt the air with Passion.

"I wouldn't," she said, meeting his eyes.

He swallowed, his entire throat shifting with the effort.

"Maybe just a chat," he said. He tilted his head, waving for the other guard to go inside. "Tell Maegin he has a guest."

732 kept her hand on her sword, though she relaxed her stance. As Viden always said, it was important to remind your enemies that surrender was possible.

"Like I said, I only have a few questions."

———

As the guards led her through the warehouses, there was a feeling of superficial quiet, the ghost of a place that should have been busy. Warehouse doors were closed and lamps unlit despite the shade cast by the morning sun. She usually found herself sad at the passing of Sund-z'ar and the summer fog, but she was grateful there was none this morning to hide enemies. Between that and first and second meals being so close together, it seemed Curis-gan really was just around the corner.

She tightened her grip on her sword. She wasn't here for idle thoughts about the weather. And as badly as her mind wanted something else to think about, the knot in her chest told her the truth: a fight was near, and that required attention. The guards led her around an L-shaped corner where a half-dozen men were waiting for her. All of them looked as wary as the guards save one, a bearded man at their center.

"Are you Maegin?" she asked, stopping short to put a few extra feet between herself and her escorts. The gate guards looked over their shoulders, starting as they realized she was no longer directly behind them. They joined the others, holding their clubs.

"I am," the bearded man said. He was the only one without a weapon. Two had spears, and another two had staves. A man at his side held something wrapped in cloth. She looked back to Maegin, nodding.

"I've just come from the Cobalt Bridge Guard; we received a tip a child may have been here?"

Maegin laughed, stroking his beard.

"Cobalt, eh?" he asked. "I was wondering who sent you. You sure aren't the one we usually deal with."

732 frowned.

"I believe there's been a misunderstanding," she said. "I work for the crown, and as I said, we're looking for—"

"Yes, lass," he said, "we *all* work for the crown. But that never explains who lines our pockets, does it?"

Some of his men began to chuckle, though it was short-lived, the tension in the air seeming to choke off their humor like a net.

"Lord Curan, if you will," she said quietly. "And I'm obliged to remind you that harboring an asset of the crown is punishable by death."

Some of the men shifted their stances, but she kept her eyes on Maegin. Even as the gravity in the courtyard shifted inward, pulling them toward violence, she waited. She would give this man his chance to make a different choice, to keep his men alive. And if they didn't cooperate… She could always do what Viden called a 'wet' investigation after.

"Sure, sure," Maegin said, smiling. "So not such a different punishment from being poor in this damned basin."

He turned to the man on his right, undoing the ties on the cloth bundle. When he turned back, he held a sword in his hand. It was short, with a thick band of metal running up its center, catching the light with a rainbow shimmer, it— *Serosine.* Her stomach knotted at the sight of it, reminding her of darker times. Only Pen'dil Deyn made swords like that, and she thought she'd seen the last destroyed after the war, melted down in a fire she'd helped light, surrounded by the corpses of friend and foe alike. She felt her teeth clench, remembering Viden's hand on hers, the regret in his voice when he told her they'd been called up.

"I know your kind gets greedy," Maegin said, bringing her back to the present, to the fight before her. "But I draw the line at interrupting my business. You either tell Dek'rc the kid ain't here, or we can settle this now."

Part of her wished it wasn't so, but resolve had settled in. This was why the High Priest had selected her for this job, after all. She had always sensed a darkness — a rot — in those around her, but this was something else entirely. A vessel missing, one of her own possibly helping them escape, a man in the warehouse district with a sword that shouldn't exist — a sword designed to stop her sacred gifts. There was no telling how much the others knew, how involved 151 was with the Cobalt Duke, but she was here now. She would find what this trail was hiding, and she would burn every trace of it away.

Without shifting her stance, she gently eased the wax pouch from her cheek, biting down on it. The sharp tang of raspberry juice filled her mouth. It was getting harder to swallow, raspberry almost lost to her, but she was glad for it all the same. Against this many men, she would need violence that shocked, and nothing was better for that than ice. With her hand on her sword, she slowly filled its banded blade with power. Made with a mercury amalgam, it could hold fifteen chul'uns. She poured every ounce of the raspberry's Remembrance into it until the hilt began to throb beneath her hand. She felt a chill, her mind getting heavy with memories, but she blinked them away, pushing away the Remembrance as she held to the other Principles.

"Very well," she said, pulling her sword.

Perhaps they'd thought she would back down — had seen others of her kind back down before. But as she moved in, the first man's face showed surprise. She stuck his feet with Permanence and spun, catching him in the neck with the unimbued side of her blade, his body crumpling while his legs stayed put. He'd never had time to lift his cudgel, though the others weren't quite so slow.

She immediately danced back as the ones with spears moved in front of Maegin, their blades thrusting for where she had been moments before. Still, the other guard with a cudgel had overextended, moving several feet in front of his fellows. She kicked against the air, shooting herself forward with Identity. He, at least, raised his weapon in time, but she struck it with the imbued side of her sword, instantly cleaving it as the cudgel turned to ice. With the force of her swing, the sword tore him across the chest, his entire body freezing over to a ghastly gray.

She heard Maegin curse, but the spearmen didn't wait, both of them charging her with a paired thrust. She put out a hand, burning one of them to ash, though the other caught her on the shoulder as she tried to spin away. She ignored the pain, grateful to have avoided being pinned, though she felt blood seeping into her cloak. Sensing an opportunity, the man stayed on her, forcing her to parry. He aimed for her hands, keeping her from snapping his spear with ice as she was forced to block.

It was lucky she was attuned to the Principles as she was because she was almost too focused on the spearman to notice the shift in the air. Still, the moment she sensed it, she ducked on instinct, a roped blade slicing through the air where her throat had been. She came up from the ground in a swing, just in time to block a diving thrust from the spearman. So he knew he wasn't fighting alone… She glanced to the front, the man at Maegin's side now swinging the rope. She could feel herself running out of time, the growing need to finish things.

She surged Flow, pushing in on the spearman. There was no water nearby, but she felt herself gain control of the water inside her, becoming even more flexible as she dodged the spear with ease. Still, she committed to her attack, trying to look like she was growing desperate. Finally, when she felt the rush of air again, she batted away the spear, dashing in and grabbing the spearman by the throat. She spun him in front of her, the rope blade lodging in his chest.

The man at Maegin's side cursed, trying to pull the blade back out, but she had already dropped the body, summoning a massive burst of Passion. She felt it burning in her stomach, her heart racing to keep up with it as she tore apart the air around her and pushed it toward the last two men. As the inferno reached them, Maegin held up his sword, the serosine seeming to bend the air as the flame warped around him. His friend, however, wasn't so lucky, the man's screams echoing off the walls as he died.

Maegin roared, surging through the smoke on the attack. She cursed, bringing up her sword to meet his. As they met, the metal let out a sharp crack, the sword vibrating in her hands as the serosine absorbed the Remembrance of her amalgam. Not only was his sword genuine, but Maegin apparently knew his business, attacking in a flurry of sword forms. She knew every style of fighting in the valley, but he was still hard to track, seeming to switch between the clean strikes of a palace guard and the firm jabs of a Deynen. So he'd fought in the war, then, but perhaps not on her side?

She dashed back, nearly taking a blow to the chest. She'd grown too complacent in the years since the war, her mind still looking for opportunities to use the Principles that weren't there. She could call for help, but with Maegin on the offensive, she'd likely never get her flare lit before he ended her. And besides, if she lost this trail, if the child escaped, everything could be lost. Suddenly, Viden's voice was in her mind, the first thing he'd told her when they were finally sent to the front.

"Sword fights are only luck, son. If you can't finish it with magic, find a gut and stick something in it."

It could have been the Passion, but she felt a burning rage building in her chest. The forbidden sword, everything she honored teetering on chaos, all of it surged inside her heart, threatening to burn her away. She had given everything to this basin, would give even more the moment it was asked of her. And this man thought he could silence her, could hide the truth from the crown? She swung with all her might, pushing Maegin back with a blow that shook her hands. She danced back a few feet herself, letting the Principles fill her. She couldn't use magic on him while he held the sword, but that said nothing of herself or the world around her.

She sucked in a breath, letting her mind attune Identity. The warehouses were like a cavern, a wind tunnel for the air to dance along. She soaked herself in that breeze, like dipping her hands into a river of air. She felt a calmness washing over her as the Passion faded, and still, she felt a *rightness* to this fight, to doing whatever it took. She launched herself on the wind, whipping through the courtyard like an arrow. Maegin lifted his sword, but she was already swinging, knocking his blade to the side as she barreled into him. They rolled on the ground, but she had already found his throat, clearly better at tumbling than this man who had never known the air, had never lost his bearings in the wake of the Passing.

She rolled on top of him, yelling in spite of herself as she struck him again and again. Her chest heaving, she finally pulled out her belt knife, putting it to his throat.

"Tell me what you know," she said.

Maegin's eyes fluttered open, and he smiled, his teeth slick with blood.

"To the caves with you," he said.

She slit his throat, her lungs throbbing as she watched the light leave his eyes. When he stopped breathing, she rolled off him, fumbling at her belt for her flare. For a moment, she almost couldn't remember how to light it, the wave of Identity crashing back down on her as it combined with her aching muscles and lost blood. Somehow, though, she found enough Passion left in her belly to light the fuse, the flare shooting into the sky like a star. She used what was left of her magic to touch her shoulder, sealing the wound with fire. It wasn't the same as being healed, but the priests could deal with that later.

She went to one knee and reached for her sword, the blood of the dead men rippling along the strip of her mercury amalgam. She wiped it on Maegin's shirt and was about to put it back in its scabbard when she heard a voice.

"Excuse me," it said from the shadows.

732 spun, her hand on her belt pouch as she held her sword warily, ignoring the throbbing in her limbs.

"Sacred One," a willowy man said, stepping into the light with his palms raised, "I mean you no harm." He bowed, putting one thumb to his forehead. "I'm Small Jerin; I left the tip for you."

She blinked, slowly easing her stance as she put her sword back on her belt.

"I thank you for your tip," she said. "And my condolences for your friends."

He ran a hand through his hair.

"Nothing to be sorry about," he said, looking around at the warehouses. "When the ants stop crawling over this place, I figure I'll have come up a few rungs in the world."

He was an odd man — and not so small, in truth — but she would not question the gods if this was their way of helping her reach the child. She took a breath, ignoring the sharp pain in her shoulder as she reached for her notebook.

"Wait," he said, looking at his dead companions as if for the first time. "Do you have to write this down?"

"You speak to a vessel of the Elders, Small Jerin," she said. "I can choose to not write if you wish, but everything that passes my ears becomes a record of the state all the same."

He stared down at the cobblestones, licking his lips.

"Alright," he said. "I'll tell you what you want to know. But I want to see 151 before they search the place. And then we can talk through my reward."

16

26th of Sund-z'ar : After 2nd Meal : 984, 22nd Year of Iron
14 days until the 163rd Voting

Keroes nir Sen'l walked along the tiled hallway, feeling like a boat surging down the river. And in many ways, he was… Flanked by four priests and led by two Masked Ones, the tiles below him were a beautiful blue, a pantomime of the river that led between his throne and the king's. He took a breath, starting his prayer again from the beginning. This was no time for frivolous thoughts. Not that he was afraid — never that! — and least of all of Bital nir Föhr. The Iron King could puff and rage all he wanted to the others, but in this kingdom, they were equals. Even if the king owned every cobblestone in the city, every wheel and blade, Keroes served the gods.

But in that, perhaps, there *was* room for fear… This was no ordinary weekly meeting with the king. He knew already from the ritual in the cave the immense task the gods had set before him. But the voting was only fourteen days away, and without the king, it would all mean nothing. With the damage Bital nir Föhr had already done to the basin, he could almost feel the urgency of the gods, their desperation to bring this vessel to their people. And unfortunately, guiding that man was worse than turning a raging bull.

Unfortunately, before he could finish his prayer, they reached the throne room. A pair of royal guards bowed, opening the giant metal doors as his arrival was announced. He would never be awed by the halls of man, but it was easy to see why this place cowed so many weaker beings. Where the hallway was merely pretty with its tiles, the throne room was resplendent. Tall windows brimmed with light on either side, sparkling off every shade of blue as the replica river spun and frothed toward the center. There, the king sat surrounded by advisors on a statuesque throne, shaped like Sen'el'seng itself with crags and peaks rising behind the Iron King.

Keroes walked a quarter of the way into the room, stopping on a raised dais, a sort of island in the faux river. His own advisors circled him, and the Masked Ones took up their guard at the side, bowing to their counterparts in the king's honor guard. It was easy to miss them — like shadows compared to the flamboyance of his advisors — but there were three surrounding the throne, their masks covered in gold leaf, a symbol that there were some pieces of the Elders kept out of his reach. Though perhaps not for long…

The king was leaning forward, pointing at some blueprints held aloft by his engineers, no doubt some fresh nonsense for his so-called 'New City.' Whether it was a blatant insult — some attempt to look too busy for the High Priest — was never certain with the Iron King, but Keroes would still show his respect. The gods had placed this man on the throne, and like a child, he couldn't be *blamed* for his shortcomings, only…improved.

Keroes turned to the right, bowing to the giant bronze statue of Bitan, the king's lost son. He towered over the room, his presence casting the same long shadow as the boy's death. The Doomed Prince… That's what the dukes called him, anyway — when they thought no one was listening. Where would their kingdom have been if Bitan hadn't found his end in the war? Perhaps the gods had sent him to the grave for this moment, the moment when they could bring him back and change everything.

Finally seeming to notice him as Keroes came up from his bow, the king began shooing away his advisors, tenting his fingers as he sat back on the throne.

"Keroes nir Sen'l," the king said, "you are most welcome here."

"The gods roam among men with purpose, Bital nir Föhr," he answered. Still, after their ritual greeting, there was a brief silence, like two animals sharing a cage, unsure if it was wise to approach.

"I have news," Keroes finally said, "but those blueprints seem fresh, perhaps you should inform me first of your plans?"

The king waved a hand.

"Nothing new," he said, "though it is all rather pressing. You have my apologies for interrupting your arrival with my business. The sacred wagons are finally having their wheels redesigned, and the engineers wanted me to know of their progress."

Keroes caught himself frowning, the facade of the priestly sage cracked by the king's inadequacy. Must they give up everything for the Iron King's cursed wagons?! Still, he forced himself to take a breath. The wagons *were* nothing new, and after their success in the war, they were unlikely to ever go away. At least they were designed with the sanctity of the holy water in mind. Politics was like the river; there were tides you could fight and tides that would sweep you away. No, what he should argue against wasn't the wagons but where they would be parked.

"Perhaps," Keroes said slowly, "while we're on the subject, you could put my mind at ease. I heard talk of your scouts looking for well sites east of the Kellinh Crag. I do hope those are rumors, since as we've discussed before, the intent of the Elders—"

"Was to keep us in the bloody basin," Bital nir Föhr said, shaking his head. "I'm well aware from our countless afternoons of arguing, Keroes nir Sen'l." He reached for his wine, taking a hasty drink. "And as you've forced me to say over and over, what I do is *for* the sake of the basin. It's as if you don't remember when the Deynens built their dams. A basin without water is—"

"Just a crack in the rocks," Keroes said, grimacing as he took his own turn at finishing the other man's sentence. He felt his tongue trying to pull him into the old arguments: the expansion of 690, the uprising at the Broken Arch, the assassination of Kerol nir Irmun. But for once, with such an essential task before him, he saw the pride — no, the *vanity* — in continuing to argue in the same way. Bital nir Föhr knew all that history, and still, he attempted to abandon the old ways for his idols of progress. He was no longer meant to make those arguments, but he wasn't meant to fail either. He had prayed long and hard, and the gods had *answered*.

"My…apologies," Keroes forced himself to say, "for rehashing what we have already discussed. Today, I am here for something far more important."

Bital nir Föhr seemed genuinely surprised, leaning forward with his arms on his knees, though his eyes remained narrowed. The Iron King was not one you could flatter. If there was falseness to Keroes's apology, Bital would sniff it out. Still, he was *listening*, and it was time for the gods to do their work.

"I trust the Golden Ones in your employ still keep you apprised of the sacred ceremonies?" he asked.

The king nodded. Keroes knew, of course, what the Golden Masks were told and what they were not, but it was essential the king knew the ceremony had been performed as prescribed. The result could not be seen as his doing; it was of the *gods*.

"Well," Keroes continued, "we had a most unusual result, and one I believe to be an act of deliverance from the Elders, something not seen since the Forgotten Years and the reign of Jeon nir Sen'l."

"And?" Bital asked.

"The crypt of the returned spirit, my king, was that of your son, Bitan nir Föhr."

The king somehow kept his composure, the sternness never leaving his face, but his eyes gave him away. They darted immediately for the statue of his son. Everyone agreed the Doomed Prince was the only thing Bital nir Föhr had ever truly cared for, war nothing more than a pretext to keep him busy, a way to kindle his rage while he waited to join Bitan in the grave. But this showed the power of the gods, the wisdom in their sending. When the Iron King's heir was voted upon in fourteen short days, it would be a vessel, *his* vessel, at the front of the line.

"We seek," Keroes continued quietly, though his voice now echoed in the silent chamber, "a vessel for your son's soul, a child."

The king looked back, his eyes now wide, frenzied even.

"Unfortunately, it appears someone is trying to help the vessel escape, an ugly reminder that you have true enemies in this kingdom, Bital nir Föhr, enemies that go beyond our little…disagreements. Enemies who well know that time is precious."

The king blinked, nodding as he seemed to understand, the implications of the voting spreading across his face. No king liked to be handed an heir, but the iron fist of Bital nir Föhr? He could select his own if the candidate was good, even more so if that person was the hero of the Deynen campaign. Electing a vessel wouldn't be simple, but with the assurances of House Sen'l that he would be guided by wise hands?

The king turned to the Golden Mask on his right, the one they called 'The First,' the numbers of the other vessels meaningless among their ranks.

"Ensure the High Priest has whatever he requires," Bital said. "And use as many palace guards as you need."

The First bowed, his hand never leaving his sword.

Keroes opened his mouth to speak again, but there was a clamor in the hallway behind him. Raised voices pushed through the doors, muffled by the metal, until they cracked open, the hallway suddenly quiet as a new Masked One entered, their mask thankfully of porcelain instead of gold.

"Keroes nir Sen'l," the man said, bowing. "There's been an emergency flare from the northwest. The vessel, 732, said you were to be notified immediately."

"My king," Keroes said heavily, inclining his head. "I will take my leave. It seems the spirit may be at hand."

"May the gods protect you," the king said, putting a thumb to his forehead. The Iron King had never once shown such deference, but Keroes held back his smile, nodding again as he turned to go, his retinue beside him. For once, he felt his boat was on calm waters, anticipation filling his stomach instead of dread. As the ancients said, the river held many tides, but the only one that mattered was the deep.

17

26th of Sund-z'ar : Before 5th Meal : 984, 22nd Year of Iron
14 days until the 163rd Voting

Borash sucked in a sharp breath, his leg throbbing as the wagon rumbled over the cobblestones. When were they going to get to the bloody end? They'd already crossed the whole damn city, circling to the south until the palace was visible again from the back of the wagon. They may as well have walked, nearly back where they started with nothing much to show for their journey but an aching leg and a bunch of wasted time.

He took another hasty sip of the vodka, though it didn't seem to be doing anything for the pain. He'd been nervous at first, surely enough, barely wetting his tongue after the magic had frozen him up like a bloody stone. But now, even if the liquor tasted…off, he couldn't rightly sit in this much pain and do nothing about it. The wagon turned, and suddenly the southern guild rows were visible, men and women off for the day moving about the little cottages, no doubt ready to eat fifth as a family. He'd had one of those cottages once… He could still picture it: a bit of moss in the garden, smoke from the chimney, a chair to sit in.

A searing pain shot up his leg again, a tear coming to his eye as he clamped his teeth together.

"Yeah, yeah," he said under his breath to his leg, "you wouldn't want me going and remembering nothing good now."

"Are you alright?" Teros asked, looking up from his book again.

"Fine," Borash said, wiping his eye with the back of his sleeve. At least the robes they'd stolen weren't as rough as his usual bloody worm wool. "Absolutely fantastic."

It was quiet for a moment, the kid looking away, though he didn't go back to his book.

"When did your leg start hurting?" he finally asked, his tiny voice barely louder than the wagon wheels.

Borash frowned. When *had* it started? It was so mixed up in his mind. He'd always been a drinker, hadn't he? But he certainly needed more as the leg got worse, the bad days closer together and the memories mixing up. Still, a single memory floated up in his mind like the night mist itself. The night before he graduated from the merchant school, his leg had suddenly given out, the priests without a clue how to fix him.

"I guess..." he said slowly, "it must have started when I was finishing school. One day it just seized up, and it never got better."

"But you were walking earlier, right?" Teros asked, looking between Borash and the leg.

"Comes and goes," Borash said, sighing. The kid looked so damned bashful that he somehow found himself forcing a wan smile to his face. "You don't have to look so scared; it's alright to ask."

Teros nodded, looking at the leg again, staring as if he could see something through his robes.

"It's not a war wound or nothing," Borash said, "if that's what you're thinking."

Teros looked up, blinking. He set down his book, kneeling forward to have a closer look.

"Did you ever have a priest look at it?" he asked.

"Plenty," Borash said, "load of good it did me. They gave me all the hoity-toity foods, but they said it was up to the bloody gods. They said magic can plug a wound, but the body has to heal itself."

"Maybe," Teros said quietly, his face barely a foot above Borash's knee as he stared down intently. "The book says the Elders could heal people — really heal them, but I guess we forgot. Still, I feel like..."

The kid reached over to his bag, pulling out the remains of one of the rough biscuits the drivers had given them for third meal. He shoved it in his mouth, his little teeth grinding away before he swallowed.

"I don't know why," he said, "but there's a lot of Remembrance in your knee. Does it feel cold?"

"Cold?" Borash asked, leaning forward and rubbing his leg. "Feels fine."

The kid narrowed his eyes and shuffled closer, putting his hands on

Borash's knee. He started to move, to ask the kid what in the bloody cave witch's name he was doing when a rush of heat filled his leg. He pulled his leg back on instinct, snapping it away from Teros, but as he did so, he realized…the pain was *gone.*

"Warn a bloke before you use magic on him, eh?" he asked sharply, rubbing his knee.

"Sorry," Teros said, biting his lip as he sat back down against the other end of the wagon.

Borash eased out his leg again, turning it this way and that.

"Sorry, lad," he said, sighing. "It…helped, so thank you. Just a bit of warning next time."

Teros nodded, though he looked pleased. Borash was about to ask him how he did it — how he could bloody repeat the process himself — when the most godforsaken smell poured into his nose, like a pack of cave bats in musking season. Just then, the carriage came to a stop, the horses' reins jangling.

"What *is* that?" Teros asked, coughing with tears in his eyes.

Borash leaned out the back of the wagon to look, though he already knew. There was only one place in the basin capable of smelling that awful.

"Lily Well," he said as he caught sight of a bunch of workers wading through the muck in their leather breeches, dragging sticks through the dark pool as they wove through the lily pads. "Never heard of it?"

Teros shook his head.

"It's the end of the canal," Borash said, "keeps anything unseemly from going back in the sacred river."

"Not sure a lily could keep you out," one of the wagon drivers said, coming around the back. "Hand me that," he added, pointing to a large jute sack full of garbage. Borash rolled over, gratefully able to hold the weight on his knee as he slid the bag over. The driver hefted it over one shoulder as he walked away.

"Want me to ask if they got a job for you while I'm over there?" he called back without turning around. "Real easy on the leg to wade through shit."

"See if I get you a bloody job," Borash muttered under his breath, crossing his arms as he stared into the wagon bed.

The driver spent a few minutes haggling loudly with the workers at the Lily Well to take their trash, but soon after, they were on the move again, heading south toward the far end of the city. Once the wagon was making noise again, Teros looked up toward the drivers before speaking in a low voice.

"Why don't those other men like you?" he asked.

Borash scowled.

"As if I bloody—" he started, but the kid's eyes actually looked earnest — like he really wanted to know. It was an odd feeling, and not a comfortable one at that. When was the last time someone had asked him a question about himself and actually wanted to hear the answer? Besides, it wasn't like the kid was wrong. He wasn't a bloody merchant anymore, but only a fool kept pretending when everyone knew his barrels were empty.

"They…don't think I'm all that good of a bloke," he finally said. "And I guess they might not be wrong. I haven't always been easy to work with, and merchants don't forget so easy. Nothing worse in their mind than somebody they can't trust."

"I don't think you're bad," Teros said. He looked out the back of the wagon before turning back with a shy smile. "Maybe a little grumpy, but not bad."

Borash chuckled despite himself.

"Yeah, alright, lad," he said, shaking his head. "Just keep that to yourself."

Finally, they reached the Un'weil, the giant stone blocks of the Zi'yun arch passing overhead as they left the city behind. No wall ringed Pen'dil Zenn — not like the one they said circled Deyn — but the city stopped all the same, the cobblestones immediately giving way to the dead rock of the moss barrens. From the back of the wagon, he watched as everything he knew slipped away until they passed over a hill that hid the basin completely. If only his problems could vanish so easily… Perhaps he should be frightened leaving home, but it was time for a new start — if only he could be sure the streets wouldn't pull him right back in.

Maybe it was his time with the kid — or the jabs from that bloody wagon driver getting under his skin — but it got him thinking all the same. Was he really as bad as Maegin thought? He saw his own side of things, sure enough, and knew he'd only ever done what he had to do. Even if some of what he'd done had been caused by drink… Maybe he didn't deserve to start over, shouldn't have been hoping for something different, but he couldn't help himself. The kid, with his fancy robes and books, was a reminder of what he'd been denied, of what he might have again with the magic on his side. And even if that magic came at a price, it was one he found himself willing to pay. Even with the awful dreams and the memories he'd rather forget…

He shook his head, trying to focus on the positive. But sure enough, as they left the city behind, the road grew bumpier, and with each and every jolt, the pain in his leg seemed to come back. Whatever the kid had done didn't last, but why had he expected it to? His pain was a river, and just like the basin, it never stopped flowing. Anything he put in its way was just a pebble, ready to be swept away. If only he hadn't drunk the last of the vodka…

At least it wouldn't be long now. As their surroundings grew more desolate, he knew they were getting close to the outpost. Not that he was excited about facing the Stone Forest… Even for bloody Zi'yun soldiers, there was nothing to live on outside the basin, and every foot you stepped into the stones was asking for trouble. Between the outpost and Irmun Pond, there would be no water to speak of and bears lurking besides. But it was a start, and a better one than he deserved.

When they finally reached the outpost, the wagon drivers swung the carriage in a wide arc, facing the horses out so he could see the barracks in all their sodding glory. Already, he could tell the place belonged to a duke, the entire thing built of a forest of wood, likely imported from Pen'dil Sohn and worth a fortune on its own. It was shaped like an L, the short side holding a stable and armory, while the longer edge was several stories tall, no doubt to house the men. There were Zi'yun ducal guards scattered all around with their cream-colored tunics and spears. It didn't feel very bloody smart to be around armed men so soon after the incident with those Cobalt bastards, but if Maegin said it was fixed, it was usually so. And it wasn't as if they'd be sticking around long…

Unfortunately, as he clenched his teeth and struggled off the back of the wagon, he caught sight of the Stone Forest itself. Rising beyond the barracks, it was impossibly empty, the chalky ground blank save for a few patches of dry-moss and the ghastly rock formations that gave the place its name. The nearest hill looked like a skull, and maybe it was, the head of some beast from the Giant Lands slain centuries ago. If the gods were really in the river, then they were nowhere to be found in this place, the water trapped below the rock, winding its way in secret toward the duke's pond.

He reached out just in time to grab the wagon post, closing his eyes as his head swam. The drivers came back around, looking for anything they had to drop off at the barracks.

"I…" Borash said, gulping, "think I'd better wait 'til morning."

The men stared at him, his mouth suddenly dry.

"I'm sure my leg will be better in the morning, but I don't think, uh…Maegin would want the lad walking the stones at night, eh?"

The lead driver sighed, wiping a hand across his forehead. He looked into Borash's eyes, a sharp remark seeming on the edge of his lips before he simply nodded, waving at a nearby guard.

"Oy!" he called. "Grab us Sernil, yeah?"

The guard nodded, disappearing into the barracks. The drivers kept on with their unloading, taking a bunch of glass water jars out from where they were hidden under a tarp and lining them up along the wagon wheels. Eventually, an older man with a mustache came out, looking like a thunderhead with captain's epaulets on his shoulders.

"What's this?" he asked, walking up. "You men forget how to unload?"

Apparently unfazed, the wagon driver turned to face him, his hands on his hips.

"Got something sensitive to discuss," he said, "from Maegin."

Sernil seemed to soften up at Maegin's name, standing a little straighter.

"Well," he said, "I'd be happy to help, then." He waved for his guard to go back to his post just out of earshot.

"Got this kid here," the driver said, jerking a thumb at Teros. "Maegin needs them to reach Duke Irmun at his pond, but they need a place to stay tonight. No questions, no problems, yeah?"

The captain met Borash's eyes for a moment, sizing him up. Recognition seemed to bloom suddenly, his men no doubt given the same warning as the bridge guards earlier, but he simply nodded.

"We got a poster inside about 'em," he said, "but if I tell the men what's what, they'll keep quiet. No love lost between our lord and the bloody Iron King, I'll tell you that much. Besides, out here there's better money in keeping your mouth shut."

"Alright then," the driver said, nodding as he turned back to his work. "Maegin will be pleased."

"Come on, then," the captain said, waving for them to follow. "We got a nice empty room, and fifth is almost on."

Borash nodded, turning briefly to the drivers.

"Thank you," he said.

"Wasn't for you now, was it?" the man said without turning around.

Borash frowned, but he followed the captain inside, the wood of the barracks finally shutting out the view of those awful empty hills. He'd be able to walk them in the morning; he just needed time and something to drink.

18

26th of Sund-z'ar : During 5th Meal : 984, 22nd Year of Iron
14 days until the 163rd Voting

732 followed two other Masked Ones down the steps of the tower, the stone damp compared to the summer heat outside. They descended in silence, the choreography of the interviews already well-rehearsed. Would she be punished for what happened at the warehouse? She was within her rights as an Elder to fight those men, but as a vessel… The priests could be funny about violence, some rejecting it while others almost relished in its expediency. But any punishment mattered little compared to the information she had and how badly she needed it to get to the High Priest.

They reached the bottom of the steps, the torchlight of the stairs giving way to the dream-like glow of the crypts. Tiny dyed stones in the domed ceiling glittered like stars, shining off of dozens of silver rings inlaid into the floor. The priest who was to interview her was already there, his back to her as he sat by the widest ring in the center of the room, where the city was drawn in miniature, the stars above glowing brightest as they split into the Diagram of Calling.

She followed the others across the room in silence, though she couldn't help herself from looking at Viden's ring as they passed it. How long until his vessel gave out and he was buried there, his body abandoned by the Elders? She was mostly beyond crying now, though she felt…heavy. As she came around the center of the crypts, standing at attention, she realized the priest awaiting her was Keroes nir Sen'l himself, the High Priest's stole loose around his shoulders. He held the Cyran Stone already, turning it over in his hand, its three outer pieces — titanium, cobalt, and zinc — dancing in the light as its smaller veins of silver and gold shimmered.

"Thank you," he said to the guards, ignoring her, "you may go."

The other Masked Ones left without a word until there was no sound other than the breathing of the crypts, the musty air whispering as it flowed between the burial chambers.

"I trust you spoke of your task to no one?" the High Priest finally asked, looking up at her.

She nodded.

"151 took over at the warehouse," she said, "but I think you should know, those men had—"

"Irrelevant," he said, waving a hand. "A bit of grain always goes to the rats."

So, he knew of the corruption, then? Although, a bit of 'grain' as he said could hardly explain why those men had a sword that should not exist. It paled in comparison to a stolen vessel, true, but whoever brought that serosine to the basin was powerful, frighteningly so. Still, she only nodded again. Priests never listened to you until they felt like it, and Keroes nir Sen'l would know everything soon besides.

"For now," he continued, not noticing her distress, "we need to act quickly on the child. To your circle. It's best I hear it for myself."

She bowed, walking backward to her ring, her feet having memorized the path long ago. For some reason, her own crypt bothered her less than Viden's. Even knowing she was likely only ten years from the final Passing herself, at the moment, the thought of having her bones folded up under the stone felt…restful.

She reached the center of the ring, kneeling on her heels. She looked up at the star pattern above her, taking a deep breath, but Keroes nir Sen'l seemed too hurried for tradition. Before she had a chance to say her prayers, he was already standing before her. He placed the Cyran Stone in the shallow bowl just inside the ring so that it was touching the silver, gesturing for her to awaken it. She nodded, reaching for her knife. Her left thumb had still not healed from her last interview, so she used the right, pricking it with the blade. When there was a good-sized pool of blood, she placed her thumb atop the stone.

Immediately, it began to hum, waking the silver of the ring as the air began to vibrate with its rhythm. Could Keroes nir Sen'l feel it? No one, not even Viden, had ever spoken of the interviews. She knew such thoughts were useless, knew what was coming, but she thought them anyway. Why was it that her vessel's mind seemed most active just before it was lost? Whether he could feel the vibrating or not, though,

Keroes nir Sen'l seemed to know it was time, finally joining her in a seated position with his hand on the Cyran Stone.

The moment he touched it, her entire body froze, even her lungs stopping for the span of a heartbeat before he gave her permission to breathe again. Her eyes locked on his, but it was hard to see, the stone already dredging up all her memories, the images blending together with what was right before her eyes. She both remembered and forgot herself at the same time, the zinc and cobalt working alternately until she felt like she was watching her own life from above as if she were at the top of a well, the truth deep and dark below.

"What is your name?" the priest asked quickly, eager to be done with the pleasantries.

"Zi'yun nol Curan," she said, the answer forcing itself from her lips, the bridge between thought and word shortened to nothing by the Cyran Stone.

"And who lies beneath you?" he asked.

"No one," she said. "An empty vessel, though it once held my spirit. A vessel known as 731."

"Very well," he said, clearing his throat. "Now, what did you see at the warehouse?"

As he asked his first question, the memories flooding her mind seemed to multiply, darting like birds around a tree as they coalesced around the warehouse. Every detail came back to her, the images piling up until she was drowning in them. Still, some seemed to shine brighter than others, and she eagerly described them to him, her mind suddenly desperate to share what it was seeing in its lost state. She could hardly make the High Priest out through the haze of memories, but at the end of her story, as the images dispersed, she saw him frown.

"Why did you fight those men?" he asked.

"The sword," she said without hesitation. But the answer didn't seem to his liking, a searing pain rocking her spine, her teeth clenching.

"What of the child?" he asked.

"They hid the child," she said, struggling to speak. "They deserved to die. But I know where."

The pain disappeared as if it had never been, the memories swimming before her mind again like fish rising from the bottom of a pond.

"Who did you share this information with?" he asked.

"No one," she said. "I was to speak only to you."

"Good," he said. He reached down and snatched up the Cyran Stone, releasing her bonds. She gasped, her lungs suddenly desperate for air. She blinked, shaking her head, but Keroes nir Sen'l was already standing.

"I have called up a contingent of palace guards," he said, folding his hands behind his back. "They will be ready in an hour, and you will lead them. Tell no one where you're going until it's time to leave, and no matter what, return with the child."

———

Teros made his way up the narrow stairs of the barracks, carefully balancing two heavy fifth meal trays. The men in the mess hall had been nice, heaping his plate with braised cabbage and thyme sauce — not to mention all the extra food they'd piled into his belt pouch. Apparently, sixth meal in the barracks was little more than a snack before the night watch started, so they'd urged him to eat up. They hadn't seemed to question Borash wanting to eat in their little room above the kitchens, even giving him a little bottle of whiskey to shove in his pocket for the older man.

It was confusing how everyone could be so nice to him and so rude to Borash. Uncle Elin had always said if you showed a friendly face, a friend you'd find. But even when Borash tried to be friendly, it seemed the others didn't care. But those same men were nice to him, so what was the difference? Couldn't they see that Borash was good? He was walking him all the way to the pond, after all. He hadn't left, hadn't quit, and he hadn't told anyone their secrets. To him, that was a real friend, and Mother always said you could only count those on one hand.

Mother… He got to the top of the landing, squeezing his eyes shut as the bad faces threatened to come back. But he was getting better at thinking of the good ones, and it only took a second before he could breathe again, moving down the hallway. When he reached their room, he couldn't work the handle with the trays in his hand, so he knocked on the door with his foot. He heard the grumbling before the footsteps, Borash's face finally appearing as he cracked open the door. He scowled at first but actually softened as he recognized Teros, with maybe even the hint of a smile.

"Well done, lad," Borash said, swinging the door wide as he trudged back to where he'd been sitting by the window.

The room was dusty and full of boxes, but it was cozy, and it actually had a fireplace where Borash had started a small fire while he was gone. For some reason, it was always colder outside of the city at night, and the sun would be setting before long. Teros carefully set Borash's tray on a nearby box before retreating to the fireplace. As he sat, though, the bottle in his pocket clinked against the floor.

"Oh," he said, scrambling back up, "they wanted me to give you this."

Borash raised an eyebrow as he took the bottle, pulling the cork and smelling the whiskey.

"Guess if they wanted to poison me, they could just put it in the food," he said, taking a long pull from the bottle.

"Bloody gods on the mountain," he said, coughing. "Still tastes like nails."

Teros tried to do some calculations in his head to figure out how much longer Borash had before he couldn't stomach the whiskey, but truthfully, he didn't know enough about alcohol. More importantly, he didn't know how many chul'uns were in the fire he'd wielded earlier, though it had to be a lot to burn those men to bones.

"I think they seem okay," Teros said, returning to his tray.

"Maybe," Borash said, running a hand through his hair as he finally took up his tray. "But if I can give you any advice, lad, it's to not trust the people where you're going. There's plenty of snakes in this basin, but the dukes are the worst bastards of the lot."

Uncle Elin had been a duke, and he'd been a good person, right? They had left the farm suddenly for Uncle Pesrin's, but Mother had never had a bad word to say. Still, Teros only nodded.

"Maybe," he said quietly to himself, but now he was thinking of Mother. He stared into the flames, dully spooning his food into his mouth as he tried to imagine Irmun Pond. He shook his head, remembering the other things he'd slipped into his belt pouch.

"They make overnight rice balls in the kitchen here to go with fifth," he said, pulling them free and lining them up by the fire. "Since they have a little bit of everything but sixth in them, I figured they'd be good for us to practice with."

Borash perked up, rubbing his eyes.

"Well, isn't that something?" he said. He scooted toward the fire, picking one up and turning it over in the light. "Haven't seen these in years. And they aren't half bad-looking either, tenth acre at least, lucky sodding guards. My Mems used to make 'em for the high holidays, would cook like a bloody demon from morning 'til night."

Teros smiled, picking up his spoon again. They ate in silence for a while. He'd noticed they were tenth acre, too, which had given him the idea for the practice. When they were done eating, only a single rice ball remained, and Teros picked it up, showing it to Borash.

"So," he said, "we worked on Permanence in the wagon, but I figured you should practice the others, make sure you can call them all."

Borash took a sip from his whiskey bottle, shrugging.

"I found the fire sure enough," he said. "But I guess it wouldn't hurt — so long as you don't turn me to stone again."

"You should be alright," Teros said. "You did Passion already, and Permanence is only *really* scary the first time. The others just feel…odd. I'll teach you to flare the opposites though, to keep the Passing back."

They started how they had in the wagon, with Borash staring at the rice ball as he tried to guess which Principle was which. He actually remembered Permanence from before, and with the book in front of him, he was able to find the others easily enough.

"And what about Place?" Borash asked. "We don't have any sixth meal, but shouldn't I learn that one, too?"

"Eventually," Teros said, nodding. "Every Principle's important. Like the book says, 'the Mother's secrets whisper equally.'"

"Sure, sure," Borash said. "But what is it? What's it for?"

"For movement," Teros said. "But… I haven't actually done much with it. Uncle Elin had me move things across the room and all that, but I've never moved myself with it. They say the Masked Ones can send messages, travel to another basin if they want — though that would probably set you back a ways with the Passing."

"Another basin…" Borash repeated, shaking his head. "Sounds like bloody paradise."

"Anyway," Teros said, pointing at the book again, "you need to find them in your stomach like earlier, only separately. If you listen, the humming will sort of match those lines in the book."

Surprisingly, Borash closed his eyes without being told, rocking gently back and forth with the whiskey in his hands.

"I feel the warmth," he said. "I remember that from before."

"That's good," Teros said. "Now you have to pick them apart. Feel the Permanence first, just like the stone."

He rummaged in his belt pouch, coming out with the practice stone again. He'd rejoined the halves after Borash broke it, a brand-new line shimmering in its center.

"I…think I feel it?" Borash said.

"You feel the others?" Teros asked.

"A bit," Borash said.

Teros held out his hand, cupping his palm as he felt the air with his mind. Uncle Elin had said the air was actually full of all sorts of things — strangely named gases all mixed together. He felt for one, listening for its voice as he told it to burn. He held the flame constant, not letting the Passion escape as the fire flickered over his hand, sucking in new gas to keep itself lit. Borash opened his eyes at the light, blinking.

"You see the pattern?" Teros asked. "This one's Passion, though I guess that's obvious since it's fire."

"Right…" Borash said, squinting at the book again. *Obvious.*

After a few more minutes, though, Borash *could* feel the Passion, and by the time their fire burned low in the grate, he was holding his own flickering flame in his hand.

"Incredible," Borash said, looking years younger as he stared at his palm. His wasn't as stable, the fire quivering as it danced across his palm, but it was under control, at least — far more than when he'd burned those guards. After Teros showed him how to counter the Passion with Identity, Borash finally closed his hand, taking a swig of whiskey as he rubbed his eyes.

"Thank you, lad," he said, looking up. "It's a kind thing you're doing for me."

"I had a teacher," Teros said. "And you should too."

Borash nodded. He slowly reached out his hand, patting Teros on the shoulder like Uncle Elin used to do. They were quiet after that, watching the fire burn low, but for the first time in days, he didn't feel so afraid. He pulled his cloak around him and lay on the floor, listening to the crackling moss until sleep came.

———

732 leaned against the statue of Elder Zi'yun, her forehead touching his chalky lithium robes. She breathed out, listening to the whispering voices in the dark. The Cyran Stone always left her struggling to return to herself, the memories of her vessel swimming up. Usually, it was benign things, memories from her training before she'd quieted her mind. But tonight, for some reason, she found herself remembering the before. They were useless thoughts, and so deeply buried she had all but lost their meaning, but one of the faces she still knew: her brother.

His face was a blur after two decades without him, but if she strained, she could still just capture it. What would he look like now? She had been so young when the priests divined her; would he recognize her without her mask on?

"My lord," a voice said behind her.

She turned slowly, finding a palace guard watching her warily. She'd heard his footsteps approach, hadn't she? Why was her mind in such a fog? At least she hadn't jumped. The guard bowed hastily, shrinking under her gaze.

"They're ready for you," he said.

She nodded, waving for him to lead the way.

They crossed the grounds, the crops glowing golden in the setting sun. As they reached the reflecting pool, she found what were meant to be her troops, some twenty palace guards, a half-dozen of them with epaulets on their shoulders. Standing to the side and speaking to 151 and two other Masked Ones was one of the king's Golden Masks.

"Zi'yun nol Curan," the Golden Mask said, nodding. "I am the King's First. I hand-selected these men for you."

"Thank you," she said, nodding in return. He may work for the king, but she didn't bow. The Golden Masks were said to be empty vessels, chosen for their purpose with no way of determining their true rank.

"It wasn't done for your sake," he said matter-of-factly. "You should know your task is as important to the king as it is to Keroes nir Sen'l."

"Very well," she said, nodding.

"I have also brought two for your task," 151 said, gesturing to the other Masked Ones. "They can be trusted."

"Will you be joining us?" she asked, though she already knew the answer. She would like to know what 151 had done at the warehouse after sending her back to the tower, of course, but that was no longer her concern. All that mattered was the child.

"This is not where I'm needed," 151 said simply. "I'll stay with the First; we have much to plan."

"And we should begin without delay," the Golden Mask said. He raised his hands, turning toward the palace troops. "This is Lord Zi'yun nol Curan," he said, his voice ringing out as if projected from his mask. "You are to obey him as you would me. When he attacks, attack. If he retreats, protect him with your life. Do you understand?"

The men all bowed, their thumbs to their foreheads.

"The men are yours," he said. "I will eagerly await your return."

With that, he disappeared back into the palace with 151, leaving 732 with her men. She still felt unmoored, like a tiny piece of herself might float away, but she put her hand on her sword and turned.

"We march south," she said, leaving the others to follow. The guards moved quietly despite their armor, following her through the shadow of the wall as the sun slipped beyond the city. Hopefully, they enjoyed the quiet now because where they were going, darkness alone would fail to hide them.

19

26th of Sund-z'ar : After 6th Meal : 984, 22nd Year of Iron
14 days until the 163rd Voting

Borash woke to a scream, his body lurching upright before he was truly awake. He listened, staying absolutely still. There was a lot of noise from the courtyard, but no more screaming. Some disagreement between the night guards, then? When had he fallen asleep anyway? He remembered drinking, staring at the fire as the kid slept, but he didn't remember lying down himself… The fire was nearly gone now, nothing more than embers in the grate, though there was still a strange orange glow to the room.

He groaned, getting to his feet before shuffling toward the window. What he found below looked like the bloody cave of demons. The Zi'yun troops were fighting a battalion of palace guards, the clang of swords now clear. The glow of fire was everywhere, the carriage house turned into a pillar of flame. He stood for a moment, frozen as he watched, until he saw something even more terrifying: a flash of porcelain in the darkness. The masked killer stopped, looking up at the window as it met his eyes.

He spun, crouching down. For a moment, he couldn't move, his heart pounding before he finally crawled back to Teros, shaking him.

"Lad," he barked, "get up, get up!"

Teros was somehow immediately on his feet, his eyes wide and terrified.

"What?" he gasped, looking about as he seemed to only then realize he was awake.

"They've come," Borash said, "we have to go."

He had already grabbed the boy's belt pouch and shoved it around his shoulders, pushing him toward the door. It would be cold out in the stone forest, but there was no time for the bedrolls.

"Come on," he said, more to himself than Teros, "come on."

————

732 pulled her sword from a man's chest, her eyes already probing the air in front of her for another wave of arrows. The lithium guards were proving more effective than she expected, and every moment she spent fighting outside gave the vessel another chance to slip away. Her own soldiers had been regrettably hesitant at first, seeming to lose their nerve when they realized who they'd be fighting. That only lasted until the first one took a spear to the neck, of course. But now…

Just like the cursed sword at the warehouse, this battle was raising questions she didn't think she'd ever have to answer. The ducal guards seemed as if they had trained to fight her kind. They didn't have any forbidden swords, but they knew how to group up, using their shields to defend against fire, moving in tight knots and forcing her to split them off one at a time. Even worse, the Golden Mask had only given her twenty men, and they had already burned through half of her forces, the other Masked Ones forced to hold her flanks.

She scanned the barracks, the bowmen at least looking like they'd all been killed, their bodies either dangling from windows or mangled on the ground below. She was about to join the Masked One on the right when she saw movement in one of the windows. She readied a hand to shield herself with Identity when she saw a hazy face through the glass, the figure immediately disappearing.

There! The battle immediately forgotten, she was pulled toward the barracks as if on a string, launching herself into the air. The vessel would be in that room, she could feel it in her bones. She moved quickly, killing the two men guarding the door, their cries lost to the din of fighting filling the courtyard. No one else seemed to spot her as she slipped into the barracks, pausing to listen. There were stairs in front of her and a long hallway to her right, voices carrying through a thick set of doors.

"Bloody caves, man, where are the city troops?!" a man shouted.

"Sir," another man said, his voice shaking, "they said they'd need at least an hour. I-I'm sorry."

"You're gonna be real bloody sorry with a sword through your gut!" the first man said. "Now grab a damned bucket; if the barracks catch like the carriage house, we're finished."

The man clicked his heels, his footsteps coming toward her. She raised her hand as he came through the door, the man's eyes wide as she filled the hallway with fire. She would not be stopped now, not when she was so close to the vessel. Shouts came through the doors, but she was already running up the stairs, anyone who could have chased her trapped by the flames. She felt a twinge of pity, but just as quickly, it was gone. These men who'd been arrogant enough to build their barracks with pricey wood from Pen'dil Sohn were the same ones harboring the child.

As she reached the top of the stairs, she heard footsteps running off to her right. She gave chase, trying to keep her bearings. The barracks were split in half by the stairs, with each side holding a long hallway that ended in a T. As she entered the hallway, she saw someone going around the corner at the other end, a flash of color amidst the smoke already filtering through the floorboards.

"Stop!" she shouted, sprinting after them.

She came around the corner, the next hallway ending abruptly in a window. The child was there, attempting to climb out. But as she turned to the man beside him, they locked eyes, and time seemed to stop. It had been so many years, decades already, but it seemed the memories dredged up by the Cyran Stone hadn't failed her. Even changed as it was, covered in lines and a scruffy beard, she could never forget it. It was the face she still saw in the darkness, the memory deeper than any other, of the last time she was human, his eyes meeting hers in her hiding place. Her brother, Borash.

But was it real? A *trick* of the stone perhaps, or something more sinister, some demon sent to steal her nerve? Regardless, time would not be still forever, and there was precious little of it besides. Whatever it was, her body reacted, her training taking over. They raised their arms at the same time, Borash's eyes widening with fear. Even as she read the air, knowing he would use Passion, somehow her own mind could only choose fire in return. Two massive flames met between them, the fire spinning together in a furious tangle of light before it erupted, blasting outward with a force so intense she felt her mask crack as its power flung her back.

Suddenly, she felt only fear. This was not meant to be. Like the sword from Deyn, that face should not exist. And it should not be attached to such raw power. She scrambled to her feet, her mask somehow holding to her face despite the gash down its center. She spun Identity, pulling in a black cloud of smoke from the burning hallway to cover her. She dropped from the window on the other side, her hand already on her whistle. And even as her men died around her, as the child no doubt escaped through the window, she blew her whistle with all her might, signaling their retreat from a battle they had already won.

20

21st of Curis-gul: After 2nd Meal : 961, 14th Year of Copper
23 Years Ago

Borash moved slowly through the Wist Ristare, his mind fuzzy from hunger. The guards would get on his case eventually, shuffling about like an urchin, but it was everything he could do to keep moving. He'd tried seven different restaurants, and all of them had shooed him away. Even the man from Seln had turned him down, though he'd at least looked sorry about it. Not that an old man's guilt would keep the wind out…

A sharp breeze blew up, cutting through his threadbare robe like a knife. He had to stop, clutching his arms as his bones shook. It felt cold for the end of Curis-gul, though it could be the hunger, too. Everyone else on the street seemed fine, most of the rich folks not even bothering with shawls. Still, he had to keep trying. Paps wasn't much better — though the other foreman let him get wheeled over so he could watch, even if they wouldn't bloody pay him for it — and Mems's fingers seemed fit to bleed from all the needlework she'd taken in. They kept arguing late at night, fighting about something he couldn't quite grasp — not that it seemed to solve anything.

The night before, though, the fighting had been worse than ever. The banging had woken his sister, and she'd crawled into his bed, crying. When Paps finally stopped slamming his hand against the wall, he'd gotten her to go to sleep, though the arguing continued. He'd left Eyri sleeping and crept toward their door, putting his ear to the reed-wood just as Mems screamed.

"You even speak that about Eyri again, and I'll open your bloody cave-digging throat myself!"

Mems's footsteps had pounded toward the door after that, and he'd run to his bed for all he was worth. But he couldn't stop thinking about it… They really were hiding something about Eyri, and if Mems had gotten riled up enough to curse, it had to be something bad.

He reached the northern end of the Ristare, nearly crying as the smell of the Bake Helm floated over to him. He thought about trying to find some work over there — hauling grain, anything — but the gate guards gave him such a dirty look he got scared they'd break his legs for fun. As he crossed the palace road and wandered into the park, though, he started to see a crowd, all of them gathered around a priest who'd climbed on top of a box.

"—if you have any knowledge of such a child, the reward is more than just a spiritual blessing, my friends! To anyone who gives information leading to the vessel's safe collection, the reward is one hundred fullers. For any family who makes the sacrifice on their own, the reward is one thousand!"

Borash ran into the man in front of him, apologizing as he stepped back, eager to avoid a slap. But as he stopped, he couldn't seem to move, his mouth hanging open. A thousand fullers… He couldn't even begin to imagine that much money. A single-ring coin was enough to feed his family for a week, and the most money he'd ever laid eyes on was the two-ringer Paps gave him on his name day, though that was years ago now.

"Hey," he said to a woman standing next to him, "what's the priest want?"

The woman clucked her disapproval at the priest, shaking her head as she marked her forehead with her thumb.

"Nasty business," she said, turning to him with the same look of disgust as if she'd just noticed him. "Looking for children what know the magic. But anybody who'd sell their own kin is good as a cave worm if you ask me."

She eyed him as if he might be just such a cave worm, but he simply nodded his thanks, disappearing into the crowd.

A thousand fullers… That would be enough for Paps to never work again, for Mems to never get another bruise under her eye. It would be enough…for anything.

———

It can't be real. That's what he kept saying to himself in his head. He knew what the Masked Ones did down in the palace, but that wasn't the stuff of regular folks, and certainly nothing he'd ever heard of someone doing on Mer'n Hill. But the longer he thought about it, the more it made sense. What else would Eyri have to offer that Mems would be so mad about? She was a girl, true, so they could sell her to Pauper's Palace, but Paps would never stoop that low. He'd open Paps's throat himself if he even suggested such an awful thing, but his sister wasn't big enough to earn more than scullery wages there besides. But even if it was impossible, he found himself praying to the Elders, wishing for something, *anything*.

When he finally got home, it seemed the Elders had seen fit to hear him. As he walked into the garden, Mems was coming out, her basket in hand.

"Oh, good," she said, rubbing his hair. "I'm just leaving. Your Paps went to the mill and the tailor said he has something for me today. Be a good lad and watch Eyri, alright?"

He nodded, though as she walked away, he simply stared at the house for a while. This was a good thing, right? If he wasn't wrong, if it was what he thought it was, it would be better for everybody. Eyri could live in the palace, never hungry again. Besides, if they didn't do something, how long until one of them got sick? Soris, just on the other side of the hill, had lost his mother and his father both, their family too poor to pay the priests. He took a deep breath, pushing his way inside.

Eyri was there, playing by the kitchen with her dolly. The thing had seen better days — its moss hair getting raggedy and its worm-thread smock split in a few places — though Eyri didn't seem to mind. She looked up, smiling.

"Hi, Borash," she said.

"Hiya," he said, sitting on the floor next to her.

He watched her play for a while, talking to herself as she jerked the dolly around the floor. She really was a smart one, always coming up with her little pretends.

"Listen," he finally said, her eyes darting up and back. "Eyri, listen to me."

She stopped, blinking as she dropped the dolly, watching him.

"I need you to tell me something, and tell me true, alright? Have you ever done anything…magic?"

She pulled her legs to her chest, staring at the floor.

"No," she said, starting to pout.

"Eyri," he said, "I know you, and that face says you're hiding something. Tell me the truth."

She looked up at him, frowning.

"Mems said to never tell," she said. "And Mems—"

"It's alright," he interrupted gently. "I'm your brother, Eyri. Just tell me."

"I…I don't know," she said. "Mems said sometimes I just get dizzy, that I don't know what I'm doing."

He thought of the stories, what they said the Elders could do. He'd never seen a Masked One at work, but everyone talked about their fire. He gestured to the grate, where they hadn't been able to afford a fire in weeks despite the chilly weather.

"Why not make a fire?" he said gently. "It's chilly, and I've been out all morning."

"I'm too hungry," she said, not looking up from the floor.

Too…hungry? But did that mean she *could?* They said the Elders lived in the holy acres, but was that how it worked? They'd never be able to afford anything good enough like that, unless… He looked up at Mems's prayer jar in the kitchen.

"Mems said I could feed you," he said. "Said to give you something nice, like from the jar."

Eyri looked up at that, her eyes giving her away as they stared longingly at the prayer jar hiding at the top of the cabinets. It had been forever since they'd been allowed to dip their hand in the jar on holidays, but it seemed she remembered still. And who could blame her? On his hungriest nights, his stomach making him toss and turn, he would sometimes dream about the jar, the cinnamon plums mocking him in the darkness. But even with everything they'd been through, Mems was firm on keeping it intact. They'd never be able to afford another, for one, but he knew it was fifth acre, and when things got dark enough, they'd probably sell it. But with a thousand fullers, they wouldn't have to, could have cinnamon plums every night if they wanted.

"Come on," he said, standing and offering Eyri his hand. "Mems said you've been a good girl, and she wants you to have a treat for once."

She looked doubtful but took his hand, following him to the cupboard, her mouth hanging open as she stared at the jar. He carefully crawled onto the counter, setting the jar down before he dared climb down. As he lifted the top, there was a gasp of air, the intoxicating smell filling his nose. Still, he only took one, unwilling to risk Mems's wrath should he be wrong.

As he held it out to Eyri, she took it like a treasure, staring at it for a time before she shoved the whole thing in her mouth, closing her eyes as she chewed. When she finally swallowed, she gasped for air, smiling like she had on her name day.

"Good?" Borash asked, smiling back.

She nodded, and he tousled her hair, pointing her back to her dolly as he returned the jar. When he got back to her, she was muttering to herself again as she played, though the dolly's dances were more lively than before.

"Eyri," he said, crouching down. "I need you to show me the magic now."

She looked up, frowning.

"But Mems *said*," she stressed, pouting as she turned back to her doll.

"Eyri," he said, "I know you're too young to understand, but Mems and Paps are in trouble. If you can show me the magic, you'll be able to help everyone. We need food, and you can get it for us."

She didn't look back at him, but she sniffled, her back quivering as she started to cry. She never said as much, never complained about anything, really, but their fighting clearly kept her up too.

"Eyri," he continued, "come on, we need—"

"*No*," she said more firmly. "No, no, no."

"Eyri," he snapped, growing angry. "We're gonna bloody starve. Is that what you want? You want Peps to never get better?"

She clamped her eyes shut, shaking her head, her dolly clutched tight in her hands.

"You want Mems to get sick? You want me to get sick? I need you to do—"

"No!" she shouted, her dolly suddenly bursting into flames. He fell back, barely catching his fall as his eyes widened. Eyri dropped the doll, clutching her legs to her chest as she cried. He watched as the doll burned, the stale cloth turning into ash. Slowly, he reached for Eyri, taking her in his arms.

"Well done, lass," he said, stroking her hair. "Well done."

The air filled with smoke as the dolly shriveled to nothing, his sister's tears soaking his shirt. But for the first time in months, it felt like his family had a chance.

21

27th of Sund-z'ar : The Small Hours : 984, 22nd Year of Iron
13 days until the 163rd Voting

Teros followed Borash up the rocky slope, his lungs searing as they climbed. They'd been hiking for hours, and he was going too slow — the older man cursing under his breath — but he couldn't stop looking back. Even after they'd hiked over the first hill and the flaming barracks were hidden from view, something kept pulling his eyes toward the north. Maybe it was because he finally understood… The men crying for help as they died, the blood boiling in the flames, the moon blotted out by smoke — *he* had done that.

He thought he had been doing the right thing, doing what Mother had wanted. But for once, both the faces in his mind seemed false. She was gone, smoke and ash, just like those men. And it had been his fault. Everyone who tried to protect him died. Mother's voice still tried to spring up in his mind, calling him her precious boy, but he held it back. Even as it put a knot in his chest, he held it back. This was *his* fault.

"Borash," he said, his own voice sounding strange to him. "We have to go back."

"Back?" Borash asked, stopping for the first time in miles to glare at him. "Kid, look around you, we're in the middle of nowhere running for our damned lives. We go back, we're both sodding dead, you understand?"

Teros looked around the Stone Forest. He had no idea where they were. They'd been walking for so long, climbing through the hills, but everything looked the same. Massive stones loomed in the darkness, growing like fingers from the hillside. They'd climbed high enough that they were above the night fog, like they were floating on a pond. There was nothing but dust and dry-moss, the closest water locked away somewhere in the river far beneath the surface. He didn't like when Borash was angry, but something in him hardened.

"They were nice to me," he said, "and we should have stayed to help."

"Help?" Borash asked. "You saw those things crawling around the flames. What are we gonna do that a bunch of bloody soldiers can't?"

"I don't know," Teros said. A lump formed in his throat, but he refused to cry. "At least we have magic, same as them."

"Yeah, kid," Borash said, "we have magic, sure, but not enough. They burned the whole place down like it was nothing, and they were looking for you anyway. You want to help those poor bastards? Then keep walking and get as far away from them as you can."

With that, Borash turned, continuing his march up the hill. But Teros could only look back. He'd already known it was his fault, but somehow what Borash said made it even worse. The Masked Ones were looking for him, and wherever he went, there would only be more fire.

"*Teros*," Borash said sharply, looking down from the top of the next rise. "I don't know how many miles left to Irmun Pond, but if we don't get close before sunrise, those things could be on us again."

Teros glared at him but started walking again. As soon as he reached the top of the hill, Borash started back down the other side. Why was Borash walking so fast? He could barely move earlier, and if he hadn't made them stay the night, none of those men would have had to die.

"How are you able to walk so far anyway?" Teros asked, the words sounding more bitter than he'd meant.

"Because I have to," Borash said, "just keep up and we can—"

He suddenly slipped, crying out as he hit the ground, rolling a few feet down the hill. Teros scrambled after him, his eyes wide.

"Bloody cave witch's teat!" Borash cursed, baring his teeth, his eyes clamped shut. Eventually, he looked at Teros through tears, his face a storm cloud.

"Why'd you have to go and bloody say something?" he asked. "We were doing just fine until you opened your big mouth and made me remember my leg. You want me to get bloody killed too? Let the sodding white masks rip me apart? Bloody *mero relin*, as if I ain't been put through enough."

"I'm sorry," Teros said, no longer able to hold back the tears. "I didn't mean to, I was just asking."

"Bloody gods above," Borash said, squeezing his forehead. "Don't add crying on top of the rest now." He took a deep breath, pushing himself to his feet.

"Look," he said, pointing to a shadow on the ridge line where there was a gap between two rocks. "We may as well camp for now until my leg feels better. You just better hope your duke is bloody waiting for us; I think we've been through enough for that bastard."

"Okay," Teros said, trying to keep his voice from cracking. He followed Borash through the darkness, the older man hobbling forward. He didn't want to sleep in the Stone Forest, probably wouldn't even be *able* to sleep. But at least for one night, no one else had to get hurt.

———

Teros woke to the sound of voices, lurching up from the cold stone. There was nothing to cover him but his robe, and he was freezing. He wiped his eyes, looking around him. Borash was the one talking, muttering in his sleep.

"No, please, no," he said before his words fell into mumbling. He looked like he was still in pain, though, a grimace on his face.

Teros watched him for a long time, suddenly feeling very sad. He'd been angry earlier, but now he just felt guilty. Borash was like everyone else, putting himself in danger because Teros was too afraid to face what waited for him. And what if the Masked Ones did find them out here? They would almost certainly come with others, and Borash's fire wouldn't be able to save them then. Without wanting to, he pictured Borash's face covered in blood, lying dead next to all the men from the barracks, their eyes open, blaming him. He squeezed his eyes shut, holding his breath as he tried to force them away.

"I'm sorry," he whispered, though he wasn't sure who he was talking to. Mother tried to come to him, but he pushed her away, too. He could no longer listen to her voice. He opened his belt pouch, leaving his book by the older man. It wasn't much of a thank you, but keeping him alive would have to be enough.

Before he could change his mind, Teros got up, walking back toward the north. Enough people had died for him. It was time for him to face what he was and protect what he had left.

THE END OF PART TWO

A Respite

Pen'dil Seln - Time Unknown

—:—

Theiral carried the lamb over a small rise in the highlands, finally spotting the rest of the herd below. He'd found the little creature hiding in a crack in the stone, whimpering and shaking. Perhaps it, too, knew a storm was coming? Reading the weather seemed so obvious to him — he was always more surprised when someone told him they couldn't — though father still insisted his abilities were rare. Father even talked about him splitting the tents and starting his own tribe when he was older, but who would want that? When tents split, you never got to see your friends anymore, and the sheep got split up besides.

He made his way back to camp, the others already hurrying about their tents preparing for the storm. The sky was still blue, though, so apparently Rikosh had told everyone. When he finally reached the tiny copper statue of the forefather, he stopped, putting the lamb down outside the garden gate. The creature didn't run off to join the others, though, instead staring up at him as if waiting to be picked up again.

"Fine," he said, shaking his head at the lamb. "You're a little *minosek,* but at least you're cute."

He held up a finger, hoping the lamb would understand to wait as he went into the garden. The plants looked rather small as he wove between them, but they'd stopped at this field a week before, and that was the garden mothers' business, not his. The forefather was in a state of repose today, the statue tilted down in the grass with a blanket covering it. Theiral placed his forehead on the ground a few inches from the forefather's and placed his right hand so it was covering the statue's eyes, blocking its views of the heavens.

"Father Serimin," he prayed, "please grant me the horizon's sight. To know what the wind knows, and think what the rain thinks. Protect us from the coming storm."

Then, he simply breathed, waiting until he felt he could hear the statue whisper. He still didn't know what it said — and no one else in the elders' tent even believed him that the whispering was real — but he was grateful for it all the same. In some small way, it felt like the gods were responding, saying: 'We hear you, Theiral nin Cusak.'

Finally satisfied, he got back to his feet, returning to where his lamb was waiting for him. Funny he was already thinking of it as his. It belonged to everyone, of course. But just like a tent wife, when something chose you and you chose it, you were connected somehow. He would look after this lamb, and maybe one day the lamb would return the favor.

He continued on into camp, the others smiling when they saw him carrying the tiny creature. Still, he pressed on, not stopping to talk. Father would be waiting for him, and now, just on the horizon, he could see the first storm cloud. Towering and dark with rain, it was a reminder that what was promised would always come.

Pen'dil Sohn - Time Unknown

—:—

Auyd walked through the grove, humming the song of stillness. He hummed it exactly as his father had, and his father's father. For whatever reason — perhaps because it was how he'd been trained — the song made it easier to do things properly. Walking barefoot, the slower you moved, the more easily you could attune the trees and the soil around them. Walking along the intersecting lines of metal, it allowed him to feel their needs, to know who needed what.

And the trees themselves proved how important it was to do things the right way, the old way. His family's were the tallest in the basin, taller even than the First Son's — though no one would dare mention it in the Forest King's presence. Still, even if it was only in secret, there was much pride in that. Most of the other groves came to his family for advice, consulting them on illnesses and new growth alike. Most importantly, though, everyone knew how much they honored the trees. His family took only the minimum allotment each year, and no one in his grove-kin had ever taken the full cut to move south amongst the unshaded. Not like Tek nir Irmun, may the spirits curse his name…

He stopped, suddenly feeling distress from a nearby tree. Perhaps it was *him* the spirits should be cursing in his carelessness… If you could not carry stillness in your own mind, you could never hope to urge your grove toward the light. He left the metal line, moving slowly across the soil so as not to lose his hold on the tree. Finally, he found it, a young arendin tree. He remembered its name — *kesperwen* — as he had chosen the planting spot himself.

He looked up at the canopy, tracing the light as it filtered down. It *was* a good place, but this was indeed the tree who had called to him. He put his feet carefully on the metal nodes set between the roots while his palms caressed the bark. The problem was immediately obvious, the tree's pain pouring into his mind. It was wordless, but he could sense it through every fiber of the tree, the meaning running along the lines of metal twisting through its rings.

He moved quickly around the trunk, easily finding the hole in the bark, clearly the work of a borebug. He moved more quickly then, his heart wrenching as he thought of how much pain the tree must feel. He took his stone cup, filling it with cinnabar from his pack. Then, he lit the reddish paste, blowing the smoke into the hole with his cherin fan. For a moment, there was nothing, but he kept at it, his years in the grove teaching him the wily tricks of the borebug. At first, they would always play dead, hoping you would think them gone. But they could not play forever, and he had the song of stillness on his side.

Finally, he heard a scratching noise, the borebug frantically moving its hundred legs as it tried to escape its ill-gotten home. When its head appeared, Auyd was ready, moving suddenly as he turned his hands, filling the poor creature with so much Permanence that it would never move again. He took the bug by its neck, easily pulling it free from the tree now that it was little more than a rod of stone. Still, all creatures were worthy of his respect, and he laid it gently on a patch of moss by his feet. It would have a place of honor in his collection, another token of their vital work.

As he patched the hole with kern sap, he began to hum again. But this time, he hummed the song of joyfulness. There was nothing to disturb him now. Only himself, the wind, and his grove.

Part Three

22

27th of Sund-z'ar : The Small Hours : 984, 22nd Year of Iron
13 days until the 163rd Voting

732 followed the others into the crypts. There were three Masked Ones this time, 151 among them. He was afraid, she could tell, but it hardly mattered — she was *terrified*. She could barely remember the retreat, running through the night as the barracks burned behind them. All she could see was that face, a face that should not be, shrouded in flames that should not exist. Still, they were not the same. 151 was afraid of the torture waiting for them below. She was afraid of the truth, and the unmooring of the world it caused.

Keroes nir Sen'l was waiting for them again, but he too was changed. There was no meditating now, his eyes afire as they landed on her.

"Leave us," he said to the others, pointing to the stairs. They stared at him for a moment, but he was in no mood. "I said leave us!" he bellowed, the others hurrying away.

He grabbed her by the shoulder, nearly dragging her toward her grave. When they reached the silver ring, he shoved her to the ground. The Cyran Stone still had her blood on it, the cleansing ritual ignored in the few hours since their last interview. Instead of placing it in the bowl, though, he ripped off her broken mask, shoving the stone against her forehead. She gasped, her heart skipping a beat as the magic bored into her core, her lungs no longer seeming to work. She tried to work her mouth — to tell him he was killing her — when it stopped, Keroes nir Sen'l finally taking control of her spirit and allowing her to breathe again.

For the first time, he seemed to actually notice her, frowning as he

"

met her eyes, no doubt seeing the fear in them. He blinked, shaking his head, perhaps realizing he had manhandled a god. Still, it was only a moment of weakness, his anger returning even as he began the ritual as he should.

"What is your name?" he asked, nearly spitting out the words.

Eyri, she thought suddenly, the name coming unbidden to her mind. She had to bite her tongue to keep it from leaving her lips, the force of the stone making it nearly impossible to withhold the truth. Where had that come from? It was forbidden to even think such a thing, of course, but that name should have been buried too deep to retrieve. It was irrelevant, useless, gone from the world. She was not that person. Regardless of what she had seen at the outpost, the face she had forgotten, the magic that shouldn't exist, she *was not* that person anymore.

"*What* is your *name*?" he said again, more harshly. A flash of pain shot into her spine, forcing her toes into the floor, her feet curling with the pain.

"Zi'yun nol Curan," she said, the correct answer thankfully forcing its way out, the practice of thousands of interviews finally correcting her like grooves in a riverbed.

But as the memories welled up in her mind, the Cyran Stone pulling up everything that had ever passed through her vessel, she saw that face again. And in that moment, she knew she wasn't wrong. It *had* been Borash. Even with the passing of the years, she knew that face. And she saw him again now in another memory, decades younger, finding her beneath the bed. She remembered running, the men at the door, the end of herself — her life. If that face was real, though, then so was the magic. But her brother was no vessel. It was still something that should not be, *could* not be.

"Keroes nir Sen'l," she tried to say, "I—"

"Silence," he said. He pushed the stone harder against her forehead, though it only forced her back onto her haunches, forcing him to cup a hand behind her head, the gesture completely out of step with his anger. Still, it did not stay his hand for long, another wave of pain forcing bile into her throat.

"Why did you call the retreat?" he asked.

Suddenly, she knew. Whatever this truth was, it was her own.

"The one with the child," she said. "He wields the Principles; he nearly killed me when he cracked my mask."

"Who was he?" the priest asked, the pain letting up a fraction as his focus drifted, mumbling to himself. "Perhaps if the king…" he muttered, "the others…"

He shook his head, focusing on her again.

"How could that be?" he asked. "Who was he?"

"I don't know," she lied, her veins threatening to melt away as she fought the power of the stone. It would never let her betray her oaths, but somehow, she forced herself to find the truth in what she said. She *didn't* know how Borash came to be there if that was even really him and not some demon with his face. "He was maskless. But Keroes nir Sen'l, this should not be, something is wrong here, very wrong."

"It's like the damned Forgotten Years," he said. "The dukes grow too powerful. Still…"

He turned away from her, her limbs sagging as the stone left her forehead. Still, he didn't seem to notice, not bothering to set the Cyran Stone in its basin as he paced before her, talking to himself. She worked her jaw, forcing herself to breathe.

"You have failed me," he said, finally returning to stand before her. "The king is aware of the attack on the outpost, and your inability to finish things properly has made things uncomfortable for us. If we lose the child…" He took a deep breath as if the thought were painful to him. "If we have nothing to show for our efforts, the cost will be immense."

"I'm sorry," she said, bowing her forehead low to the ground, the cold of the stone unfamiliar to her naked face.

"You may serve our kingdom yet," he said, rubbing his chin as he stared up at the false stars on the ceiling. He muttered to himself, only the word "Dek'rc" getting past the ringing in her ears. "You are forgiven," he finally said, "for now. Get yourself to the infirmary; I need you well. When you've been healed, you can fix your mistake."

He left her, uncaring how she got herself to the eighth floor. As she watched him go, a tear rolled down her cheek, though she wasn't sure if it was for herself or the girl she only just remembered being.

23

27th of Sund-z'ar : Before 1st Meal : 984, 22nd Year of Iron
12 days until the 163rd Voting

Borash started, coming to on the cold ground. His nightmares still clung to him, enough to make him hug his cloak tighter. One of those masked creatures, reaching for him with a ghostly hand, getting closer as he realized he couldn't run. Even worse, it brought back memories that made him wish he'd stayed asleep, ghosts be damned. He clamped his eyes shut, trying to will them away. He'd never seen one so close, but it only made him think of that little girl, screaming as she was dragged away. If only he hadn't finished his bloody whiskey…

He coughed, sitting up as he tried to clear the dust from his throat. Sodding Stone Forest, might as well be—

"Teros?" he asked, his voice sounding like someone else's. But, of course, no one answered. There was no one *to* answer. The camp was empty, and now that the sun was up, he could see for miles around the blank hillside. He was instantly on his feet, turning in all directions. Had they taken him? But then, why would they bloody leave him sleeping there? And how could they do it silently? Unless it was those bloody things… He—

His foot kicked something in the dust as he turned. He looked down, finding the kid's book sitting next to where he'd been sleeping. He picked it up, wiping the dust from its cover. Staring at it in the blue light of dawn, he immediately knew what it meant: he'd been left behind. He dropped to the ground, his legs splayed in front of him as he stared at nothing.

Why? They'd argued the night before, surely, but he'd only been protecting him. They got lucky with those masked devils, and they weren't likely to again. Still, if the kid went back… He sat up, looking for footprints on the hillside, but the wind had blown the stones clear of dust. But there was no way he would've gone back. The kid was sentimental, sure, but he wasn't a fool. A bit of time to think, and he'd have realized the outpost was finished. But then, that meant…

It felt like a lance to the heart, and he squeezed his eyes shut, refusing to cry. Why was he bloody surprised? He'd been let down by every other bastard in the basin, so why should the kid be any different? Just 'cause the kid had taught him a few tricks and said some nice things? As if that changed the fact that they were all devils, from the sodding gods on down. And now, surely blaming him for the fire, the kid had bloody walked to the duke's on his own, keeping everything for himself but a useless little book.

Well, too bad. The kid *had* taught him some things, and he'd be a cave witch's kindling before he slunk off without the prize. He got up, throwing the book to the ground as he walked off, heading to the south.

———

After everything — walking through the darkness, screaming at the faces in his mind, turning himself in — now, there was only waiting. Teros sat in a guard house just beyond the palace walls, a cold mug of tea in his hands. He'd forgotten to drink it. The guards kept coming and going, giving him strange looks as they ran about, trying to find where he was meant to go. But he didn't pay them any mind, hardly even noticing them really.

Still, he was more sure than ever that this was the right thing to do. As he'd walked, every step had brought a new face to his mind. The guards from the outpost, the wagon drivers, Maegin. But especially Borash. He could only imagine how angry he would be when he woke up, but he couldn't lose him, too. By the end, when he'd finally reached the city, there were so many faces chattering in his mind, he could barely hear his footsteps any longer. Even if there was only one whose voice he could make out… He saw her now, Mother's bad face, begging him to run, demanding he stay free.

"I'm sorry," he said, clamping his eyes shut. "But I don't want it, not if this is what it costs."

He shook his head, opening his eyes to find a guard staring at him, his hand on his sword. And finally, he realized: they were afraid of him. It was a good reminder of what he was here to do, what Mother had tried to save him from. He was here to become a Masked One. He would wield the Principles for the king, and he would cease to be himself. But he was here now, and they could stop chasing him. The dying could stop, and Borash would be safe.

24

27th of Sund-z'ar : During 1st Meal : 984, 22nd Year of Iron
12 days until the 163rd Voting

732 sat on a bed in the infirmary, waiting for the priest to return to take her poultice off. It stung something awful — cherry juice mixed with alcohol and something else — but he'd said it had to sit on her shoulder for an hour before he could stitch her up. He'd blown out the candle, no doubt hoping she'd sleep, but even with exhaustion boring into her bones, she couldn't bring herself to close her eyes. Doing so would only bring the memories back.

Instead, she stared at her mask on the table, its porcelain somehow glowing in the darkness. They had brought her a new one, her sigil already engraved on it. It was probably her fifth or sixth mask, though only the second one she'd broken. The others had grown too small, resized as her vessel left childhood behind. She picked it up, turning the cool ceramic over in her hands. Suddenly, she remembered the first time she'd put it on. It had felt like a relief then, the same coolness soothing the bruises of her breaking. But even now, she couldn't feel regret. Her ascension had saved her family from starvation or worse, the gods caring for them while she saw to her duty. Every Masked One knew that, and finding any semblance of peace meant learning to be grateful for it.

But then, why would Borash be at that outpost? He didn't look safe or well-fed. Her heart suddenly ached for her family. She even thought of her mother. After twenty-three years, she couldn't picture the woman's face any longer, but she somehow remembered the shape of her. What had become of them? She feared something awful, something evil. The legends all agreed the maskless were no better than demons. But why would a demon wear that face? How would it know her weakness? It put a pit in her stomach, making her feel that the evil coming for her home was greater than she could imagine.

There was a knock at her door, and she straightened, putting the mask down. She could have worn it, but the doctoring priests never seemed to mind, and it would be better if he could inspect her cuts first anyway. But as the door opened, the soft glow of a single candle revealed the shining face of Pelona from the armory.

"Oh, my lord," she said, quickly covering her eyes, "I'm so sorry. I didn't realize you were indisposed."

"I'm fine," 732 said, quickly pulling the mask's straps over her head. "Please, be at ease."

"My lord," Pelona said again, bowing. She turned, pulling a hand cart in from the hallway. "I was up with the hospital rations, and I heard you were here." She began to busy herself with some dishes, clearly relieved now that the mask was on. "Anyway," she continued, "I haven't seen you in a few days — hard at work, I'm sure — so I put something special together for you."

She turned back around with a streaming bowl on a tray, laying it gently across 732's lap. It was a lovely first meal spread, with bright yellow mustard potatoes and a bowl of shaved leeks.

"I triple-checked your register," Pelona said, "and it's all things you can eat with no trouble. Just enjoy and rest, alright?"

"Thank you, Pelona," 732 said, smiling under her mask. "It means a lot."

"It's nothing compared to what you do for us, Sacred One," she said, though she looked pleased, her smile deepening under the praise. Still, it faded a moment later, the woman stepping closer with a somber look.

"And…" she added, slipping a rice ball onto her tray. "I'm afraid your friend, Lord Viden, wasn't able to keep anything down the past two days. Still, I thought I'd better drop this by since you're here in case you'd like to try."

732 took the rice ball, hefting it in her palm as she stared at it.

"Thank you," she said again. "I will."

———

Viden was awake when she reached his room, though he could have just as easily already been gone. He was staring at the ceiling, his mask off and his eyes glassy.

"Father," she said quietly. His eyes finally moved, swiveling toward her. He blinked at first as if unseeing before a small smile came to his face.

"Son," he said barely above a whisper.

She crossed to the bed, taking his hand.

"Where is your mask?" she asked. It was like seeing him naked, the times he'd been maskless around her less than she could count on one hand. Still, she didn't dare shy away from it, not at the end. If he needed her to change him, she would — anything to give him the dignity he deserved.

"I told them to take it," he said, though he wheezed from the effort of putting so many words together. "My vessel is finished."

She nodded, holding his hand tighter as she felt a tear come to her eye.

"I'll carry you to the crypts myself," she said, the only thing she could offer him now, the food from Pelona as useless as his mask.

"Don't bother," he said. "Just…a heap…of bones."

"Bones that are precious to me," she said, which at least earned her another smile.

She sighed, finally taking a moment to stare out the window. The mountain was ringed by the rising sun, its shadow no doubt hiding the spirits of the gods. When it was her turn to go, would she really make it to Sen'el'tul, to die in the grass staring up at the peak? She heard a sniffle from Viden and looked down, finding his face covered in tears.

"What is it, father?" she asked, running a hand along his forehead.

"I wish…" he said, his voice straining, "I had let you die."

"What?" she asked, starting. "Surely you don't mean that."

"Both of us," he said. "It should have been finished…in the war. Not…like this. It isn't…real."

"Isn't real," she repeated, frowning. She suddenly thought of Borash again, the memories still floating in her mind, mixing with ones of Viden. She still feared it was a demon, but if it wasn't… The war, the Passing, the rivers of blood they'd spilled in the name of the crown. What would any of it mean? What would it have been for?

"Viden?" she asked, even his name forming a question as her mind struggled to stay afloat in a sea of doubt. "What if we aren't the only ones?"

He squeezed her hand tighter, his eyes softening. They were no longer glassy, his gaze returning to its old intensity, to the way he'd been when he trained her.

"Run," he said, his voice barely above a whisper. "Go."

Just then, a knock came at the door.

25

27th of Sund-z'ar : During 1st Meal : 984, 22nd Year of Iron
12 days until the 163rd Voting

Borash felt the pond before he saw it. The dry air of the Stone Forest was suddenly heavy with moisture, and his tongue no longer felt baked into his mouth. He had no idea how long he'd been walking. Caught between the throbbing of his head and leg, he'd had no choice but to carry on, slumping forward at an odd rhythm, moving as far as he could between bursts of pain. Still, even in his barely conscious state, his anger had pressed him on. They thought a bloody bum couldn't walk to their precious little pond? Well, they were in for a surprise. Those bastards probably never went an afternoon without their comforts, but he'd gone without his whole sodding life.

Despite all that, though, when he finally came out of the final pass and saw the pond, he stopped short. The night mist had cleared, and the water looked like a sapphire glittering beneath the sun. It was the most water he'd ever seen in one place, like they'd flooded the whole Wist Ristare. It was jarring after the grey of the forest, the entire place impossibly green, with acres and acres of crops stretching up into the fields beyond the water. It was…incredible.

Not that the feeling lasted long. As his eyes adjusted to the sun, he noticed the wall encircling the place. It went the whole way round with sharp pikes at the top, and as his eyes followed the road, he caught the glint of spears. Squinting, he could make out at least a dozen guards at the front gate, with more no doubt patrolling the grounds. Bastards, keeping the garden of the bloody gods to themselves while the rest of them rolled about in the filth like worms. He straightened his robes, marching onto the road.

It took the men a long time to notice him, far too long for men who were supposed to be on watch. Still, even a cave witch would eventually notice a hand in front of her face. A captain-looking bloke with a feather in his helmet and a sword on his hip was the first, throwing a hand in the air when he was just ten feet away.

"Halt!" he yelled. Shooting a harsh look at his men, he waved for them to follow as he walked up.

For a moment, he almost softened, his training no doubt opening him to the possibility of a guest. But Borash was no such guest, of course. He hadn't arrived in a carriage, was certainly unexpected, and one look at his robes had the man frowning again.

"What business do you have here?" he asked. "This pond is private."

As two guards came up beside the captain, they wore the same frown, though one spared a look for the desolate hills behind him, clearly surprised he'd walked there through the night.

"Here to see the duke," Borash said, standing firm. "Owes me an audience for getting the boy here."

"The…boy?" the captain asked, tilting his head. He looked at his men, who shook their heads. "Listen, friend, I think you may be confused. There's no boy here. Just turn around and we can leave it there."

Borash ground his teeth. The boy had been at the pond all of six hours, and they were already playing games with him?

"I'm seeing the bloody duke," Borash said, meeting the man's eyes. "Tell him I know what the boy can do, and I can do it too. He's gonna wanna meet if he knows what's good for him."

The spearmen shifted their stances, preparing to fight, but the captain held them off. He ran a gauntleted hand over his face, sighing.

"My old man was a drinker, too," he said, "so I'm trying to be patient. But this isn't the place for you. Leave, *now.*"

He thought of the letter in his pouch, the ring the kid had left behind, but he was done being told where he belonged. Done with being shooed to the bloody shadows like a rat. A fury leapt inside him, and before he could think, he raised his hand, ready to burn the man to ash. But nothing happened… Of course, nothing *could* happen. He hadn't had a drop of whiskey in hours. He…

The spearmen laughed, and the captain shook his head, waving a hand for his men. Before Borash could even drop his arm, the man on the right stepped up, punching him square in the jaw. He dropped to the ground before the sharp kick of a boot followed, his lungs emptying as his ribs pushed inward. He lost track after that, but when the beating finally stopped, he was being dragged up the road where he was finally tossed into a ditch. He rolled to a stop, blessedly facing up. He felt the men rooting around in his pouch, heard them laugh when they found the ring, but he couldn't stop them. It hurt to breathe, hurt to think even. But as he stared up at the perfectly blue sky, he was just glad it was over.

26

27th of Sund-z'ar : After 1st Meal : 984, 22nd Year of Iron
12 days until the 163rd Voting

732 struggled not to run as she hurried through the tower. It seemed the gods *had* heard her prayers, and they'd answered precisely when her doubt was at its fiercest. The child had returned. The messenger had been from Keroes nir Sen'l, and while his message had been simple — written in her own cipher — its implication was clear: *Child returned. First Ceremony. Only trust vessel's blood.*

She knew there were factions in the tower, but for whatever reason, it seemed the High Priest wanted the child in Zi'yun hands. It dredged up other uncomfortable questions in her mind, of course — who had helped the child, and how had they stolen her brother's face? — but she could stew on that later. *The child had returned.* Perhaps her fight at the outpost hadn't been for nothing, had frightened whatever dark forces were at work to steal the boy. Even if that face…

She shook her head. It was more important now to serve. A pile of flimsy memories were nothing compared to training, and what was this nebulous truth she was seeking compared to serving the kingdom? And she *could* serve now, find a way to undo her shame. If she succeeded, perhaps she could put behind her doubt, forget the things Viden had said and the loss that filled his eyes.

Her hope carried her through the halls, all the way through the priests' ward, right up until the guards showed her through the door. But then she saw the child from behind, sitting at a desk as he looked through the window, and suddenly, her memories came surging back again. It seemed like another lifetime when she was in this room herself, Viden taking her hand and drying her tears. Still, she'd needed him then, just as this child needed her now.

"Hello," she said quietly, slowing as she reached him. She sat gently on the edge of the bed, smiling beneath her mask as the child turned around.

"Hello," he said. She'd expected tears on his face, but he was calm, far calmer — on the surface, at least — than she felt herself.

"I'm 732," she said, "but you can call me Curan."

"I'm Teros nir Zi'yun," he said. "Or…I guess I was."

She nodded. He seemed older than she had been when she arrived, old enough to know something of what awaited him. His accent seemed educated, too, so different from her, afraid and alone, her voice hoarse from screaming. But she'd had Viden, and he would have her.

"They didn't tell me which spirit has chosen you," she said, "but I'm a Zi'yun, too — Zi'yun nol Curan. So for now, we're like family."

"Thank you," he said. "You seem…nice. Do we have to go now?"

"We do," she said. She looked at the desk, where he'd pulled a copy of The Laws of Faith from one of the shelves. But it was unopened, its gold leaf cover gleaming in the morning light. She wanted to ask him how he had found his way back, what had happened after her retreat, but the words wouldn't come.

"You'll have some time to yourself after the first ceremony," she said instead. "I'll tell you about it on the way. If all goes well, we'll likely do the second ceremony tomorrow night, and you'll receive your mask."

"Alright," he said, standing. He'd seemed much older as he sat meeting her eyes, but now he looked small, his robes much too large for him.

"Come on," she said, taking him by the shoulder, "I can show you the grounds on the way to the cave."

As they walked through the grounds, it was almost too easy to forget where they were going. The sun was shining on the crops, and Teros even seemed like a child again. He didn't smile, but he took a genuine interest in the fields, his eyes suddenly wide as they stared at all the plants.

"They're all like this?" he asked, reaching up to touch a sunflower. A farmer a few rows over opened his mouth to object before he met her eyes. The man bowed, no doubt realizing this was no ordinary child.

"They get even bigger by the river," she said, pointing. They were making their way down the Zi'yun aisle, and they were only in the sixth acre. By the bottom of the hill, the crops were enormous, the cattails reaching almost to the statue's waist.

"I can show you all the aisles this afternoon if you'd like. In the Cosk aisle, they have watermelons bigger than your chest."

"I'd like that," Teros said, nodding his thanks.

She smiled again under her mask, gesturing for him to follow. He asked a few more questions, his voice seeming brighter, but they still couldn't forget their purpose for long. As her eyes passed over the northern wall, she caught a glimpse of Sen'el'seng, the god mount rising above the city. She couldn't help but remember the Elders then, and every question from the night before rushed back into her mind. She stopped, glancing across the field at the caves where the priests were already waiting for them.

"Teros," she said, kneeling beside him. "The man you were with last night... Who was he?"

His face hardened, his eyes turning down to the dirt.

"No one," he said.

"His name..." she said. "It's Borash, isn't it?"

Teros looked up, frowning.

"How do you—"

"I knew him once," she said quickly, "or thought I did... Tell me, his powers, are they real? Is he...human?"

He looked into her eyes, though what he saw there she couldn't tell.

"Yes," he finally said. "But I'm here now, and if you want me to stay, just leave him alone. Besides, he's just like the others anyway."

"Others?" she asked, her head suddenly swimming as the blood pounded in her ears.

"Adults who use the Principles," he said. "Like my Mother. They can all do it, at least a little. But please," he added, his eyes desperate, "just leave him be."

"I... Alright," she said, nodding. For whatever reason, she believed this child. There was no artifice to him, none of the falseness so common in the tower. What his words meant for her, on the other hand, was impossible to fully fathom, like a dark stone hiding at the bottom of the river. Whatever this secret meant, whatever questions it raised, she could never mention Borash's part in it. But in that moment, Viden's voice was also in her mind again, urging her to run.

"Come on," she said, shaking her head. "They're waiting for us."

They continued, passing the statues. She could make out the priests clearly now, Keroes nir Sen'l first among them.

"Can I ask you a question?" he whispered, staring straight ahead.

She nodded. "Why are they so sure it's me?"

"There is another ceremony," she said, thinking of the crypts. Her pulse quickened, and her muscles tensed with the memories of her interview so recent, but as she focused her thoughts on the stars, she somehow found a sort of calm.

"It's rather beautiful, really. There are stars in the crypts, stars that match those in the sky. And this ceremony, it tells the priests where in the basin a soul might be. It helps the priests know which tips are true, but more importantly, it helps us know a vessel has arrived. A vessel is a sacred thing, but it's dangerous, too. A vessel *must* serve or else we face disaster. I can show you the crypts after the ceremony. It's quiet, and… I suppose I feel hopeful knowing I was chosen, that the gods wanted me to serve."

His faced hardened.

"Tips?" he asked.

"For the stipend," she said. "I…" For the first time, she realized who had turned her in all those years ago. She felt a fool, though it changed nothing. She couldn't undo the nights of crying or the whispers from Viden that had made it easier to bear. "The crown pays a thousand fullers to the families of Masked Ones. It saves many of them from starving; it's one of the greatest legacies we leave behind when we end our lives as people and begin them as vessels."

"From the stars," Teros said, shaking his head. He met her eyes, looking sad. "Thank you," he added. But they had reached the priest, and before she could say anything else, the child was taken from her side.

No one said she was to leave, so she followed, the weight of tradition carrying them all forward. She let it sweep her along, grateful for even a moment without having to think. The priests shepherded the boy into the caves, Keroes nir Sen'l singing at their head. They passed the ancient graves, moving toward the grotto. She joined the other Masked Ones in pulling back the river, allowing the priests to cross with the child. The burden was lessened with so many hands, but she was still grateful to release Flow as she crossed herself, the power of the river reasserting itself.

As she joined the circle around the grotto, however, the crutch of tradition fell away. Teros sat on the floor, his legs folded as the High Priest swirled around him. Keroes nir Sen'l's voice was exultant, his hands shaking as he sang the prayers, but the boy… Teros's face was blank, his eyes empty as he stared straight ahead. This was not the look of a sacred vessel. Neither was it the tear-streaked face of a worried child, something easily fixed through training. This was…a corpse, a lamb awaiting slaughter.

She glanced at the others, but their eyes were closed, their voices joining the High Priest's as they echoed off the stone. She looked back at the boy, hoping he would meet her eyes, hoping she could give him an ounce of strength. But the singing stopped, and Keroes nir Sen'l stepped between them.

"This is a sacred day," he said, "a holy day. The gods have granted us a spirit in our hour of need, a spirit of noble courage, sent from Sen'el'seng to answer our prayers. What say you?"

"Entodash rikal," the priests chanted in the old tongue, raising their hands in exultation. *"Entodash mishtal."*

The Masked Ones were silent. In this place, at least, they were part of the spirit world the priests were calling down from on high. But as Keroes nir Sen'l lit his incense, circling the boy with smoke, she finally realized what came next, and her heart began to pound.

Handing his incense to another priest, he reached into his robes, revealing the Cyran Stone. It was not aimed at her, *could* not be under the law in this most sacred of places, but she felt the breath leave her lungs all the same. Whether it was the power of the stone or the recency of her interview, she couldn't say, but she found herself reaching for the Principles, needing to feel their touch.

As Flow and Passion poured into her, she sucked in a quiet breath, the numbness leaving her limbs. But then her heart wrenched, remembering Teros. She hadn't warned him… Of all the things that shook your soul during the first days, the Cyran Stone was the worst. She only vaguely remembered her own initiation, but the feeling of drowning, unable to move, was still with her every time she saw the stone.

Keroes nir Sen'l stood before the child, handing him the knife as he ordered him to prick his thumb for the first time. Teros's eyes narrowed, but he did as he was told. He touched the stone, gasping as his muscles spasmed. And in that moment, she knew what the priests never could. He didn't yet have a mask, hadn't undergone the countless hours of training to turn himself into a blade, but Teros was gone, his body no longer his own. From this day on, he would forever be a Masked One.

27

27th of Sund-z'ar : Before 5th Meal : 984, 22nd Year of Iron
12 days until the 163rd Voting

When Borash finally reached the city, the sun was hot, his face a mess of sweat and blood mixing with the dust from the forest. He got even more stares than usual, but why shouldn't he? Let the bastards look. Hopefully, they enjoyed seeing a man on his way to the gallows. He'd thought he'd hit bottom, but it seemed there was always further down to go. But now, at least, he truly had nothing to lose. What could they do? Send him to the caves? His *life* was a cave, and he didn't need a bunch of rocks to live in darkness.

He used that feeling to his advantage, coasting on a boldness he hadn't had just two days earlier. Had it really only been that long? It felt like he'd been with the kid for a year. That's what hope could do to you, lull you worse than drink and make you think you were on your way to a new place, a better place. But now he was free, free to stop pretending. His only coin was spent, the ring was gone, and he was back to being no one. Even the letter the guards had left behind was worthless now, the fancy words empty in his belt pouch.

He worked his way toward the Wist Ristare, stealing a large bottle of whiskey from the back of a wagon. He could've been caught — would've been damned if he was — but no one saw him. Perhaps there was a lesson in that. After all, it's the man looking over his shoulder who catches the guard's attention. But there was no point in thinking such thoughts, the cork coming out easily and the whiskey pouring in even easier.

Everything hurt, but the drink took care of that well enough. And before long, he was walking like a lord, swaggering through the streets as if he owned them. It seemed he was in between meals, but based on the sun, it looked like the bells would ring for fifth any minute. Odd that he could miss the rhythm of the city after such a short time. He found himself looking forward to the fifth meal crowds, the voices and the hum of people, even if they would only stare at him like trash beneath their carriage.

He finally made his way past King's Square to the Menagerie, catching sight of the looming sign of the Peacock. Bloody bird. But at least it got his stomach rumbling. The only thing that could make whiskey taste better was a bit of food. He didn't much care for fourth — usually some kind of rice drier than the sodding forest — but food was food, and there'd almost surely still be something on the altars, fourth and fifth too close together in the summer for the restaurant owners to clean them properly.

As he came up to the ivy-covered lattice, he saw exactly what he needed, a pile of baked rice balls sitting on the upraised hand of old Irmun. He marched right up to the statue, not even noticing there were still patrons on the patio until he met their eyes through a gap in the ivy.

"Go find the bloody witch," he said, giving them a dirty look as he started shoving food into his mouth. Why were they at the restaurant between meals anyway? They'd probably go tell the owner, sodding princes, but he suddenly felt a surge of confidence, without a care in the world. After all, he had a belly full of whiskey, and the restaurant guards would probably think twice once he brought his fire out. Eventually, though, he heard voices through his chewing, realizing the men inside the patio hadn't run off after all.

"*Anyway,*" one of them said pointedly, "I'm just surprised Old Iron Teeth is going in for it."

"I know," the other one said, sighing. "Seems Sen'l's got him twisted around his finger. But can you imagine the lucky bastard they choose?" The man lowered his voice, and Borash found himself leaning into the ivy. "Do a bit of magic and they make you the king's own son. Mask or not, I just can't believe it — and a Zi'yun, of all people."

Borash realized he'd frozen with his hand in mid-air, a rice ball dripping sauce onto his foot. The kid's surname was Zi'yun, wasn't it? Anger welled up in him again. As if abandoning him for the duke's pond wasn't bad enough, they made it sound like the kid was being made a bloody prince! He met one of the men's eyes again through the lattice. Apparently unable to bear his presence any longer, the man raised a hand, signaling to an incredibly large carriage guard waiting by the curb.

Borash dropped his rice ball, turning into the alley. Part of him knew he could have burned the whole restaurant to the ground, but he wasn't running away. He simply had somewhere better to place his anger now, the top of the palace appearing over the rooftops. The king wanted bloody magic? He'd show him that and then some. He'd spent so many years afraid of his memories, but what had he really done wrong? Eyri was probably still living in the palace, eating like a queen while he rolled around in the filth. It was time for him to get his own mask and everything that came with it.

Of course, there was no palace gate on the west side, just the wall and a steep drop toward the river and the fields below. Even feeling like he could have flown down on his powers, he still headed to the north where he could ask to be let in. But he marched like a drunken soldier, stomping past the Bake Helm into Bitan Park, feeling like he was headed for battle and the glory that would follow after.

As soon as he arrived, though, he could sense something was different. Normally, Bitan Park was an empty place, the poor shooed away so the rich could look at their beautiful flowers in peace. But today, there were crowds forming — and of normal folks, too — stopping to hear palace criers spread around the square. The criers would stop, shouting their message before moving down the row to shout it again. Borash stopped beside a bunch of merchants who had paused with their handcarts just as one of the liveried men passed.

"Glorious news!" he shouted, gesturing to a long scroll in his hand — as if the bloody palace script were legible to anyone but a courtesan. "The king's son has been returned by the gods! Tomorrow, at sunset, after the holy ceremony, there will be a parade. All the king's people are invited to attend, with feasting and dancing. Sunset! Tomorrow!"

With that, he moved on, already assailing the next pocket of passersby with his 'glorious news.'

"Sodding cave witch's brood," Borash cursed. The merchants turned, frowning at him, but he glared back. Pious bastards. Didn't they get how unfair the world was? They were out here hauling scraps while the lords inside were sipping wine. And not only would the kid keep all the riches for himself, but he would get a bloody parade in his honor! His hands formed into fists, and he walked on, weaving through the crowd of fools toward the palace.

As he reached the gates, he found a dozen guards fanned out across the paving stones. They were eyeing the crowds, no doubt displeased at the peasants idling in their precious little square. If he thought he'd get close like he had at the pond, though, he was mistaken. These men were no slouches, and the moment he crossed onto the stone, the man at the head of the formation put out his hand.

"Halt," he said, his voice carrying without him raising it. "State your business."

Borash stopped, his hands on his hips as he met the man's eyes.

"I have important news for the king," he said.

The man frowned, his hand tight on his sword.

"And that would be?"

"It's about the boy," he said, "the one they're throwing a bloody parade for."

The guard waved a hand, and two others came toward him, pikes on their shoulders. He whispered to them, turning and pointing at the stone turrets behind him. As Borash followed his hand, he finally noticed one of the masked creatures standing in the shadow of the gate. He gulped, but why should he? He had the magic himself, didn't he? He'd fought one off at the outpost, and if all went well, he might actually *become* one before the day was done — and get pampered like one, too.

"Approach," the guard finally said, his men adjusting around him into a triangle under the gate. "State what you know."

"Well," Borash said, "I know the kid you got in this little parade deal, and the thing is, he doesn't really know the magic all that well. But I do, and I'll gladly wear a mask for the king if you let me in."

Under the gate, the Masked One moved suddenly, looking him in the eyes like a statue come to life. Borash swallowed again, harder than he would've liked, forcing his gaze back to the guard. The other man's frown had deepened, and he turned his shoulder slightly, his hand still on his sword.

"You speak evil, man," the guard said quietly. "You have one more breath to tell me you're a drunkard else we treat you like a demon."

"Now, listen," Borash said, "the kid—"

"The child is none of your concern. He has been vetted by the priests and inducted under the law, while you are here in violation of palace code. Back away *now*."

Something broke in him, his rage breaking loose like bile in his throat. After so many indignities, so many bloody curses heaped on his head, he could stomach it no longer. He had the magic, he had been chosen, and the kid dumping him in the forest wouldn't bloody stand. He raised his arm, just like he had at the pond, but this time, he could feel the power surging in him, the fire traveling through his blood, making—

The Masked One moved, quicker than a man should be able to, putting his hands together in a cross. Suddenly, the fire disappeared, and he felt cold, like a winter wind had sprung up around him.

"Detain him," the Masked One said.

"No," Borash said, putting his palms up, "I—"

He tried to run but couldn't, his feet suddenly stuck to the ground. The guards were already moving, their swords and spears at the ready. He met the Masked One's eyes as the butt of a spear was thrust toward him, taking him in the forehead as everything went black.

28

27th of Sund-z'ar : During 5th Meal : 984, 22nd Year of Iron
12 days until the 163rd Voting

732 closed the door to Teros's room, nodding to the guards as she left. After only walking a quarter of the way around the tower, though, she had to reach out to the wall for support. She felt dizzy, her head still swimming. She looked in both directions, making sure the hallway was empty before she dipped into a doorway, leaning against the stones as she tried to catch her breath.

The child... She'd been tasked with preparing him for the next ritual, walking him through the necessary segments of the law, the things he'd have to learn all too quickly the moment he donned the mask. But it seemed he knew everything already, maybe even going so far as to memorize the Laws of Faith. Still, he'd nodded along, emotionless as he listened. She hadn't had such an easy time, having to force herself to say the words, to read the passages in the dim light of the room. Even as her own voice droned on, all she could think of was what he'd said about Borash in the fields: "I'm here now, and if you want me to stay, just leave him alone."

If what the boy said was true... A wave of nausea crashed over her, and she had to steady herself with an arm against the wall. She hadn't been able to absorb it earlier, not truly, the rhythm of the ceremony taking over. But if it was even *possible* that humans could use the Principles, it would destroy everything. She could accept that her own life was gone — given for her family, spent in service of the crown — but the boy was only just beginning. And who did he have to save? Why would any of them — nearly all children when they arrived — have come without the bargain?

She forced herself to stand, moving down the hallway before she was discovered. But she didn't head for her rooms. She went instead toward the stairs, unable to let the questions linger in her mind any longer. When she reached the throne room, the doors were closed for fifth meal, the guards carefully standing in her way.

"Sacred One," one of them said, "Lord Sen'l is partaking of his worship. Perhaps if you'll return…"

"I need to see him now," she said. "Tell him 732 is here. It's about the boy."

"My lord," the guard said, bowing as he disappeared through a small wooden door set into the larger metal one.

After only a moment, the larger doors were pulled open, revealing Keroes nir Sen'l on his throne. The throne room looked transformed in the evening, the inlaid tiles of the river glowing black in the torchlight as the sun prematurely slipped beyond the palace grounds. And the ceiling… There was a glowing star mosaic like in the crypts, only in a pattern she couldn't seem to recognize. Were these merely for show, completely divorced from the sky above?

Remembering herself, she hurried forward, bowing before she took her place on the floor, her sword beside her. The High Priest was still not looking at her, scratching notes onto a letter in his hand. There was a vast feast before him, laid out on a tray that seemed custom-built to straddle the breadth of the throne. There were offerings from the first four meals of the day as well, a dizzying abundance of things she would never eat again.

"Tell me," he finally said, putting down his letter to meet her eyes, "what is it you wanted to tell me? How are the boy's preparations?"

"He is…prepared," she said carefully. "But—"

"Good, good," Keroes nir Sen'l said, picking up another letter. "Much more is required to finalize the ceremony, and I need someone I can trust. I'm glad you are so keen on redeeming yourself."

He wrote on for a time, almost seeming to forget she was there before he looked at her again.

"Do you have some concern to share?" he asked.

She sucked in a breath. She had been trained to investigate, not influence. How was she to make him see?

"Keroes nir Sen'l," she said, "I am concerned. Some of the things the child has said, it seems….he knows of many maskless who wield the Principles."

"Hearsay," the priest said, waving a hand. "I can assure you I've never heard of anyone in House Sen'l doing such a thing. But we do know the bloodlines are sacred. I wouldn't be surprised if some of the nobility had tiny blessings, *echoes* of the Elders, but anything more would be impossible. There are Masked Ones and there are demons, nothing more."

"But you said yourself when I took this assignment that there were concerns of someone helping the child." She would keep her promise, she would never mention Borash's name to this man, but the *idea* of it, the mere possibility she could have been wrong this whole time... "You said it would be chaos, like the Age of Disbelief. What I saw at the outpost, what I wrote in my reports—"

"Your *reports*, Lord Curan, appear muddled by the fighting," he said. "And concerns are very different than reality, my lord. There was an exceedingly large amount of fire where we first confronted the child, but it is clear now that his vessel is very powerful — in need of our control, of course — but powerful all the same."

"I..." she started, grinding her teeth together. "Perhaps I was confused by the fighting, Keroes nir Sen'l, but what I saw at the outpost was no echo. And I have to believe I would know the face of a demon."

"Well," he said, holding out his palms, "where is your demon, now? The child has returned as the gods promised he would. Even if a demon — or a lesser magician from another basin — *had* tried to interfere at this most holy hour, the child is on sacred ground now. There is nothing more to fear."

He picked up his chalice, taking a sip of wine.

"A bit of advice, Lord Curan. There are plenty of mysteries in the Mother's Valley, but it's best not to think about them when you have the answers you need. When the gods speak, do you really care if they use a comma or a question mark?" He smiled, putting his fingertips together. "Now, will that be all? If you find yourself beyond recovery, I need to know. Should your vessel no longer be capable of the soul inside it..."

She met his eyes. The threat in what he said was clear. The Cyran Stone could kill as easily as it froze. And it was a reminder that there were worse ways to die than Viden's, ways that would forever keep her from the freedom of taking her last breath in the mountains. Still, as she looked at him, another thought crossed her mind: she could kill him before he reached the stone, her sword through him before he took another sip of his wine.

She shuddered, bowing low to the ground to hide her shaking hands. *What was she thinking?* Never once had she thought of committing violence against a priest. Perhaps she *was* losing her grip. It wasn't unheard of, after all, of Masked Ones losing their minds before the final Passing.

"I am eager to serve," she said, getting to her feet. She bowed once more, turning as she fled the throne room. She wanted to be far from this place before she lost her grip, before she became a demon herself.

———

For a long while after 732 left, Keroes nir Sen'l sat in silence, both his meals and his letters untouched. It wasn't that he didn't fear demons — he was too devout to ever doubt the mysteries of the Mother's Valley — but he was also strong enough to know he wouldn't be turned back by anything, least of all a shaky vessel. But the truth was, he needed 732. There were too many factions, too many whispers of Masked Ones seeking their own ends. That in itself wasn't a sign of evil — the Elders had their disagreements, too, of course — but his was the only *righteous* path. The child was proof enough of that. He just couldn't afford to leave anything to chance.

He rang his bell, his ring servant Cirot'e appearing from behind the throne.

"Go to my rooms and fetch my dagger," he said.

"Your Holiness," Cirot'e said, bowing. "Are you…sure you want it now? You did say to keep it secret. Perhaps if—"

"*Now,* Cirot'e," he said. "This is a dangerous time, and a vitally important one at that. Or have you forgotten your purpose?"

"No, Your Holiness," he said, bowing again, this time with his head to the floor. "I'll return right away."

As the servant glided away across the tile, Keroes nir Sen'l felt a flash of anger. Perhaps a week in the dungeons would keep Cirot'e from questioning him next time. Or perhaps he was overreacting… He took a deep breath, squeezing his temples. The blade *was* a forbidden object, at least among normal men. It wouldn't do to flash serosine around the tower, especially given how…sensitive the Masked Ones were about the substance. But it made him feel better, too. Without any magic of his own, even the ability to absorb a little of it with his blade would set his mind at ease.

Just then, there was a loud knock, the guards swinging the throne room doors open again. Keroes looked up, squinting through the darkness at the shadowy figure in the hall with black robes and a mask of gold.

"Holy One!" Keroes said, standing from his throne as he bowed from the waist. "To what do I owe this honor?"

The Golden One stepped carefully into the room, looking about with his hands behind his back.

"His Kingship sent me to see how your preparations are coming," he said. "The parade is ready on our end. I presume you're leaving nothing to chance on yours?"

"Absolutely not," Keroes said, bobbing his head. "His Kingship will be most pleased. The first oaths are sworn, and by sunset tomorrow, his son shall be returned."

"And the Masked Ones in your service?" he asked. "They're still… reliable? The king was most disappointed by what happened at the Duke's outpost in the south. Even if it ended with the boy's return, it's made things…difficult for us. Money can fix many things, but not everything."

"My apologies," Keroes said, bowing lower. "As I said in my letter —"

"I care little for your letters, priest," the Golden One said, waving a hand. "I asked if they're reliable. 151 and 732, if I recall correctly?"

"Most reliable," he answered, though his throat felt tight. "151 has been in my service for years, and 732 is as loyal an ancient one as the basin has ever seen."

The Golden One chuckled, meeting his eyes.

"Loyalty can be a funny thing," he said. "Rather like a ghost."

He turned away, raising a hand.

"I'll see you tomorrow evening, Keroes nir Sen'l," he said. "It would be best if you do not fail us again."

And with that, he was gone, though the throne room felt darker in his wake.

———

It wasn't until she reached her room that 732 felt she could breathe again. But as she leaned her back against the wooden door, her room felt like a place she no longer recognized. How many days did she spend here a month, two? It was meant to be hers, a haven from the troubles of the kingdom, but now, it only reminded her of where they'd locked away the boy. It was a prison, nothing more.

What the High Priest said needled her mind, but she tried to ignore it, anything to stop the pounding in her chest. She took off her cloak, hanging it with the others by the door. Then, she removed her mask, massaging her scalp as she untied her hair for the first time in days. What could she do but carry on? Keroes nir Sen'l had been clear: the truth didn't matter. She was still a Masked One, still belonged to the Cyran Stone. Could she disobey even if she wanted to? And what would she do if she did? Even if she was property, she still wanted to serve the crown, wanted to honor the family she'd left behind.

She lit some candles with Passion, crossing the short distance to her desk. With Identity, she pulled at the hidden latch in the floorboards, the wood springing up from where she'd rigged it. She knelt down, pulling out her bag of dandelion along with her distilling jars. She carefully laid out the equipment, the familiar motions soothing her. She lit the brazier, boiling the dandelion until the steam began to rise, condensing on the glass as it dripped into her beaker on the other side.

It was painstaking work, only a few useful drops produced for every bag, but it was soothing all the same. Still, it was a wonder the forward guard were able to do their jobs. The palace attendants must boil dandelions day and night to allow them to send their messages throughout the city. But even though it had taken her years of rations, soon she'd have enough to fill a flask. And then she would be free. Even if the only path for her was death, she would still have something that belonged to her and her alone. And when her final moment came, whenever it was, she would slip away to die under the stars — the *real* stars — far away from here.

———

Borash woke on his back, a searing pain in his head. He groaned, blinking his eyes open. At first, they couldn't seem to focus, only registering a hazy blue light. As his eyes finally adjusted, though, he found himself in a prison cell. But it wasn't like any of the other pens he'd been thrown into over the years... Beyond the normal iron bars, the cell was set into an arc of silvery metal, the ceiling dotted with glowing blue moss.

He winced, trying to sit up from the stone floor. How had he...? It came back in a rush: his march through the city, the palace guards. Bloody gods, what a fool he was. Who did he think he was, the king of the sodding caves, out to rule the moss worms? They'd probably hang him. He felt a spike of fear, but he was still angry, too. He had the magic. He *had* it, and it changed nothing. No matter what he did, no matter what he learned, he'd always wind up right where the gods left him, a nameless beggar swimming in filth.

He could still feel a smoldering ember of whiskey in his belly, and he feebly reached out a hand, hoping he could melt away the bars, but nothing came. He could sense the fire, the anger and *Passion* welling up, but it wouldn't budge. He looked up at the glowing metal arches. Was it this place? So, he *was* just a bum. A man again, with nothing to free him from the prison of his own bloody design.

He slumped back down on the floor, wrapping his arms around his chest as he squeezed his eyes shut. Even as he berated himself for being a child, he couldn't stop a single tear coming to his eye. For the first time in his life, he was glad his parents were dead. There was no one who cared for him, no one who would mourn him. He was nothing, and in the morning, he'd be hung before the kid's parade.

29

21ˢᵗ of Curis-gul : Midnight : 961, 14ᵗʰ Year of Copper
23 Years Ago

Eyri hadn't called for Mems or Peps when she was taken, she'd called for *him*. His parents had left the money where it was for a long time, arguing over who had done it, neither of them ever thinking to look at him, to blame *him*. He stood there, staring at the money until it got dark, until even Paps wouldn't leave money sitting out like that anymore. His father swept it up, hobbling to the market alone, returning far too late with a bundle of food and a bottle of whiskey under his arm.

"We'll…get you to school now, I suppose," was all he said.

But all he could see now was that face, tear-streaked and afraid. And when Paps passed him the bottle, he drank from it, hopeful he might forget for even a moment. In reality, though, it didn't help much. If anything, it only made his thoughts darker, forcing him to stew in the grisly details. As Mems prepared a late sixth meal, though — crying the whole time — the smell of the food finally distracted him. After so many months without a proper meal, eating his fill finally dulled the ache in his mind. He wasn't even sure if he tasted it, but he shoveled it into his mouth until he was so full he thought he might throw it all back up.

When they were finished, they stayed sitting around the table for a long time, the dirty dishes glowing dully in the candlelight. Mems had always been the type to start washing up the moment she'd taken her last bite. But tonight, she stared into space, her face ashen. What would she think when she knew what he'd done? She couldn't go forever without looking in her prayer jar. And when she did…

Paps took another long drink, passing him the bottle. Borash drank again, the fire of the whiskey feeling better this time. With some food in him, it made him feel warmer, helped him separate himself from the awful scene before him. And as his brain began to fill with a contented fuzz, he could hardly tell he was sitting on the stone floor any longer. After passing the bottle back and forth a few times, Paps rubbed a callused hand over his face, letting out a deep sigh.

"I guess we ought to pray," he said. He squeezed his eyes together as if he might actually cry. "It feels wrong, but we've been saved, and we should be grateful."

Mems shot him a look, the most hateful he'd ever seen her give anyone.

"Don't you dare," she hissed. "My little Ey—"

"Enough!" Paps said, slapping a hand down on the table. "Our little girl is a god now, and I'm gonna bloody pray to her."

He pushed himself to his feet, hobbling to the shelf in the kitchen where he kept his weathered copy of the Odes. Paps had always been proud of learning to read, but the gesture felt twisted now without Eyri sitting on his lap to listen to the stories. Still, anything was better than silence, and as Paps limped back and started reading, Borash felt calmer somehow. Paps started at the beginning, his hands trembling on the sides of the book.

"Oh, to remember the time before time, when the Mother held us beneath her waves. We knew only precious water then, and she formed us of her metal, shining like the sun in her embrace. She came for us, the lost of her children, lapping her waves against our boats. And we discovered her, the echo of her singing, waiting and perfect, timeless against the foolish ramblings of man."

Even Mems began to listen, nodding to herself as she closed her eyes. Maybe Paps was right; maybe Eyri *was* a god now. Wherever she was in the palace, she'd be just as safe and well-fed as they were, wouldn't she? The Creator had brought them from the Giant Lands so they could be happy, after all. And maybe they would be. They'd been *saved*, delivered from the hunger that had threatened to sweep them all away. Borash took another drink, folding in on himself until his forehead rested on the table. He closed his eyes, drifting in the whiskey until there was only Paps's voice.

"We have a legacy, you and I, even when the others do not see. We are a tapestry of stardust, brought here as a symbol of all that we've forgotten. We honor the sacred memory, build temples to its truth. And we will sing until the stars sing with us, until the forgotten is remembered and only light remains."

She would be safe. She would be alright. She would be a *god.*

30

28th of Sund-z'ar : After 4th Meal : 984, 22nd Year of Iron
11 days until the 163rd Voting

732 hurried across the grounds, an army of palace attendants scurrying behind her. She hadn't slept a wink, but perhaps that was for the best. Sleeping would have meant dreams, her mind circling on things better off forgotten. Besides, Keroes nir Sen'l was right: where was her demon? If it really had been Borash, he wasn't here now, and that meant he was still safe. She had a sinking feeling that watching the child's initiation would break her heart, but he had made his choice, just as she had made hers. Even if it felt as though she didn't have one…

At least her list was long and her time brief. After reviewing the oaths with the boy, she had delivered him to 151, who would take him to the High Priest for his final preparations. Now, she had to ensure that a dozen other things were seen to: flowers and food laid out, offerings burnt, a child-size porcelain mask procured. She finally stopped on the western steps of the palace, pointing to where the servants could hang the ivy they'd just collected from the gardens. With that, she left strict instructions with the head maid before heading back toward the tower. Not only did she need the child's mask, but she'd need enough first acre food from the armory for him to swear the stone again.

As she made her way through the Great Hall, she passed a small group of Masked Ones, whispering as they huddled together by the stairs. She recognized the one facing her, 331, though she didn't know the others by sight.

"Said he came with Passion," 331 said. "Maybe he's from Sing, sent to kill the king, but they say he has no accent. I don't understand it myself. I—"

"331," she said, turning toward them.

They stopped speaking, their hands subtly moving to their swords as they faced her. Violence between Masked Ones was unheard of, but it didn't mean your training simply disappeared, least of all when threatened.

"What did you say?" she asked, willing herself to approach despite the shaking in her knees.

331 met her eyes, sizing her up.

"Prisoner in the cavern cells," he finally said. "Taken by a Masked One at the north gate. Says he was about to use Passion, but he's just a regular man, far as he could tell."

"What did he look like?" she asked, suddenly struggling to breathe.

"Like anybody, I guess," 331 said, "just a bum from the west end. But it just doesn't make any bloody sense. Nobody's seen him yet, but Sen'l knows, says it should wait for tomorrow."

"Thank you," she said, "for telling me."

She turned on her heel, forgetting all about the armory as she rushed out of the tower. She moved like a sleepwalker, gliding through the fields, her eyes fixed on the prison in the distance. Built below the palace wall on the cavern slope, it hardly ever had anyone in it. Most criminals were kept at the little tower in Middle Field or the ducal outposts. This place, however, had three amalgam cells, used to strip Masked Ones of their abilities before they were felled by the stone. She'd only seen a handful of people enter that place, but none of them had ever left it alive.

It wasn't until she reached the outside of the prison that she finally stopped, staring up at the building. Made of a strange black stone, it was unlike any other place in the basin. They said it had been built by the Elders, but why would they have built a prison? She could still turn around, go back to the tower, and get on with what remained of her life. But could she forget? Borash's face appeared in her mind, the fire he used at the outpost. And for the second time, she remembered her name. *Eyri.* She forced herself to move, stepping toward the prison. She had to know.

———

Borash lay on the stone of his cell, staring at the ceiling. He felt numb. How long had he been there? At first, he'd been afraid, but the longer he was locked up, the more the boredom took over. It still put a pit in his stomach to think about dying, of course, but all this waiting made a part of him just want it to be over with. At least they were feeding him. It was little more than gruel — the bastards were probably afraid he'd get his powers back otherwise — but at least it was consistent. He couldn't remember the last time he'd had all six meals in a day. But in between those meals, the hallway holding his cell was completely empty, the guards scurrying away once they dropped his tray.

He sighed, closing his eyes. He was still sore from the beating he'd taken at the pond, but at least the cold stone felt good. Maybe he could sleep a little while, and fifth meal would be soon. Life had been content to kick him in the teeth every chance it got. He should at least take his little pleasures now. Maybe they'd even give him a drab of whiskey before the end, something to ease his way to the beyond.

"Borash?" a voice asked quietly.

For a moment, he thought he was dreaming, but the voice spoke again.

"Borash," it said more urgently.

He cracked an eye open, turning his head toward the hallway. There was a Masked One standing in the shadows just outside his cell, watching him. He jolted, sitting up too fast as he backed against the wall. His heart raced, his calm from just a moment ago vanished. Was it already the end? Were they here to end him, trussed up in the caves like a common thief?

"It's alright," the creature said, stepping closer. It had a woman's voice, far...gentler than he'd expected it to be. Now that he thought of it, had he ever heard one speak? "I don't mean you any harm."

"H—how do you know my name?" he asked. "Are you here to hang me?"

The Masked One looked over her shoulder, stepping up to his cell. She eyed the glowing moss above him for a moment before gently laying a gauntleted hand on the bars.

"No," she said. "I'm here because there's...something I need to know."

A glimmer of hope. However foolish, his mind suddenly focused on getting out. It would be like making a deal with a cave demon, but he *was* a merchant, after all, and if someone wanted something from you, the battle was already half-won.

"What do you need to know?" he asked carefully, his throat suddenly dry.

She met his eyes. Hers were dark, like the caves themselves, just like his sister's had been, reminding him of that awful day when she'd stared out at him from under the bed. He suddenly felt exposed, like she could tear apart his soul with nothing more than a thought.

"Are you really…" she started, shaking her head. "Can you really use the Principles?"

"Yes," he said, suddenly unable to lie beneath that gaze. He could barely even speak the word.

"Are you a demon?" she asked.

"N-no," he said. "A demon, you—"

"Are you from Pen'dil Sing?" she asked, not waiting for him to speak.

"No," he repeated. He swallowed, finally managing to clear his throat. "I'm from Mer'n Hill."

"Mer'n Hill," she repeated slowly. She turned suddenly, putting her back to him. She paced the small corridor, talking to herself, though he couldn't make out what she said. She stopped, putting a hand to her mask as she shook her head. He finally noticed the sword on her hip, and he felt afraid again. What was that about a demon? He'd had those same fears, of course, but now… Wasn't that why they wanted the boy?

"Why did you come here?" she asked, her hand on the bars again as she met his eyes.

"I…" His mind wanted to dredge up the anger again, but it seemed he couldn't. "I just want what I'm owed," he said quietly. "I helped the boy, and now he gets a parade. Why can't I have what he has?"

"He came here to *save* you," the Masked One hissed, her stare unmoving.

"From what?" he asked. "Six meals a day and a pile of gold? Sounds like a pretty good life to me."

"This is no life," she whispered, her chest suddenly heaving as if she was straining to breathe. "Spilling blood and starving to death, nothing more. When he puts on that mask at sunset, his life is over."

She squeezed her eyes shut, whispering to herself as if she'd forgotten he was there again. This time, though, standing next to the bars, he could make out what she said.

"Viden was right," she whispered.

He'd always heard the Masked Ones weren't all there, but this… It made him think of his sister again, his chest tight as he realized what he'd *really* done to her, what he'd done to Teros. All this time, he'd told himself her life would be better, repeating the lie until he could sleep at night — even if he needed whiskey to sleep soundly. His anger disappeared completely, replaced by a sorrow so heavy he had to bite his lip to keep from crying. Suddenly, it all made sense. Teros hadn't left because he was angry, he'd left because he was scared, because he didn't want anyone else to die. And Borash had let him. The Masked One looked at him again.

"If I let you out, will you leave this place?"

He blinked in surprise, narrowing his eyes.

"Let…me out?" he asked.

She reached into her pocket, pulling out a key.

"If I let you out," she said more slowly, "will you *leave*?"

"I…" He imagined himself climbing the palace wall, wandering the streets again. But for what? To sleep on the street while the boy lost his life? Could he really live with that? "What about the boy?"

"I don't know," she said. She turned again, looking at the empty corridor. "I don't think I can help him, my oaths… I don't think I'd be able to fight them."

"Then why come here?" he asked. "Why let me out?"

She met his eyes.

"You remind me of someone," she said. "And we all wish for a way to replace the things we've lost."

She tossed the key at his feet.

"Wait for nightfall," she said, "and go far from this place. I can't save the boy, but I promise I'll look after him."

She turned, disappearing as quickly as she'd come. He stared at the key in the glowing blue light, unsure if he'd ever be able to pick it up.

31

28th of Sund-z'ar : Before 5th Meal : 984, 22nd Year of Iron
11 days until the 163rd Voting

Teros followed the Masked One down the corridor, his new robes trailing behind him. They were heavy, the gold thread perhaps really made of gold, with the fabric covered in gems and sigils besides. The man, 151, was quiet, not like the woman before. She had been…kind, not at all what he'd expected. He wished she could have taken him to the ceremony, but she'd been sent away. Would he see her again at the temple? He was ready, he just…hoped he'd see a friendly face when sunset came.

They reached a pair of giant metal doors, the Masked One kneeling beside him.

"Remember," he said, "bow when you reach the circle, and only speak when spoken to. You may call him Keroes nir Sen'l, High Priest, or 'my lord.'"

Teros nodded.

"Very well," 151 said. He nodded to a pair of guards outside the doors, and they pushed them open, revealing a gigantic throne room. It was beautiful, full of blue like something Mother would have painted at the pond. Thinking of her brought her face to his mind, but he was ready for it, had spent the whole afternoon banishing her away. *I'm sorry*, he thought, squeezing his eyes shut.

They followed the blue tiles on the floor until they reached the center, where he bowed as instructed. After bowing himself, 151 left, leaving him alone with the High Priest. He seemed young for his position, and he smiled, waving for Teros to approach a tray of food laid out on the floor below the throne. It was the biggest meal he'd ever seen, with even more dishes than Uncle Elin's birthday. There was a steaming risotto surrounded by cups of side dishes: lilac ends, roasted asparagus, corn soup, and a dozen other things he couldn't name.

"Thank you for joining me," the High Priest said as he sat. "This is a momentous day and one worthy of celebration."

Teros didn't feel hungry, but 732 had said he'd need to eat to swear the Cyran Stone again. He shuddered at the thought of not being able to breathe, but it would all be over soon. He picked up his spoon, forcing the risotto into his mouth.

"You see," the priest continued, "we normally don't discuss this until the ceremony, but you have a very specific honor as a vessel, and I wanted to tell you personally. The gods have chosen you to carry the spirit of Bitan nir Föhr."

Teros froze, his eyes wide. Everyone knew the Doomed Prince. Even when he lived on the farm, the workers who'd been in the war would carry coins with his face around their neck. He didn't know if the part about the spirit was true, though. He knew from Mother how normal it was to use the Principles, but would he really trade his soul for Bitan's when he wore the mask? If it wasn't true — if he was still himself — then maybe it would be an opportunity. If he could do more than just stop the killing, if he could change things…

"I see you can appreciate the gravity of your task," the priest said, nodding. "Now, we must talk of what comes after."

Teros nodded, forcing himself to continue eating. The priest droned on about his place in the king's court, the possibility of being selected heir at the voting in eleven days. Before long, the meal was over, and the priest was standing, taking him by the shoulder to lead him to the ceremony. The High Priest chattered on, and Teros let the words wash over him, nodding along as he thought of the only thing that mattered: He may have failed Mother, but he didn't have to fail his people.

32

732 finished her preparations just as the bells began to ring. Her stop at the prison had delayed her, but she'd still managed to be on time, the sun just sliding behind the palace walls. The path to the temple was lined with candles she'd lit, their lights twinkling like stars in the darkness of the gardens. Her hands shook as she lit the final wick, her mind spinning, but she was grateful too. Perhaps she couldn't run, would never disobey her training, but she had saved her brother. Even if he never knew it was her, never knew what had become of Eyri, he would be alive and free, and that made every other sacrifice worth it. As for the rest…

She stopped, reaching around the edges of her mask to squeeze her temples. He was no demon. And if that were true, then the child was right. But why continue the charade? Surely someone else must know the truth. The priests continued to hold up the Age of Disbelief as the ultimate evil, the moment when the border between men and Masked Ones last blurred. Could she continue to serve knowing there was a hidden truth? She couldn't leave the child, not after she'd promised Borash to protect him. But what of Viden? He had told her to run, and could she really leave him to die alone, without a hand to hold?

She retrieved her sword and cloak, carefully fastening them as the time for the procession arrived. She could hear them before she saw them, though it wasn't long until the lanterns appeared, a river of humanity chanting as they streamed down from the tower. The priests were in the front, led by Keroes nir Sen'l and the king's Golden Mask, the boy between them. They all sang, humans and Masked Ones, their voices rising in the Chant of the Elders. She waited silently by the crops until the procession was only a few yards away. She met the boy's eyes, bowing her head in respect before joining at the front of the Masked Ones' column.

Ahead, the temple sat on its wedge of grass beside the river, lit up like a feast day, its windows shimmering in the evening light. She sang the ancient words, though they sounded hollow to her now. Was this really what the Elders wanted? They'd followed the river farther than any others, building their basin in the promised land. But if they saw them now, would they be proud? The Principles lived on, but it seemed they had little else to show for their centuries of struggle. Still, her questions could wait. Tonight, she bore witness to the child's sacrifice. She could decide what was left for her when it was over.

———

Borash stared at the key for a long time, until the sun passed over the wall and the light faded from the prison windows. His mind felt adrift, passing over all the memories he thought he knew so well. Every lie he'd told himself, every promise he'd made and broken. Who was he really? At the bottom of his soul, when everything was scraped away, what could he show for himself? He thought of Teros, of the light in the kid's eyes, the *hope* he'd felt for the first time in years. Could he really run? But what if he *didn't* run? If even a Masked One said there was no hope, what chance would he have of saving the lad?

He was about to give up, to roll over and wait to die — anything to not make a decision — when he heard it. It sounded like singing, like the feast days when priests wandered the streets. It was eerily beautiful in the darkness, as if the cave spirits had come to take him after all. He stood, his feet unsteady as he walked over to the window, straining as he pulled himself up to look out. There were hundreds of people outside, walking through the fields toward the river. And at their head, wearing golden robes, was Teros. The lad didn't sing, his face unmoving as he walked between two priests. The Masked One's voice returned to his mind:

"This is no life," she said. "Spilling blood and starving to death, nothing more."

His rage came back a hundredfold, a century of anger pouring from his heart like the river from the caves. But this time, he wasn't angry for himself, he was angry for *all of them*. Himself, the boy, Eyri. He'd thrown his own life away, sure enough, but gods above had those bastards taken their bloody share. He'd been kicked down, beaten, left to starve, and now they wanted Teros, too. They wanted this quiet, brilliant lad to give up his life so the sodding king could shine his crown. And finally, he knew the truth. If he let them have that boy, if he let them pry one more thing from his bloody hands, he'd never be able to live with himself.

He grabbed the key, wrenching open the door as he stormed into the hallway. He'd lost the drink lying in the cell, but even with nothing but gruel in his stomach, he felt the magic the moment he stepped free of that blue glow. He wasn't sure what drove it, couldn't remember the foods from Teros's book, but it had to be powerful. The magic felt like it had always been there, wrapping around his anger like moss around a rock. He reached the stairs, moving slowly down as he let the fire fill his mind. For once, it felt like he knew who he was, what he was meant to do.

It wasn't until he reached the ground floor that he heard the men, a half-dozen guards crowded in a doorway. The parade was past the tower, the chanting distant, but the men still watched, chattering as they craned their necks to see. Borash stepped off the stairs, his boot thumping on the stone. A guard looked, opening his mouth in surprise, but Borash gave him no chance to scream. He lifted his hand, swallowing them all in fire, their bodies ash before the others had a chance to turn.

He stepped through their bones, turning left where he saw the glint of metal. It was a break room of sorts, part armory and part mess hall, with swords hanging on the walls and fifth meal still on the table. And in the corner, he saw what he was looking for: a mishmash of glass bottles filled with liquor. The kid said alcohol was powerful, dangerous even. Maybe it would kill him, bringing on the Passing until he couldn't stomach another drop, but he needed every ounce of power he could get. And luckily for him, he could stomach more liquor than any sodding man in the basin.

———

732 entered the temple, forced forward as the others swelled around her. They were still singing, their voices echoing off the stone, but she couldn't seem to join them. Her eyes wouldn't leave the child, wishing she'd had the strength to make a different choice. But how could she? Least of all in this place… The temple was even more enormous than she remembered, its ceiling held up by thick columns like the trees of Pen'dil Sohn. It had two streams running along the walls — borrowed

from the sacred river — the water joining beneath the altar before it flowed back through matching grates on the other side. Light flooded into the atrium from above the palace walls, the stained glass seeming to pool the sun onto the altar. It was like the gods were mocking her, showering her with light even as they aimed to snuff the child's out.

The priests split off, standing along the streams on either side to make room for the Masked Ones. They marched forward in their ranks, stopping in formation just short of the atrium's light. A half-dozen palace guards waited beside the altar — another symbol of the king's approval — bowing to Keroes nir Sen'l as he helped the child to the altar, the Golden Mask at their side. And then, finally, there was silence, the temple seeming to hold its breath as the High Priest turned to speak. 732 felt her stomach turn, desperate not to watch even as she knew she'd never look away.

"My friends," the High Priest said, holding up his hands, "this is a truly glorious day."

————

Borash crossed the river, following the bridge the Masked Ones had taken to the temple. He held a sword in his hand from the prison, his knuckles bulging as he gripped it tight. He could feel the alcohol seeping into his veins, but his mind felt oddly clear, his anger spurring him on. He stopped in the shadow of the building, looking up. Shaped like a bloody spear, its top was lit up like a torch in the setting sun. They'd closed the doors behind them, leaving the grounds eerily quiet. How in the bloody cave witch's tit would he get in there without being killed on the spot? He couldn't very well walk in the front door…

He finally noticed the glitter of water. Pure and blue, a stream flowed through the temple, going in the front before trickling out the pointy end on its way back to the river. He walked toward the temple's point, finding two old grates built into the stone. He straddled the water, peering at the metal lattice and the dark tunnel behind it. It didn't seem to have a weak point, no lock or hinge he could force with the sword. He closed his eyes, trying to remember what the lad had taught him when he thought of the practice stone, the lines of Permanence glowing in the wagon.

"Tell it," the kid had said. Tell the stone to break and it would break. He closed his eyes, breathing as he felt for the power in his stomach, the vodka he'd forced down his throat just moments before. When he opened his eyes, there was the faintest glow to the metal. It was clearly different from the setting sun, like morning light, a pure white against the darkness of the tunnel. He put his hand against the grate, and he felt that strange pulse, the same one from the stone. He could see the grate in his mind, sense its outline, the way it wanted to be and the way it *could* be.

Break, he thought, and the vodka burned in his stomach with a jolt, his head spinning as the power rushed through him. A giant crack rang out, and he fell back, landing in the stream with a thud. He shook his head, the stiffness already in his limbs. But just as the kid promised, it wasn't as bad as the first time. He closed his eyes, imagining himself as part of the stream. Flow, the kid had called it, and that one went with wine. He felt for the wine in his stomach, pulling at its power as the stiffness left him.

When he stood, he realized that the grate had cracked, a thousand lines zigzagging through the metal from the place he'd held his hand. He kicked it with his boot, the metal cracking like an old loaf of bread. His head was beginning to throb something awful, but he pushed through it, dropping into the tunnel on his hands and knees as he crawled toward the light.

———

Even after the child turned toward the altar, 732 kept her eyes glued to him. If only she could lend him her strength, hold his spirit with her own. The High Priest held his face to the light, his eyes closed in ecstasy as he recited the *Ode to the Distant Star*. But as he repeated the ancient words of the Wise Father, they seemed twisted. Was this a song of love? Was *this* the Sea Mother's promise?

As Keroes nir Sen'l finished the recitation, the other priests began to sing again, leading them in the *Hymn of Leaving*. This time, she joined them, but she sang for the child. This was the Sermon of Loss, the words Entodal nol Serim had used when he realized he would forever leave his home. This was the end, the moment when the child would cease to be. As the song reached its climax, Keroes nir Sen'l came around the child, holding the tiny porcelain mask aloft.

"Take this mask, the promise of the Elders, and as you wear it, wear the Mother's blessing, so the lost may return while their spirits remain."

He placed the mask on the child's face, the porcelain casting a pool of light onto the stone. The singing continued, the Golden Mask approaching the altar. It was time to swear the stone and bring Bitan nir Föhr into the world again.

———

He'd known he was a bloody fool for coming, but what Borash found on the other side of the tunnel was nothing short of a nightmare. There were hundreds of Masked Ones — probably the whole lot of 'em — and they were all chanting, a low, pitiful sound like a dirge. Even worse, damn near everyone in the room had a sword — and they likely knew how to use them a good bit better than he did. Still, when he finally saw Teros, kneeling on the altar in a mask, his blood boiled. So much so that he had to heave in lungfuls of air to keep himself from erupting into flame then and there.

His fear burnt away, and he leapt to his feet, climbing up the steps of the altar as he pointed a finger at the priest.

"Oy!" he yelled, somehow louder than all that chanting, his voice echoing off the stone walls.

Suddenly, there was silence, the air becoming frighteningly still as hundreds of eyes turned on him at once like they were a single thing, a cave beast from a bad dream. Hands were somehow already on swords, everything tightening to the breadth of a string, with little standing between peace and violence.

The old man lowered his hands.

"How did you get in here?" he asked, his voice cold. "This is a sacred day, and I will not have it ruined by some—"

"I came for the lad," Borash said, his anger growing at the bastard's tone. "He's my friend, and you can't bloody have him."

The old man motioned to his side where another Masked One — this one's mask in gold — stood with a handful of palace guards. The gold mask pulled his sword from his sheath, stepping forward.

"I wouldn't," Borash said, holding out his palm where a pool of fire appeared.

The room itself seemed to suck in a breath, the hundreds of Masked Ones below suddenly undulating like a ripple in a pond. The gold mask slowed, looking to the old man, who only nodded. The gold mask turned back, his eyes seeming to smile beneath his disguise. Suddenly, there was a ripple in the air, only a second's warning coming before a peal of fire arced toward him. Borash raised both hands, his own fire exploding off the other as the fighting began.

———

As the streams of Passion met above the altar, they shook the air, their force throwing Teros on his back as they blasted outward. He sprawled across the marble, the mask thrown from his face as he gasped for breath. It took a moment before his lungs stopped aching, the air itself seeming to have been burnt away before it came rushing back.

He crawled onto his hands and knees, his eyes locked on Borash. The older man was fighting for his life, his own magic barely rising in time to meet the blows from the Golden Mask, who was dropping blast after blast of power: Identity, Passion, and Flow. Borash continued using flame, though it would never be enough to counter the other Principles. The Golden Mask stepped closer with each blast, his sword gleaming in the fading light.

Tears came to his eyes, his teeth grinding as he watched. How had it come to this? He'd thought things would be better if he stopped fighting, but Borash had come anyway. He would die like the others, all because of him. Die like Mother. Her face came to him, not the good face but the bad, covered in blood, her eyes glassy against the stone hearth. Was this what she had wanted for him? He'd disobeyed her, chosen to serve over being free, and still, he would lose everything. With or without this sacrifice, his friend would die, and for what? He sucked in a breath, his hands balling into fists.

"I'm sorry, Mother," he said, the tears flowing more freely. "I'm sorry."

Every choice he'd made had brought death, his life like a vortex swallowing the light. Freedom, bondage, they ended the same way. He had to choose something different, something of his own. He could see the threads the Golden Mask was pulling, feel the next line of Flow about to rise from his hand. He could stop this. He could save Borash. Teros lifted his arm, about to cancel the Golden Mask's magic, when the priest was there, taking him by the shoulder. His own robes looked singed, and there was a darkness to his face Teros hadn't seen before.

"Come, child," he said, holding the fallen mask. He gestured to the guards who were waiting in the water by the altar. "We'll escape through the tunnel and finish the ceremony when this dog has been put down."

"No," Teros said, taking the man's hand from his shoulder.

"No?" the priest asked, his face growing darker. "You serve the gods, child, not yourself!" He reached for his pocket, where he'd seen him place that awful stone. "I'll break your vessel if I have to, but you *will* obey."

Teros surged Permanence, the power of the stone floor suddenly coming into his hands as he froze the priest where he stood. Then he lashed out with Remembrance, freezing the palace guards in the water. He turned just in time, lashing out with a stream of Identity that canceled the Golden Mask's flame. The Golden Mask froze, turning to look behind him as Borash ran forward, his sword in the air.

———

732 watched in horror, her hand frozen on her sword, unable to move. Like all the other Masked Ones, she stood like a statue, watching as the Golden One and Borash fought, their power dancing across the ceiling each time it met, forming cracks in the stone. Was it training or shock that kept them still? Each one of them surely knew the price they'd pay for interfering, for stepping onto the altar without an invitation. Or was it Borash himself? Their fears made manifest in a maskless man wielding the Principles?

But what of her? She knew the truth, had set Borash free, and still, she couldn't move. Why had he come? There was no way he could defeat the Golden One. But would she help? *Could* she even help? She was resigned to die, but she'd taken solace in knowing he'd be free. Even in the brief minutes they'd shared, after decades spent apart, without him even knowing it was her, she had felt peace. But could she live with watching him die, or had the stone broken her so completely there was nothing left? Still, as she watched her brother fight for his life, something stirred in her. Something forgotten, like a giant awakening from a deep slumber.

"Fight, damn you!" Keroes nir Sen'l yelled from where he'd been frozen, his voice breaking through the blasts of the fighting. "Fight!"

She looked down at her hand, her knuckles tight around her sword. The others began to shift, too, as if waking from a dream. They would move now, attacking her brother, overwhelming him, unable to ignore a command from the High Priest. She heard the stone, speaking to her through twenty-three years of pain. *Obey*, it seemed to say, demanding her to move, *obey*. But for the first time since she was a girl, there was another voice, too. Even as it whispered, it was somehow louder, more urgent. *Save him*, it said. *Save. Him.* She knew that voice… It was *her* voice. A voice she'd forgotten. Not 732's, not Zi'yun nol Curan's, but hers. Eyri's. And for once, there was nothing left to hold her back.

Eyri pulled her sword from its sheath, coming out in a swing as she put it in the neck of the Masked One to her right. She twisted, dropping the other on her left as the rows behind her started to react, their shock swept away by blood. She dropped to one knee, pulling up a giant mound of earth behind her, blocking the bursts of fire that finally came from the others. In the span of a heartbeat, she was jumping, launching herself over the mound with wind, the air still shimmering with heat from the fading fire.

The moment she landed, there were seven Masked Ones within reach. She put her sword into the one in front of her with one hand while she immolated the two on her left with a massive burst of Passion. Part of her knew she had already burned through all of her food, but it didn't seem to matter. Somehow the magic was still coming, forcing its way into her soul like a river against a dam. It felt like she could hear the voices from the statues, the whispers that had soothed her all these years. They felt like an echo of the world, the Principles swirling inside the things around her, soft to the touch of her mind. She had never fought so well, had never truly had anything worth fighting for.

She pulled down the pillar to her right, the building groaning as the stone fell on her closest attackers. Seven dead, but so many more, dozens and dozens. A moment later, she lashed the room with wind, a thunderstorm's worth pushing against the others, their ranks rippling as they rushed toward her. There were too many. Even fighting as she was, she could never kill them all. But if she could slow them somehow, buy her time to save her brother…

She leapt back over the pile of rock, pulling down on the roof with all her might. The building lurched, a thousand years of stone finally giving way as she landed, the roof caving in as she slid into the atrium. A massive cloud of dust blasted around her, the temple effectively cut in half with the Masked Ones trapped — as well as stone could trap them — on the other side. She blinked the dust from her eyes, looking up to find the glow of the setting sun coming through a hole in the roof, centuries of history gone in a moment. She picked up her sword and walked toward the altar, the voices of the statues flooding her mind.

———

Shouts were erupting throughout the temple, but Borash barely had enough room in his mind to register them as he fought against the gold mask. Even with his enemy's attention divided, it was taking everything he had to avoid being run through. Now, the gold mask was slowly moving backward, keeping Borash at bay as he inched toward Teros. The gold mask's eyes were filled with rage, and even with the lad pulling down a good amount of his magic, Borash struggled to block the peals of fire and wind that made it through. Each time he got close, they met with either swords or magic — or both — almost always ending with Borash pushed back a few feet.

Still, he had to attack, had to keep that sword from finding Teros, the lad's face dripping with sweat as he focused on his magic. And he had to do more than survive — he had to escape with the lad in tow. Escape before the rest of the Masked Ones came and skewered him. But where were they? Why hadn't they attacked? He was beginning to get woozy from the magic, his mind sluggish. But even with his thoughts clouded, he knew they should have come by now, especially after that bloody priest had screamed for them to fight.

Still, watching Teros, he could feel the other Principles, could somehow match the boy and find something other than fire. He shook his head, preparing another blast of power, this time of Flow, when there was a giant cracking noise. He looked over just in time to see a Masked One soaring through the air like a bird as the roof came down. The entire building seemed to groan as it hit, the giant slab of stone erupting into a massive cloud of dust. It hit them like a storm, his vision gone for a moment in the haze of silt. Still, he kept his sword up and was glad he did, the gold mask lurching through the haze toward him, his sword coming down hard just as Borash got his eyes open.

They traded blows, each fall of the sword feeling like a hammer on an anvil. He felt his sword quivering in his mind, its shape growing feeble, but he held it together somehow with Permanence, *willed* it to stay together. Then, he pushed back, his arms aching as he swung himself wildly, anything to take the pressure off so he could prepare more magic. He found more whiskey in his stomach somehow and was about to seize it when he heard a voice.

"Stop!" a woman yelled, the dust clearing to reveal a Masked One walking toward them, sword in hand.

————

The moment she yelled, everyone on the altar froze. Borash and the Golden One had continued fighting through the dust, but the priest only stared, his eyes wide as he considered his ruined temple. The guards looked on horrified, their hands still trying to pry their legs free while the child looked as if he might collapse.

Eyri walked steadily, her sword raised as she rotated around the Golden One, placing herself between him and Borash.

"732?" the Golden One asked, chuckling as he read the sigils on her mask. "The *keroshai?* I thought you were a good little dog."

She pulled the mask from her face, cracking it with Permanence as she dropped it on the ground.

"My name is Eyri."

She pushed hard with Identity, the air shifting underneath her as she launched toward the Golden One. Their swords and magic met as one, the fight immediately entering a deathly dance. She had never fought without her mask, but it felt…freeing, the magic rushing into her mind as it arced about the room. Still, the Golden One was good, far better than any she'd ever faced. Their swords were identical, the steel marked with the sigil of the crown, and yet, they were completely different. His seemed to move of its own accord, spinning as he ducked and turned, edging closer as he sought her throat.

And yet, there was desperation in his movements. He was so aggressive that she missed it at first, putting all of her energy into controlling the tempo of the fight. But as he swung for her again and again, he began to growl like a wild animal. It had to be the magic… The child pulling down his power for so long, fighting Borash, he must be nearly out. But she could still feel the Principles, the statues whispering in her mind. She should have been done long ago, and yet her magic held.

She reached for those voices, letting them in as she *changed*. The magic filled her, taking over until her arms no longer felt like her own. They moved through sword forms on instinct, her consciousness devoted elsewhere, straining to guide the flood of magic filling her. The Principles moved so quickly they almost seemed to weave together, lashes of power rising like the sun, the physical world barely able to contain them as Flow turned to Passion, Identity to Remembrance, all of it little more than a voice echoing in her mind.

The Golden One seemed to sense the rawness of her power, if not its form, and he backed away, warding with his sword as he tried to launch a massive wave of fire — probably all he had left — directly at her. Still, under the surge of her power, it was nothing, stripped away by a river of Identity even as it wove into the others. For a moment, she saw fear in his eyes, and she knew the fight was finished. She launched herself into the air again, carried more by power than wind, easing the weight of gravity around her through Permanence more than Identity. And when she landed, there was almost no resistance left, her sword slipping into his chest like a stone into water, its force inevitable.

The Golden One coughed as he fell to his knees, his eyes wide as blood filled his robes. She couldn't explain it, but the voices in her mind felt…sadness at his death. Even as the rawness of their power had destroyed him, they seemed to mourn. She took him by the shoulder, easing him to the ground where she took his hand, squeezing it as the light disappeared from his eyes.

"Eyri?" asked a voice, quiet, fearful. She pulled her sword free and turned, finding Borash looking at her, an arm raised toward her, seeking.

She turned, smiling at him.

"It's me," she said. "I'm back."

———

Keroes nir Sen'l strained against his bonds, a new panic seizing him as the Golden One fell. But his body and his mind felt out of sync, the immensity of the child's magic holding him to the stone as if chained. Still, he was close, tantalizingly close. Before the vessel had turned to wickedness, his hand had reached the serosine dagger hidden in his pocket. Had he not, perhaps there would have been no hope at all. But it seemed the gods still saw fit to save him, to salvage what they could of this kingdom despite the evil before his eyes.

Through his hand, the serosine of the blade was removing the Permanence from his limbs, slowly pulling away the weight that threatened to crush him. And yet it moved so slowly, like emptying a pond with a ladle. But it *was* working. As the Golden One had fought, he'd felt one of his toes move. And now, he could freely move his foot. The dagger could only take so much, but all he needed was an arm, and he would be free, free enough to stop this chaos.

Suddenly, he felt his hand around the blade, his fingers no longer like stone. His eyes widened, a smile coming to his lips. He moved slowly, careful to still seem frozen, but he pushed his hand deeper into his pocket, finding the Cyran Stone. Deliverance from the gods indeed…

He looked up, finding the broken vessel of 732 turned around, talking to that horrid man from the gates. They were close, her mask off, a smile on her face despite what she had done. She seemed to… know him? He felt a knot in his stomach, the realization filling his veins with fire. He had trusted her above all others, given her access to plans that none save 151 had been granted, and yet she had betrayed him. Had she been working for the demons all along?

He forced his legs to move, the joints cracking as if made of ice. He stepped forward, raising the stone above his head.

"You cursed thing!" he roared. "You. Will. Bow!"

732 turned, her eyes filled with fear as the stone took her, her limbs spasming as she fell to her knees, the veins of her neck bulging. He didn't turn away, though a cry to his side told him the child had been similarly detained. He turned instead to the beggar, his eyes wild as he looked between 732 and the stone.

"I don't know what you are," Keroes said, "some demon perhaps, but I will not fear you. You are *not* of the gods, and you have no power over me."

The man raised an arm, perhaps hoping fire would spout from his hand again, but the stone held, its metal heating as it vibrated. Keroes chuckled, squeezing the stone in appreciation.

"You may not know to bow before the stone," he continued, "but it will stop your magic all the same."

The beggar gripped his sword tighter, though the motion now looked rather foolish, like a child with a plaything. Thankfully, his predecessor had long ago taught him not to fear demons. As Salin nir Cosk had always said, "A snake without teeth is just a worm."

Keroes turned toward the guards. Their eyes wide as saucers, they still looked on uselessly. He turned the Cyran Stone toward them, its surface cool to the touch as he willed it to absorb the ice around their legs.

"Come, men," he said, beckoning. "Be worthy of your crown and detain this man. He's no longer of any danger to you."

Their hands went back to their swords by instinct, but they still looked dazed, their eyes moving from the fallen Golden One to the beggar.

"Now listen," the beggar said, his voice strained, "I'm a regular bloke, same as you. There's no need for you lads to get caught up in this."

He motioned toward the broken grate on the other side of the altar.

"Just go right out the way I came in," he continued, "no trouble." The beggar patted his shoulder, miming the patches on the soldiers' shoulders. "I used to sell cloth for those very uniforms. Yellow means you're from Cosk, yeah? I grew up just west of there, Mer'n Hill. Just leave and you can be back with your families tonight."

The guards looked at each other, and Keroes felt his blood boil. This was the best the king had to offer?!

"Seize him!" he yelled. "Now! You want to see your precious families again? Then move, or be hung for cowardice."

The soldiers looked at him, their eyes still wide like children's. They finally moved, and he breathed a sigh of relief. But then, they dropped their swords, dashing for the stream as they left through the grate. Keroes looked back at the beggar in horror as the man began to laugh.

"That's the problem with you rich folk," he said, stepping closer with his sword, "you always think somebody else will do your work for you."

Finally able to fully feel his legs, Keroes scrambled to his left, grabbing the child as he pressed the dagger to his neck.

"Now, now," Keroes said, watching the beggar, "careful."

A fresh horror came to the man's eyes, but the child, at least, was easy. Under the spell of the stone, he could do nothing to struggle, his small body nothing more than dead weight.

"Now," Keroes said, "we talk."

———

"Alright," Borash said, "alright. Whatever you want, let's talk."

His eyes were glued to the priest's hand as if he'd be able to see the muscles as they tensed, anticipate the dagger before it slid across the boy's throat.

"Drop your sword," the priest said. He did so, slowly kneeling as he placed the steel onto the marble.

"Alright," Borash said, nodding. He stayed on his knees, putting his hands in the air.

"Now, I want answers," the priest asked, narrowing his eyes. "What are you, demon?"

"I'll tell you what you want to know," Borash said slowly, his eyes still on the priest's wrist. "But I want a trade. The boy for my answers. Hell, you can even hand me over to the king if you want, just get the knife off his throat, alright?"

The priest laughed.

"A trade? As if your lies could be worth this vessel. This child *is* the kingdom, demon."

"Okay," Borash said gently, like soothing a horse. That was good, though; it meant the priest didn't *want* to kill the boy. He just had to treat him like a merchant would, find what he wanted and pretend he was giving it to him. He'd give himself up if he had to, so long as the kid didn't die, but what of Eyri? He turned, looking at where the Masked One — his own lost sister — writhed in pain.

"I'll answer now, then. Let's just bring down the temperature. You want the boy, he's yours, alright? But nobody has to die. You want to know what I am, yeah? I'm a man, like any other."

"Lies!" the priest bellowed, the veins on his neck bulging over the top of his robes. "Truth or the boy dies. He's valuable, but I will find another. The *gods* will send another. If he dies, his blood is on your hands."

"Okay," Borash said quickly, "okay." He wracked his brain. What was he, really? And then, the sad truth of the answer finally came to him: He was nothing, a curse on every life he'd ever touched. The priest was right. This was his fault, the boy's blood on *his* hands. Since the beginning, all he'd done was take from Teros, or try to, anyway. And even in trying to save him, perhaps he'd just ended the lad's life. The fact was, he hadn't done the right thing twenty years ago, and he wasn't doing it now.

"I honestly don't know," Borash said quietly. "I'm nothing, or should be, anyway. I have the magic, that much is true. And maybe you missed me, maybe I was meant to be the one. My sister," he said, motioning toward Eyri, "maybe you took her and not me, and nobody realized. I didn't even know myself, but I wish I had, gods how I wish I had. I'm sorry for coming here, but please, let the lad go. At least give him a chance to set this right and live."

The priest looked between him and Eyri, his brow furrowed.

"A missed vessel..." he said to himself, no longer listening. "But not under my watch. If I could tie it to another..."

Borash didn't understand, but he nodded anyway. He knew that face, the face of a customer who fancied his bargain won. There was something there. All he had to do now was get the kid free. He forced his eyes away from the knife and toward the strange egg-shaped thing in the priest's hand. Maybe he didn't need a trade...

"I have papers," Borash said, nodding to his belt pouch. "Birth records, I can prove it all."

The priest narrowed his eyes again, coming back from whatever vision he was having for himself.

"Bring them," the priest said, "slowly."

Borash reached into his pouch, pulling out the kid's letter. He slowly crawled toward the priest, holding it above his head. The priest reached out with the hand that held the orb, his knife still tight against the kid's neck. But a moment was all he needed. The priest's eyes left his, turning toward the paper as Borash lunged. The priest fell back, and his strange stone flew into the air. Borash dove for it, even as his leg gave out, throwing all his weight into the jump, his fingers closing around it as the priest cried out.

Borash could feel the stone's power, but even as it hummed, he could feel now how soft it was, the metal more delicate than an egg. He crushed it in his hand, the kid gasping from where he'd sprawled across the ground. The priest stood, his knife in hand, lunging for the child. Borash cried out, reaching for the child, but he would be too late. But then, there was a whir in the air, the priest suddenly falling as a dagger sprouted from his chest. Borash turned, finding Eyri on her feet, her chest heaving as her arm stayed in the air, her hand empty where it had thrown the knife.

———

Keroes gasped, looking down to find dark blood — his blood — running into his robes. He met 732's eyes, coldness on her face. Suddenly, he felt weak, slumping to his side. He felt…cold. Where were the Elders? Where were…the gods? He closed his eyes, the lids too heavy to hold open any longer. But in the darkness, he heard…a voice. Or voices maybe. Singing? Or maybe speaking, as if from another room. But it was beautiful, so beautiful. He smiled, his muscles weak, and he was gone.

———

Eyri sucked in a breath, her lungs finally free of the stone. Keroes nir Sen'l lay dying, her aim truer than she'd hoped, unsure at first if her arms would even work. Borash looked at her, fear in his eyes, and for a moment, she thought she'd lost him, his love unable to remain now that he saw her for what she was. But then, as if waking from a dream, he ran to her, hugging her. When they separated, he held her by the shoulder, staring at her face.

"Eyri," he said breathlessly as if he didn't believe it was her name, "are you alright?"

She smiled, nodding.

"Never better," she said.

He smiled back, still holding her, his grip delicate but tight as if he didn't trust himself to let her go. She heard coughing to the side and turned, finding Teros on his knees, the effects of the stone surely wreaking the same havoc on him as they were on her.

"Lad," Borash said, stepping over as he picked him up. "What about you? You alright?"

The child nodded, blinking as he shook his head. Eyri was about to join them when a giant crash came from beyond the rubble, the temple shaking again. She closed her eyes, sensing Permanence and Identity weaving through the air. Of course, with the Cyran Stone destroyed, the Masked Ones would free themselves.

"Borash," she said, turning. "We have to go."

He nodded, following her toward the stream. Still, she had a sinking feeling. Where would they go? Even if they got out of the city, how far could they run with nothing to eat and an army behind them?

Borash urged the child first, looking over his shoulder at the rubble. Teros crawled into the grate, his hands and knees in the water, but not a moment later, he returned.

"Soldiers," he said, his eyes wide. "A lot of them."

Eyri ducked down, dozens of armored legs visible through the tunnel. It was lucky they hadn't come in yet, but they were still surrounded. She met Borash's eyes, her own worry reflected back at her.

"Is there any other way out of here?" he asked.

She looked around the ruined temple. The sun was gone, leaving only the stars, twinkling through the damaged roof.

"Dandelion," she whispered to herself.

"What's that?" Borash asked.

She pulled the flask from her pocket, decades of work aimed only at a good death. Until this moment.

"I have distilled dandelion," she said, "and an anchor to travel to in Pen'dil Deyn."

The wall of rubble shifted again, shouts now carrying through the thinning pile of stone.

"It leaves a ripple," she said. "They'll be able to follow us, but it's better than nothing."

Borash looked at the wall and back at her.

"Hey, kid," he said, turning to Teros. "Which one are dandelions?"

"Place," the kid said, frowning.

"And Remembrance cancels Place?" he asked.

Teros nodded again, though a pit was forming in her stomach.

"Borash," she said, "no. We can't—"

"Shhh," he said, stepping up and hugging her. Instantly, she was a child again, her brother holding her as she cried, their parents gone to work. "It'll be alright," he whispered. "I'm just doing what I should've done a long time ago, alright? It's my turn. My bloody turn. Just help me save the boy."

She felt his tears on her neck, but she nodded, squeezing him tighter. It felt like she could stay that way forever, but another crash from the rubble woke her from her dream. Borash stepped away, kneeling before Teros.

"Thank you, kid," he said, tousling his hair. "For everything."

Teros looked between them, only just seeming to understand.

"You're not coming?" he asked, his voice small. "Borash, no. My mother, the priest, I—"

"It's alright, lad," Borash said, looking up at Eyri as he smiled. "You'll be with my sister. Just be a good lad, and change this world, alright?"

Teros was crying, his face a river of tears, but he nodded.

"Quickly now," Borash said, standing. "I think our time is up."

He stepped back, pulling a bottle of liquor from somewhere in his robes. He grimaced as he downed it, coughing, but he forced a smile to his face.

"Come now," he said. "Everything'll be alright."

Eyri nodded, downing the contents of her flask. The dandelion was bitter, horribly bitter, but it was instantly replaced by a floating feeling, a surge of Place filling her. She felt hundreds of anchors floating up in her mind, but the one in Pen'dil Deyn, the one she'd made for herself so many years ago, was brighter than them all, like a bonfire signaling to her across the valley.

She looked at Borash, nodding. His smile deepened, and all the years seemed to slide off him. The room began to shake, the wall of rubble giving way.

Go, Borash mouthed. She took Teros by the hand and breathed in, letting herself go, like a dandelion on the wind. The room began to haze, but she kept watching Borash, his eyes never leaving hers. Suddenly, she felt an incredible cold as the air began to freeze, and it was followed by fire, hot enough to melt stone, enough Passion to destroy the temple ten times over. Still, through that searing heat, Borash smiled, watching as she disappeared.

Epilogue

Eyri stepped back from the ripple, the anchor already fading as Remembrance pulled it apart. She blinked, her face somehow wet with tears. Borash… Reunited and torn away in the same instant. But somehow, she felt whole, too, the family she'd secretly carried in her heart all those years proven to be real, like finding the gods on top of Sen'el'seng.

She turned quickly, suddenly remembering the boy. He was watching where the ripple had been, his own eyes as tearful as hers. Her heart ached for him anew, like it had in the cave. Only this time could be different — *would* be different.

She knelt on the moss and opened her arms. Teros watched her for a moment before he nodded, hugging her despite their tears. She held him close, feeling his heartbeat as he cried against her chest, muttering to himself quietly.

"It's going to be alright," she whispered, stroking the back of his head.

She stayed like that, unwilling to move as she looked up, the lights of Pen'dil Deyn glittering against the dark peak of Sen'el'tul. It was exactly as she remembered it when she'd laid her anchor so many years ago, and yet, it was completely changed, too. No war, no imprisonment, no Viden. There was only her, a boy, and the darkness. The stars twinkled above, and she looked up at them, only now realizing she didn't know their names. In fact, it seemed she didn't know anything at all: about herself, about their world, or about their magic. And strangely, that felt like hope.

193

THE END OF BOOK I

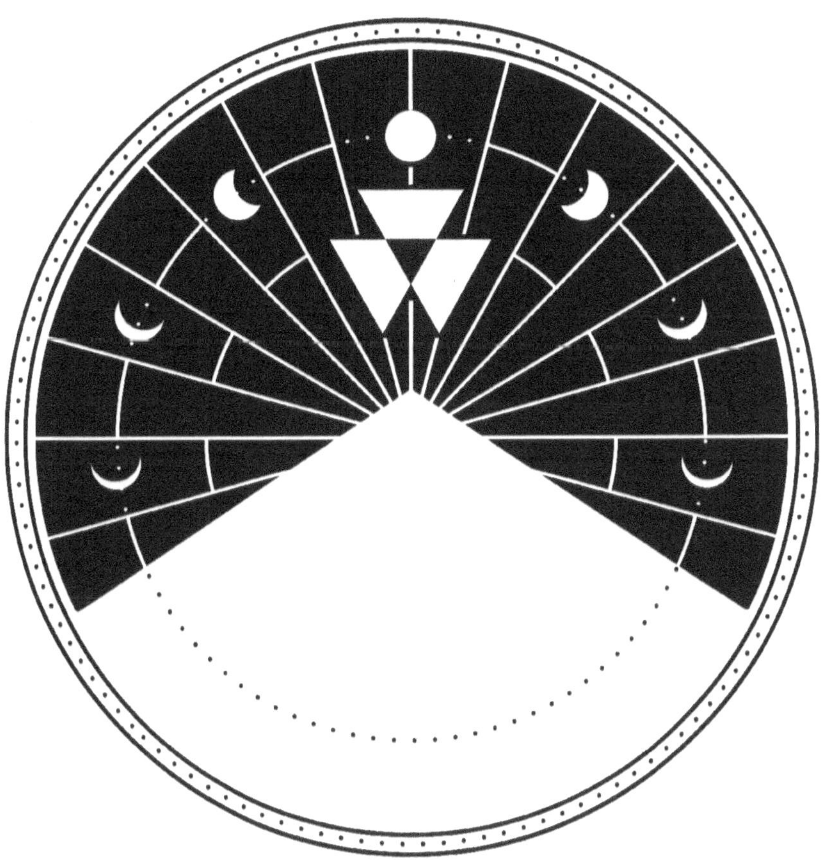